T0196519

The ✝ Second Appearance

Dr. Dahn Batchelor

iUniverse, Inc.
New York   Bloomington

iUniverse books may be ordered through booksellers or by contacting:

iUniverse
1663 Liberty Drive
Bloomington, IN 47403
www.iuniverse.com
1-800-Authors (1-800-288-4677)

Because of the dynamic nature of the Internet, any Web addresses or links contained in this book may have changed since publication and may no longer be valid. The views expressed in this work are solely those of the author and do not necessarily reflect the views of the publisher, and the publisher hereby disclaims any responsibility for them.

ISBN: 978-1-4401-4219-2 (sc)
ISBN: 978-1-4401-4221-5 (hc)
ISBN: 978-1-4401-4220-8 (ebook)

Library of Congress Control Number: 2010904093

Printed in the United States of America

iUniverse rev. date: 07/29/2010

Matthew 24:42-44 "Therefore keep watch, because you do not know on what day your Lord will come. But understand this: If the owner of the house had known at what time of night the thief was coming, he would have kept watch and would not have let his house be broken into. So you also must be ready, because the Son of Man will come at an hour when you do not expect him.

Chapter 1

The old man paused and then asked the reporter who had come to interview him, "Do you believe that Jesus Christ will return to us again?"

The reporter's face suddenly became flushed. He hadn't come all this way to answer questions. He was there to ask them. In any case, he replied, "I think so but I'm not sure."

The old man then said with a smile, "Well, he came back and he stayed here in Nelson for a few years as a child and while he was here, I was his best friend."

'Oh my God!' The reporter thought to himself, 'The editor has sent me to interview an old coot who has gone bonkers.'

The retired Anglican priest smiled and then said, "I know what you are thinking, young man. You think that I have taken leave of my senses."

"No, of course not, Sir." replied the young reporter as he tried to erase the features on his face that displayed signs of shock.

The old man looked at the briefcase by the reporter's side and then asked, "Have you got a recording device in there?"

"Yes, Sir." replied the reporter as he reached for it.

"I hope you have five hours of blank tapes also because this story I am going to tell you is going to take us past lunch and towards the supper hour."

'Jesus Christ!' the reporter mused to himself sadly, *'Five hours of listening to some old coot creating a story from his deranged mind. When I get back to Vancouver, I'll shove these tapes so far up that part of my editor's anatomy he can't see, it will take major surgery to recover them.'* Then he smiled and spoke, "I'm ready when you are, Sir."

Actually, Dave Cunningham wasn't really ready for what he was going to hear. Further, the six-foot, clean-shaven, brown-haired twenty-year-old newspaper reporter wasn't even that keen on interviewing the Right Reverend Lawrence Henderson in the first place. His employer, *The Vancouver Province* had sent him to Nelson, British Columbia where the retired Anglican minister was living. It was a long drive from Vancouver and it interfered with his plans for the upcoming weekend. Cunningham had graduated in journalism with high marks but was disappointed that he had been assigned to work in the Religion Section of *The Vancouver Province*. He had visions of being an investigative crime reporter and not simply a reporter who writes about religion, a subject that for the most part, bored him. Perhaps because he was only twenty years of age, the managing editor felt that he was too young to be a crime reporter. Further, since he was merely a trainee, he would have to be a full fledged reporter for many years before he would even be considered for an assignment in the world of crime.

The editor of the Religion Section wanted the young reporter to get as much information that he could about Rev. Henderson's life when he was a minister of an Anglican church in Vancouver. The paper already knew that the minister had recently retired and had been a very popular and highly respected religious leader in Vancouver when he served as one of the leading clergymen in Canada. The story was to be published in the following Sunday edition of the newspaper on August 20th, 1988. He had a week in which to write it.

The editor also knew that when Rev. Henderson was 18-years of age, he had chosen the Anglican Church's college, the Anglican Theological College to study theology. The college had previously moved into the Chancellor Building on the University of British Columbia campus in Point Grey, Vancouver in 1927 and it was there that he began his studies in 1956. He was well prepared for his entry into the college because as a young child and further, as a teenager, he became well versed in the text of the *Bible*. When he graduated, he was assigned to a small church in Burnaby, a city east of Vancouver, as an assistant priest. Two years later, he was given another small church in Burnaby in which he was to preach the good word, this time as a fully trained priest. Ten years later, he was assigned to one of the larger churches in Vancouver and within a year, its congregation grew in size to the point that all the pews were for the most part, always filled. As the years went by, he became a well respected Anglican priest and served on the board of directors of the Anglican Theological College. Several of his books on faith were sold by the thousands and he was considered as a profound speaker.

It took the young reporter eight hours to drive from Vancouver to Nelson, a small city to the east that is 395 miles by road. He began his drive at five in the morning. Fortunately, there was little traffic in Vancouver for him to contend with at that early hour. The route he had to take however wasn't as straight as the crow flies as the road wound its way through the various mountain ranges in the lower part of that province.

This was the first time in his life that he had ever gone beyond the vast confines of the Greater Vancouver area. He was familiar with mountains of course since Grouse and Seymour Mountains that are immediately north of Vancouver and just across Burrard Inlet from the city and a ten minute drive up the streets of North Vancouver, are where anyone wanting to climb them would begin their steep climbs that are 4,100 feet and 4,150 feet in height respectively.

As he drove eastward, there were mountains a mile or so from him on his left and flat land and farms on his right but within two hours, the highway was surrounded by hills and then mountains on both sides of him. On the eighth hour into his trip, he reached the area where the Henderson farm was located. It was on a winding road called Granite Road and was three miles east of the small city of Nelson.

Cunningham arrived at the Henderson's farm at one-thirty in the afternoon. It was on his left and was at the base of Granite Mountain, a mountain that didn't rise as steeply as the mountains north of Vancouver; however he estimated it was just as high and like those in Vancouver, it too was covered with fir and cedar trees.

He had been told earlier that Henderson's son and his son's wife were operating the farm, the same farm that the retired minister had lived on when he was a child. When he reached the front door of the farmhouse, a middle-aged woman opened the door and asked, "Are you Dave Cunningham from the newspaper?"

"Yes, I am," he replied,

"Please come in. My father-in-law is expecting you."

The reporter was taken through the kitchen and into the living room.

Sitting on a sofa chair was the man he was to interview. He appeared to the reporter to be around seventy years of age. His hair was white; he had a receding forehead, was clean-shaven and was wearing his reading glasses when the reporter entered the room.

"Please forgive me, young man for not getting up to greet you but my arthritis has been bothering me lately and it's sometimes painful for me to get out of soft chairs such as this one."

"I understand, Sir," replied the young man. "I appreciate it greatly that you are permitting me to spend an hour interviewing you about your work as a church minister."

"Only an hour?" asked the older man in a shocked tone of voice. "You have come all the way from Vancouver to interview me and you are only going to spend an hour with me? What are you writing, my obituary?"

The reporter was embarrassed. It was a stupid thing for him to have said. His desire to return to Vancouver got the better of him and he lost control of his thinking.

"I sincerely apologize, Sir, for appearing to make light of my interview with you. I will spend as much time as you feel is necessary to complete the interview."

The old man smiled and then called out to his daughter-in-law, "Martha! Mister Cunningham will be staying for supper."

Cunningham thought to himself, *'If this old coot has his way, by the time I finish this interview, it will be time for the paper to publish my own obituary.'*

"Well, Sir," began the reporter. "As you are aware, our Religion editor of the paper wishes to publish a story about your life as an Anglican minister in Vancouver." He paused and then asked, "Where shall we begin?"

The old man sat still for about a minute without opening his mouth. The reporter could only hear his deep breathing.

"I think that you should forget writing about me and instead write about Russell Hendrix."

"Who is Russell Hendrix?"

"You're not from around here, are you, young man?"

"No, Sir."

Minutes after Reverend Henderson had shocked him with his incredible pronouncement that Jesus Christ had returned to Earth and lived in Nelson and that he was Jesus' best friend, he smiled and said, to the reporter, "Just turn on the machine and lean back, close your eyes and envision what I am telling you."

Cunningham had discovered when he was very young that if anyone told him a story, within a minute, he would be sleeping as the story was being told to him. When he would wake up later, he would remember the story as if he had actually been an unseen witness in the event being told to him.

The reporter turned on the machine, leaned his head back against the back of the sofa, closed his eyes as instructed and waited for what he expected to be an onslaught of pure gibberish. He hoped that within minutes, he would be fast asleep and he could sleep through the entire interview while the recording machine did its work for him.

As the sounds of the grandfather clock in the hallway ticked in the distance, he heard the old man's soft voice as he began telling his story of Russell Hendrix. While he was drifting off to sleep, he hoped that whatever he was going to be told by the old man, the story would at least have some aspects of excitement and interest to him.

The old man started his story by telling the reporter what it was like in that era when Russell arrived in Nelson.

By December 1945, the Second World War had been over for four and a half months. It had been a five-year global war that cost almost fifty-five million lives. It was the year that the first atomic bomb was exploded in the Alamogordo Desert in New Mexico that was later followed by two other atomic bombs being dropped on Japan in August of that same year. It was the year that the miracle drug, penicillin could be given to patients orally. It was this time in history when a C-54 Douglas Spymaster circled the globe non-stop in 149 hours and 44 minutes.

The Christmas season of 1945 was one of joy and serenity. This was the first Christmas since the late 1930s when everything was looking good. Most of the fighting men of the Allied armed forces had returned home and were sharing this Christmas Season with their families and many of them were doing so in the small city of Nelson, like everywhere else in North America.

It has been said however that Christmas is also a time of sadness because there are so many who are alone during this great joyous time of the year. Many families were missing male members who were killed in the war, so sadness encompassed their families also.

By now, Cunningham was fast asleep and in his mind, he was an unseen witness to the events being told to him.

William and Beatrice Hampston were seventy and sixty-four years of age respectively. His hair was white, what little of his hair he had left and her hair was also white however, she had all of her hair. They met in Nelson fifty-nine years earlier as children and were married years later. Sadly, they were never blessed with children. They tried many times but were unsuccessful in their attempts. They had each other and that eased their pain of loneliness to some degree but having no children of their own never ceased to tear at their hearts.

Beatrice's younger sister, Mary had three children; Billy, Maria and Christina. Every third Sunday, she and her husband, Harold and their children used to visit William and Beatrice and sit down to a fine dinner. However, Harold was one of 290 Canadian soldiers who had died in December 1941 while fighting the Japanese in Hong

Kong and when their children grew up and went their own ways; Mary was left alone so she moved back to Toronto to accept a job offer that was given to her by an old school friend.

William and Beatrice had friends but no one ever asked them to join them for a Christmas dinner and when they invited some of their friends to join them, their friends politely declined saying that they had their own families coming to share their Christmas dinners with them. Despite their advanced ages, they both looked fit enough considering all the hard work they put into their farm.

Their forty-five acre farm was on Granite Road, the old highway that runs west from Nelson. Their farm was a little over half a mile from the small hamlet of Tagum Hill, which in itself was a little over four miles west of the center of Nelson.

Their property, fields and forests alike ran approximately five hundred yards north to the western arm of Kootenay Lake with a small creek in the middle of their farm running into the lake.

Calling that body of water north of them a lake was like calling a chapel by the road, a cathedral. Actually, that body of water looked more like a wide river. The lake itself is thirty miles east of Nelson, and is ninety miles long and its average width is two and a half miles.

The Hampston's farm comprised of forty acres and they had five milk cows and forty egg-laying chickens, and along with their old age pensions and William's pension from working on the Canadian National Railroad as a locomotive engineer, what they earned from farming assisted them in their senior years. The farm had been paid for years earlier so other than food, heat and hydro and of course, taxes, they managed to get by on what small income they earned and got from their pensions. Further, Williams was a good carpenter and he would be called upon to do carpentry work in the area. They had a small pickup truck but they rarely ventured into Nelson to buy anything. A daily trip to Nelson on that gas-guzzling pickup would probably have depleted whatever meager income they earned from their cows and chickens and his odd jobs as a carpenter.

The small store in the nearby town of Tagum Hill served their basic needs. They had a large vegetable garden and what they didn't eat in the warm months; they put in their root cellar for the cold months. Their root cellar was always full by the time winter arrived. Their house was a two-story house painted in white and had three bedrooms; two on the upper floor, and one on the main floor. During the winter months, they used the one on the main floor and closed the entrance to the upper floor to conserve heat from their wood-burning stove in the kitchen and the fireplace in the living room.

Despite there being a fireplace in the living room, they didn't spend that much time in the living room but they kept the fire place active in the winter months so that the heat would work its way into their bedroom with the use of a fan blowing warm air into it.

William looked after the cows and Beatrice looked after the chickens. The farm wasn't large enough to grow all the hay he needed for the cows but because of his carpenter work around the area as a part-time carpenter, that added to their joint income, and for this reason, he could afford to buy enough hay from his neighbors who had larger fields of hay, in order to feed his cows in the winter months and chicken feed for his wife's chickens year round.

The red barn wasn't much to admire (as some are) and was in need of fresh paint but it was suffice to meet the needs of sheltering his cows and his wife's chickens from the elements and wild animals. They were much too old to be farming but both were strong and experienced and although they would tire faster than most other farmers decades younger than they were, they managed to operate their farm sufficiently enough to eke out a decent living.

On December 24th, it was apparent to both of them that by the time the sun was setting; a snow blizzard was going to hit the area. The wind was at least forty miles an hour and coupled with the extremely low temperature, it would soon be a blinding storm and freezing outside. Once it began, no one with any sense whatsoever would venture outside lest he or she got lost in the snowdrifts and subsequently perish from the cold.

There was no television in Nelson or anywhere else in the Kootenays those days and their radio reception was poor, being surrounded by mountains with the exception of CKLN, which was Nelson's only radio station. That station as far as they were concerned at that time was only good for the news and weather reports and they didn't need a weather report to tell them that a blizzard would soon been encompassing the entire area.

At ten o'clock, Christmas Eve, the blizzard began in earnest. William and Bernice went to bed and after talking for fifteen minutes, William cuddled up to his wife and they both went to sleep.

Sometime after midnight, Beatrice; who was a light sleeper, woke up with a start. She could hear the cows and chickens making a commotion in the barn. She nudged her husband and said loudly, "Will! Wake up! There is something going on in the barn."

William sat up, cocked his ears in the direction of the window, and exclaimed angrily, "Those damn coyotes have probably slipped into the barn again. I'll get dressed and get my shotgun and go out there and get rid of them once and for all."

William got dressed, not unlike Scott of the Antarctic, grabbed his double-barreled 12-gage shotgun, loaded it with two shells and ventured into the cold blizzard.

It had stopped snowing but it was exhausting work as he fought his way through the deep snow while walking towards the barn. A bright light near his back porch lit his way to it. He fired off a shell from his shotgun in order to scare the coyotes out of the barn. After the echo of the sound of the blast returned from the mountain nearby, he screamed in a loud voice, "Get the hell out of my barn! If you are in the barn when I get there, I'll shoot you dead."

Suddenly, the barn door swung upon and a small figure in dark clothes ran out of the barn and up the snow covered driveway headed towards Granite Road.

'While I'll be damned!' the surprised man said to himself. 'It's a kid. What the hell is one of my neighbor's kids doing in my barn at this time of night?'

William chased after the kid with his flashlight in one hand and his shotgun in the other but being seventy, he wasn't as quick as the kid and by the time he got to Granite Road, he shone is flashlight in the direction of the retreating kid in the distance and saw him pushing a bicycle down the snow-covered road towards Nelson until the snow blowing off the snow drifts obliterated his vision of the fleeing boy.

William returned to the house and told his wife what he had just seen. Then he got out of his clothes and climbed back into his warm bed and snuggled up to the warm body of his wife.

After he lay under the covers for a few minutes, Beatrice said with concern in her voice, "Will. I am worried about that child."

William asked, "Why? He's probably one of the neighbor's delinquent children."

"William," she continued, "You said that the child was going towards Nelson. None of our neighbors east of us have children that young, at least not our neighbors two miles east of us."

William sat up and asked, "What are you trying to say to me?"

Beatrice looked at him rather sadly, "If that child lives in Nelson, he will never reach the city alive. You have to go out there and find him and bring him back here."

"If I go out there in the freezing cold air again and try searching for that kid, I won't arrive back here alive."

"Please, Will." said Beatrice in a pleading voice.

William knew that if he didn't rescue the child and the child's body was later discovered on the road, his wife would never forgive him or let him forget. He realized that the child's death would haunt him also. Those thoughts prompted him to get dressed again for the venture into the darkness and the cold.

He grabbed the keys for his pickup truck and walked to the shed he kept it in and hoped that it would start in the cold weather. It did after a few minutes and with tepidness in his heart, he eased the truck through the deep snow of his long driveway onto Granite Road and began slowly driving towards Nelson.

About fifteen minutes of slowly driving through the deep snow that covered the surface of Granite Road, he saw a glint of silver reflecting from his headlights on the right side of the road. He stopped the truck and got out. As he approached the source of the glint, he recognized it as the inside of one of the wheels of a bicycle. He then looked for signs of the kid but saw nothing.

He noticed a culvert under a driveway leading towards a farm. Because there didn't appear to him to be any footprints leading towards the farm, he decided to look inside the culvert.

The culvert was approximately two feet in diameter. He peeked inside the culvert hoping that his flashlight's beam would shine all the way to the other side. It didn't. What he saw was brown hair on a small form inside the culvert. The boy was about twelve inches or more from the opening of the culvert. He had sought shelter from the cold winds that plagued the area earlier.

William called out. "Slide yourself towards me."

Suddenly he saw the beam of his flashlight reflecting off the eyes of whoever was in the culvert. He presumed it was the boy he had been chasing earlier so he called out again. "Come on out, son. I am going to take you to my home where you can get warm."

The boy inside began wiggling about and slowly inching himself towards the opening. When his hands reached the opening, William grabbed them and pulled the boy out of the culvert. It was the boy he had chased earlier.

He helped the boy climb into the cab of his truck and when the boy was seated, the boy called out, "My bike!"

William walked back to where the bike was laying at the edge of the road and picked it up and placed it in the back of the truck. Then he got back into the truck and after making a three-point turn at the entrance to the driveway leading to the farm nearby, he headed back to his own farm. He spoke to the boy but got no response from him. When William turned on the overhead light, he saw that the boy's eyes were closed. As he kept his hands on the steering wheel and his eyes back on the road, he wondered if he was driving the boy's corpse back to his farm.

When he got to his farm, he drove the truck right up to the kitchen door and after lifting the boy out of the cabin of the truck; he carried him in his arms. His wife opened the door and as he entered the kitchen, his wife gasped, "Is he alive?" William replied, "I don't know."

He carried the boy into the living room and placed him on the sofa that faced the fireplace. His wife put more wood on the fire.

She then placed her two right fingers on his neck and said to William whose face was now showing an expression of deep concern.

"He's got a pulse. Let's get him out of these wet clothes and place him in a blanket."

The boy looked like he was only eight or nine years old. They wondered what a boy that young was doing outside on a night like the one that they were experiencing and at such an ungodly hour.

A few minutes later, Beatrice said to her husband, "I am going sit in the chair next to him and keep the fire burning. You go to bed. If I feel tired, I will wake you and you can take your turn at keeping the fire going."

William agreed and after removing his own clothes, he climbed into his bed. He thought to himself as he began drifting off to sleep. *'I'm glad Beatrice made me go out and rescue the boy. If I hadn't done this, even I could never forgive myself.'*

It wasn't until six thirty in the morning when the sky in the east was beginning to light up. William got up as he did every day at this time of the morning and after putting some warm clothes on, he stepped into the living room. Both his wife and the boy were sound asleep. He saw the boy shift his position on the sofa so he knew that the boy was still alive.

William decided that since his wife needed the sleep and he needed to milk his cows, she would be better off if he slipped out of the house without disturbing her. He looked outside his window and was pleased that it was going to be sunny outside.

The snowdrifts covered much of the area and in some parts; the snow was as much as two feet deep. William spent several hours clearing a pathway to the barn. He knew it would take many more hours to clear his driveway leading to Granite Road.

Three hours later, he returned to the house where his wife was making breakfast.

"The boy is awake." Beatrice said as her exhausted husband was removing his boots. "I told him to rest and I would make him some breakfast."

"Has he told you anything? asked William.

"No, he hasn't. Let's talk to him after breakfast," replied Beatrice.

William nodded his head in the affirmative.

When breakfast was ready, Beatrice went into the living room and after giving the boy a shirt and pants that she had bought for her nephew who was the same age as the boy, but forgot to send it as a Christmas present; she brought the boy to the kitchen. After he sat down, Beatrice and William had a good look at him in the light of day. He had brown hair, his eyes were brown and his teeth looked straight and clean for a boy his age.

William asked in a smooth soft voice. "What's your name, son and how old are you?

The boy looked up at William and said, "I'm Russell Hendrix and I'm nine years old."

William began to ask him where he was from when Beatrice interjected, "Will! Let the boy eat his breakfast before you begin pestering him with your questions."

William smiled at Russell and gestured to the ham and eggs on the boy's plate. The boy smiled back and began eating his breakfast with the same gusto as one who hasn't eaten in a long while. When he was nearly finished, Beatrice put a couple more eggs and another piece of ham on his plate. The boy thanked her and began eating his second helping.

When the three of them were finished eating their breakfasts, Beatrice led Russell into the living room where he could sit on the sofa with her next to the fireplace and keep warm. William sat in a chair across from them.

Then William asked in a quiet voice. "Russell. Where are you from?"

He didn't reply. Beatrice then asked, "Where is your home?"

Again Russell didn't reply.

William asked, "Where are your parents?"

Russell looked up and with tears in his eyes, he replied, "They're dead. They died in a car crash seven years ago."

"Who's looking after you then?" asked Beatrice.

The boy paused and then said, "My uncle." Then he exclaimed, "But I don't want to live with my uncle! He always drinks and beats me whenever I do anything wrong. I ran away several times but the

Children's Aid returned me to him. This time I decided to run away as far as I can from him."

Beatrice asked, "Where does he live?"

Russell thought for a few seconds and then responded, "Are you going to tell him where I am now?"

Beatrice grabbed his hand and softly stroked it. "No, Russell. We aren't going to tell him. We just want to know what city you are from."

"Vancouver." the boy replied softly.

William asked, "How did you get this far from Vancouver?"

Russell replied, "On my bike."

William asked with a tone of surprise in his voice, "You rode your bike all the way here?"

Russell replied, "Yes."

William asked, "Do you have any idea at all how far Vancouver is from here?"

Russell responded in an inquisitive tone, "A hundred miles?"

William smiled and then said, "How about nearly four hundred miles?"

Russell explained, "Wow! Now I know why it has taken me as much as three weeks to get this far."

Beatrice asked, "How have you been eating and where have you been sleeping during your trip?"

Russell smiled and said, "People have been generous. They have given me food and at night, I have slept in sheds and barns to protect myself from the cold."

William smiled and mused to himself, '*That's why he was in my barn.*' He thought it strange that none of the people the boy had met during his journey had reported him to the authorities. If they had, he would have been apprehended before he arrived at his farm. He then looked at the boy and said, "I am terribly sorry that I frightened you when I told you that I would shoot you if I found you in the barn. I thought there were coyotes in the barn."

Russell smiled and replied, "There were coyotes in your barn. There were three of them."

Beatrice asked, "Weren't you afraid of them?"

"No." replied Russell with a grin on his face. "I just stared at them for a few minutes and then I told them to leave and they left."

Beatrice laughed and said, "You are a lot braver than my husband. He wasn't going into that barn unless he was carrying a loaded shotgun."

William looked at his wife and said, "Oh Bea! Stop your nattering. You know that I intended to shoot them if I found them inside the barn."

Russell looked at William and smiled. "If you fired the shotgun inside the barn, I doubt that the cows would have provided you with any milk this morning. That's why my way was better."

William began to ask the boy as to how he knew that cows when frightened are difficult to milk when the boy interrupted him and asked if he could be told where the toilet was. Beatrice told him where it was and while he was in the bathroom, William began to converse with his wife. "Who is this boy? How does a city boy know that firing a shotgun in a barn will frighten the cows to the point that they can't be milked?"

Beatrice then responded, "And more important, who is this boy who can stare at coyotes and order them to leave a barn and the creatures obey him?"

When Russell returned to the living room, Beatrice smiled and said, "Today is Christmas. Would you like to spend your Christmas with us?"

"It's Christmas already?" asked Russell in a startled voice.

Beatrice looked at the boy sadly. She thought to herself, *'You poor boy. You didn't even know what part of December you were in.'*

The three of them had a wonderful Christmas. Although they didn't have any presents for Russell, they made up for that two days later on the 27th when they took him to Nelson and bought him some clothes at a clothing shop on Baker Street.

When it was time to drive to Nelson, William walked along his long driveway leading to Granite Road. The sun was out but he wanted to see if Granite road had been cleared since it had snowed quite heavily the night before.

The road leading to Nelson hadn't been snowplowed but driving to Nelson would be relatively easy as the snow wasn't deep by then.

To both William and Beatrice, the city of Nelson was a place where life was relaxed and people were friendly to one another and to strangers alike. It was a town where time had seemingly stood still. Turn-of-the-century ambiance lingered in every corner from the 350 preserved heritage buildings to the fully restored streetcars.

Nelson is situated on the southern shore of the western arm of the large Kootenay Lake to its east. Its main street is Baker Street where most of the shopping is done. Across the body of water that is approximately a quarter of a mile in width from the town to the shore on the other side is a mountain that is a bit sparse of trees with an imposing cliff (called the Pulpit) part way up the mountain. On the other side of Nelson are two other mountains that converge into a valley leading southward towards the United States border that is a mere 34 miles away.

In 1867, gold and silver were found in the area and Nelson grew quickly as a result of the mining activity. Dozens of other mining communities sprang up along Kootenay Lake. Two railways were routed through Nelson and architect Francis Rattenbury came to Nelson to design granite-hewn, chateau style civic buildings. By 1910, Nelson had its own hydro generating station, street cars, sewer system, and police force. Englishmen came to plant lakeside orchards, and Russian Doukobors, sponsored by Tolstoy and the Quakers, tilled the valleys nearby.

The Depression years saw many work projects improve Nelson's facilities and beauty, including the impressive Nelson Civic Centre: a rink - badminton hall - theatre complex which spawned the Nelson Midsummer curling bonspiel bringing visitors to the community for over 50 years.

When Christmas arrived in 1945, the population of Nelson was less than seven thousand. This time, it was a joyous one for William, Beatrice and their young guest, Russell. It was the first time in years that all three of them really enjoyed themselves at Christmas.

During the days after Christmas, the couple had to make a decision. They wanted to adopt the boy but they knew that was impossible. Besides, they weren't even sure the boy wanted to live with them.

On New Years Eve, while they were sitting in the living room after supper, Beatrice asked Russell if he would like to live with them.

Russell's eyes sparkled when he heard the question. He exclaimed, "Oh, yes. I would like that a lot."

"Well, we will see if that will be possible and if it is possible, then you can consider our home as your home also." said William as he smiled at Russell. William and Beatrice approached him and hugged him. He felt good inside. He hadn't been hugged in years. He was so pleased about their offer. Up to then, he had never lived in a home that was so grand.

Russell liked his bedroom because it was the first one he ever slept in that he could call his own. Prior to that, he slept on a cot in his uncle's bedroom in his uncle's one-bedroom house.

As Russell looked towards the front entrance of the Hampston house, he mused to himself; *At last, a door has been opened to me, just as Mathew foretold in the scriptures that it would.*

Sirach, 7, 37: Reflect on the statutes of the Lord, and meditate at all times on his commandments. It is he who will give insight to your mind, and your desire for wisdom will be granted.

Chapter 2

On January 2nd, 1946, William contacted an old friend of his who was a sergeant in the Nelson Police Department and asked him to make enquiries with the police in Vancouver to see if Russell was reported missing there.

The next day, William's friend contacted him and gave him the good news. Russell wasn't reported as missing. From that information, William deduced that Russell's uncle didn't want the boy anymore and for this reason, he hadn't report him missing. His friend also gave William the name and address of the boy's uncle.

William thought to himself, *'I think Beatrice and I can risk contacting the boy's uncle if I write him and tell him that we are willing to care for his nephew.'*

Four days later, he received a reply from Russell's uncle and in the letter; he thanked William for offering to care for his nephew.

William was able to get an abstract from Kerrisdale Elementary School in Vancouver where Russell did his grade four after writing the principal of the school telling him that he was the boy's grandfather. However, Beatrice and William suspected that there might be a problem getting him accepted into the school in Nelson because they weren't his legally adoptive foster parents.

Nevertheless, they took Russell to the Nelson Elementary School on Stanley Street on January 8th. When they got to the front office, they met the principal who fortunately didn't know them. If he knew them, he would think it strange that they had a grandson considering that they never had children of their own.

William began, "I'm William Hampston and this is my wife Beatrice and this is our grandson, Russell Roberts. His parents are dead and we have taken on the responsibility of caring for him. We have his abstract from his school in Vancouver." Within twenty minutes, Russell was taken to his grade four class.

At 3:00 in the afternoon, William was waiting for him at the entrance of the school and then they headed home in his pickup.

On the way home, William turned to Russell and said, "A mile west of our farm is a family with an eight-year-old boy. His father has agreed to pick you up at our home beginning tomorrow and take you to school and then bring you back home. He is Mister Henderson. His son, Lawrence is a nice boy. You will like him. He's going to the same school as you are and he is in grade three."

The next morning, Lawrence and his father arrived and Lawrence knocked on the door while his father waited in the car. When he was let in, William introduced him to Russell.

Lawrence was a bit shorter than Russell and had an infectious smile. Once anyone saw him smiling, they tended to smile along with him. His hair was light brown and his eyes were the same color.

William said to Russell, "This is Lawrence."

Lawrence smiled and said, "Actually, I'm Larry."

"Hi Larry." said Russell with a smile that matched that of his newfound friend.

On the way to Nelson, they talked and Russell could see that he was going to like his new friend. Later in the day, they met during the recess and the lunch hour and every recesses and lunch hours thereafter.

Russell and Larry would spend alternate weekends at each other's home. Russell began to think of Larry's parents as his second parents. Larry's mother was in her thirties and it seemed to Russell as if she was treating him as her second son. They became quite close and he often asked her for advice.

He loved William and Bernice and regarded them as his real surrogate parents but they were old enough to be his grandparents and he thought of them in that way. Larry's parents on the other hand were closer to the age of what he envisioned his real parents would be and he regarded Larry more than just his best friend; he thought of him as a brother he never had.

Sometime in April 1946, Russell expressed a willingness to attend bible study at the Anglican Church in Nelson on Wednesday evenings after supper. It wasn't long before the assistant minister Rev. James Wilson began to realize that Russell was very conversant with both the New and the Old Testaments.

One Wednesday evening, the assistant minister, asked the ten students a question.

"How did Jesus die?"

All the students; ranging in years from ten to fifteen, raised their hands with the exception of Russell.

The minister pointed to one of the students and the student said, "He bled to death on the cross."

The minister asked the others, "Is he right?"

The students, with the exception of Russell nodded their heads in the affirmative.

The minister turned to Russell and said, "I see that you didn't nod your head to confirm that you also believe that Jesus died by bleeding to death."

"That's not how Jesus died." replied Russell.

One of the students snarled, "If you're so smart, then you tell us how Jesus died."

Russell immediately responded with, "Did I ever tell you or anyone else that I am smart?"

Another student said angrily, "When the soldier stuck his spear into Jesus' side, no blood came out. That's because there was no blood left in his body. He bled to death."

Russell turned to his second tormentor and replied, "If you were to die right this instant, would you still have all of your blood inside of you?"

His tormentor replied in an inquisitive tone "Yeah."

"And if you were dead and someone then stuck a knife into you, would all of your blood run out of you?

"Of course." replied his tormentor.

Russell continued. "None of your blood would run out of your body. Your heart pumps your blood throughout your body while you are alive but when you are dead, your heart is also dead and is therefore unable to pump your blood around your body or out of your body. Jesus was already dead. His heart was dead and thus, a very small amount of his blood came out of his body when the soldier's spear was withdrawn from Jesus' side and that's why more water than blood came out."

One of the students said in a quizzical tone of voice, "Why did water come out?"

Russell smiled and responded. "Considering that the water content of a human body is as much as seventy percent, I am not surprised that a bit of water came out of the wound."

Another student asked sarcastically, "Alright Russell. You know so much. Tell us how Jesus died then."

"He suffocated to death."

The students were aghast. Some uttered statements like "You're crazy" and "He's nuts."

When it became quiet again, Russell continued, "Have you ever wondered why the soldiers broke the legs of the two thieves who were on the cross but they didn't break Jesus' legs?"

No one spoke.

Russell continued again. "Not all condemned prisoners had their wrists nailed to a cross. Many were simply suspended by their wrists with rope and if their feet were nailed to the post or tied to the post, they were left to die while suspended by their wrists from the crossbeam. Most lived for days, slowly dying of thirst in the hot sun. However, eventually, they all died from suffocation."

The young assistant minister asked, "Can you explain that?"

Russell continued. "When they were suspended by their wrists and their feet were nailed or tied to the post, their diaphragms; that which made it possible for their lungs to breathe in air and exhale; were pulled upwards as a direct result of the muscles of their arms and their sides exerting pressure against their diaphragms. They could breathe in but once they breathed in air, they couldn't exhale and if they couldn't exhale, then they couldn't breathe in anymore. The only way they could stop their muscles from putting upward pressure against their diaphragms, was to stand up. If their feet were merely tied to the post, they would have to remain awake all the time they were suspended on the cross otherwise they would suffocate when they fell asleep."

"But Jesus was nailed to the cross, not tied to the cross." said one of the students.

Russell responded with, "That's because the Romans wanted him to suffer for the four or five hours he was on the cross because they knew that they would have to remove him from the cross before the afternoon was over."

"Why?" asked one of the students.

The minister replied to the question, "The Romans went along with some of the customs of the Jews in those days and one of the customs was that no one was to remain on the cross during the Sabbath. The Jewish Sabbath begins at mid Friday afternoon and ends late afternoon the following day. Jesus was crucified during early Friday afternoon."

Russell then said, "The pain Jesus suffered was excruciating with the nails in his wrists and feet and made worse by the fact that when he tried to stand up on the small block of wood nailed to the post in which his feet could rest, his suffering even more excruciating with the nails tearing away at the flesh of his wrists and feet. He would have to stand up and pull himself up every ten or more seconds and every time he did this, the nails tore at his flesh thereby increasing his pain. It was a horrible way to die."

One of the students asked, "Couldn't he just remain standing? That would release the pressure exerted against his diaphragm."

Russell replied, "Have you noticed that every picture or statue of Jesus shows him slumped downwards with his knees protruding outward? That is because the soldiers didn't place the block of wood at the bottom of his feet with his legs straight down. By placing the block a foot up the pole, it meant that he had to exert himself to stand up to release the pressure against his diaphragm and to make matters worse, the block slopped downwards which meant he had to pull himself up also, thereby increasing the pain against his wrists also."

The room was very quiet. All anyone could hear was the breathing of everyone in it. Then one of the boys said while shaking his head, "The nails were driven in his hands, not his wrists."

Russell turned to the boy and asked, "How do you know that?"

"Because all the pictures I have ever seen of Jesus on the cross shows nails driven through his hands."

Russell smiled and said, "The painters were not there so there is no way that they would know."

Another boy snarled, "Were you there when he was hanging from the cross?"

The other boys laughed.

Russell responded to the question quietly, "The human hands would not support the weight of a body if nails were driven in between the bones of the hands." Then he paused for a moment and then added, "However, if the nails were driven in the wrists just where the two bones of the lower arms meet the three bones at the beginning of the hands, the wrists would not be torn from the nails."

The young minister sat in his chair, his eyes transfixed in wonderment at Russell. Even when he was studying at the Seminary, he had always been under the impression that the nails had been driven in Jesus' hands. Not one of his teachers told him anything that was different. What he was now hearing from the nine-year-old boy made a lot of sense to him.

Russell continued, "They didn't break Jesus' legs like they did with the other two men on the crosses next to him because when the spear was stuck into him and he didn't bleed or move, the Romans knew that he was dead and there was no need for them to break his legs so that he couldn't stand up again to release the pressure against his diaphragm."

One of the students asked, "How come Jesus died so quickly?"

Russell smiled at the student and said, "I hardly think hanging on a cross under those circumstances for three or four hours is dying quickly but one has to presume that he had the will power to simply let himself suffocate so that his death would come quickly when he was ready to die."

Another student asked, "If he had the will power to let himself suffocate and thereby end his suffering, why didn't he do that as soon as he was nailed to the cross?"

The minister cut in and said, "I think that we can discuss that next Wednesday."

When they were all walking out of the room, the assistant minister spoke softly to Russell when he said, "I think you got their attention and respect. You certainly got mine."

From then on, Russell's life was to change and that change would eventually have an effect on a great many of the people living in Nelson.

Within a couple of days, there wasn't a student in the school who hadn't heard of the kid in grade four who appeared to know more about the *Bible* than even a church minister.

In the following week during the recesses and noon hours, the students would gather around him in the gymnasium and ask him questions about the *Bible*. The questions were challenging to Russell but he tried his best to answer them. He knew by then that the students respected him for his knowledge and he was careful not to mislead them on biblical facts. Larry was always with him at these gatherings.

Another twenty-two of the students from the school joined the Anglican Church Bible Study Group to hear Russell talk about Jesus and his disciples. The assistant minister conducted the sessions but it was Russell whom they came to hear.

One Wednesday evening in March, the assistant minister asked the students a question. "Where does God live?"

Several of the students said he lived in the church because it is called the house of God. Then they looked at Russell as if to ask him to confirm their answer.

Russell looked at the minister and the latter nodded to him giving him the OK to answer that question if he chose to do so.

Russell thought for a short while and then said, "If we love one another, God lives in all of us. He is within us even when we are asleep. He doesn't need a church or other holy place to live in. He is everywhere."

"Then," asked one of the students, "why do church ministers tell us that their church is the house of the Lord?"

Russell replied, "You have to ask them. I think of a church or other holy place as a house of worship."

The assistant minister then asked Russell, "Didn't King Solomon build a temple for the Lord and call it the House of the Lord?"

Russell smiled and replied, "Yes, he did but we have to remember that in Corinthians, the *Bible* also says, "We are the temple of the living God and still do you not know that your body is a temple of the Holy Spirit?"

Russell paused and then continued. "God is everywhere and since he is everywhere all at once, his houses are the places of worship as much as our bodies are. If God is inside everyone and is also everywhere, it doesn't make sense to say that God only lives in houses of worship."

The students just stared at Russell in awe.

The next morning, the assistant minister spoke with the minister of the church. "I want to tell you about one of our *Bible* study students."

Russell, William and Beatrice were getting along just fine as a family. Russell didn't give them any trouble whatsoever. He helped them with the farm chores without being asked. They treated him as if he was their own flesh and blood. The three of them realized in their own minds that their living together as a family was the best thing that happened to each of them in a long time.

Larry was his best friend. But he was more than that. Russell thought of Larry as being like John the Baptist, preaching to anyone who would listen to him telling them that Russell was someone that should be listened to. And listen to him, the students at the *Bible* study group and many students at the elementary school did.

But the students at school didn't just gather around Russell to hear him preach about Jesus and God. They asked him for advice about love, relationships, their parents and anything else that was on their minds.

It became apparent fairly quickly to the teachers at the elementary school that they had in their midst, a very remarkable student. His marks were always 'A's but more important, he was a leader whom the students admired and followed. What really amazed them was that when Russell spoke, it seemed that he was speaking as an adult with a command of the English language. They didn't realize that when he lived in Vancouver, he spent much of his time in the local library to keep away from his uncle as much as he could and over the years, his vocabulary increased far above students who were years older than he was.

One day in May, Russell came across a confrontation in the playing field between two students. A large crowd of students surrounded the two adversaries. Russell moved past the students and was finally within a few feet of the two fighting students. The two boys stopped fighting and looked at him.

Russell then said to them, "If each of you had an opportunity to strike the other without restraint, how many times would you hit the other?"

One of them said, "Lots." The other responded in the same manner.

"If I let both of you strike me a lot, would that be suffice to reduce your anger towards each other to the point where you can walk away from this fight without either of you striking another blow to the other?"

The two boys looked sheepishly at each other. To continue the fight would be embarrassing and to strike Russell would be even worse. Russell then said, "Perhaps the three of us can go somewhere and see if we can resolve this problem between you."

As the three of them began to walk away, the crowd of students dissipated. Russell and the other two boys found a place where they could be alone. The two boys resolved their differences in minutes.

Later Larry asked Russell, "Would you really have let those two guys hit you a lot?"

Russell smiled and replied, "As hard as they want, Larry. Let me tell you something about a person's credibility."

In the last week of May, Larry got permission from his parents to join Russell for a weekend where the two of them would climb to the top of Granite Mountain and spend the night there. When the two boys reached the top, they found a small but beautiful clearing comprising of grass surrounded by cedar and fir trees. They found a flat rock nearby where they could build a small campfire.

"Those cedar trees will keep the mosquitoes away from us," said Russell happily.

They ventured outside the clearing to cut down small branches from the fir trees to build a lean-to to protect them from the rain. It didn't appear that they needed anything to protect them from the wind, as there didn't appear to be any wind blowing through the cedar trees except a slight warm breeze.

"If I ever have to be alone," said Russell, "this is where I will go." Then he added, "We have to keep this place a secret."

Larry agreed.

They watched the sunset from a nearby outcrop at the top of the mountain and after they roasted some of the meat they brought with them and ate bannock and warmed themselves with the fire, they lay down beside the fire and watched the sparks go upwards towards the stars in the sky while they talked about everything except religion.

One Saturday morning during the month of June, Russell and Larry began hiking around the woods at the base of Granite Mountain. An hour later, the boys sat at the edge of a small cliff that was twenty feet in height and talked about life in general and girls in particular. They were only eight and nine respectively but the girls in their school had not gone unnoticed by the two young boys.

Around two in the afternoon, Larry stood up and when moving forward, he tripped over a protruding root of a tree and fell down the small cliff. He banged his head on the way down. When Russell reached Larry; his friend was unconscious.

Half an hour later, Larry came too and complained that his right leg hurt. They discovered that it was broken. Also, there was deep a gash in his scalp.

"Russell. Go get some help." cried Larry.

"I can't leave you here by yourself." responded Russell.

"You must. I can't move my leg at all and you're not strong enough to carry me."

Russell knew that Larry was right. It took him an hour to get to Larry's home and when he arrived, he told Larry's parents what had happened. One of them phoned several of their neighbors and within ten minutes, there were four men at the door of Larry's home.

"Russell. Lead us to my son." said Larry's father.

Approximately an hour later, they arrived at the foot of the cliff. Larry was unconscious. The five men lifted Larry up and carried him to Granite Road and waited for William's pickup that was being driven up and down the road looking for Larry's rescuers. They laid Larry onto a small mattress that had been placed in the back of the pickup and then the vehicle carrying Larry, his parents and William and Russell sped along Granite Road towards Nelson.

They arrived at the Kootenay Lake District Hospital on View Street around five in the late afternoon. Fifteen minutes later, they were told that Larry was still unconscious and that the doctors suspected that he was brain dead.

An hour later, the doctor came out of Larry's room and told Larry's parents that their son had just died. Russell could see from the reaction of Larry's parents that the worst had happened. His best friend was gone forever.

He ran into the room and looked at Larry's face. There was no sign of pain in his friend's face. Russell knelt beside the bed and folded his hands together and cried. Then he began talking to Larry. "Larry. You cannot leave us now. You have more of the Lord's work to do."

Then Russell closed his eyes and cried out, "Lord. Please don't take my friend into your bosom at this time. I need him. Let him come back to us so that he may serve you later."

Russell looked down at Larry's face and began to cry again. Then suddenly Larry's eyes slowly opened and he called out to Russell. "I'm glad you're here, Russell. I knew you would come."

Larry's parents upon hearing their son's voice, ran into his room. His mother screamed. "Doctor! He's alive! My son is alive!"

The doctor and several nurses rushed into the room. Larry's mother pointed to Russell and exclaimed, "This boy brought my son back to life."

"Incredible!" exclaimed the doctor. "Your son's heart had definitely stopped. The heart monitor had flat-lined. It showed that his heart had stopped."

Larry's father responded. "Well the heart monitor is showing that his heart is beating now and we owe it all to Russell, Larry's best friend."

Both of Larry's parents hugged Russell and Larry's mother repeatedly kissed him.

The nurses ran down the hall telling other nurses on that floor that they had just witnessed a miracle. A nine-year-old boy had just brought a dead boy back to life.

By the end of the next day, there wasn't anyone in Nelson who hadn't heard about the miracle in the hospital. It was then that Russell had been given another name. People began calling him Jesus Boy and his best friend, Larry, was called Lazarus.

Acts, chapter 19, 11: And God did extraordinary miracles by the hands of Paul.

Chapter Three

Larry was released from the hospital three weeks after his return to life and he and Russell then became almost inseparable. But life for both of them was never to be the same after that.

Students at school began calling Russell, JB for Jesus Boy and even adults who recognized him on the street after seeing his picture in the newspaper would cross the street just to shake his hand and talk to him. And when Larry was with him, they called him the miracle boy or Lazarus.

One day when Russell was talking to a small gathering of students in the school's playing field, he was asked how he brought Larry back to life.

Russell responded with, "It was not I who brought Larry back to life. It was God. I merely asked God to do this for me."

Larry who was standing next to Russell smiled and said, "It was the strangest feeling I ever experienced. It was like I was in a dream."

One of the girls asked him, "What were you dreaming?"

"I dreamed that I was going into a dark room and then I heard Russell talking to someone and I soon realized that he was talking to me. I wanted to reply but my mouth wouldn't open. Then I heard Russell talking to someone else but whomever he was talking too, that person didn't reply either. Then all of a sudden, I felt myself leaving the dark room and I was in a room that was bright white. I wanted to see what was causing the brightness so I opened my eyes and then

I realized that I was staring at the light in the ceiling. Then I saw Russell standing by the side of my bed."

One of the boys said, "Larry. If Russell hadn't been in that room. You probably would have died."

"I know." replied Larry. "But in actual fact, I was already dead when Russell came into the room. My doctor said that my heart had stopped beating and had not been beating for at least a minute before Russell entered my room. The doctor had given me up for dead. He said that the dark room I was entering in was really my brain shutting down."

One of the boys laughed and said, "I think I will still call you Lazarus because Russell, I mean, JB brought you back from the dead just like Jesus brought the original Lazarus back to life."

Russell quickly responded angrily, "I didn't bring him back from the dead! God brought him back from the dead!"

The boy then said to Russell, "When I am dying, I hope you will be around to ask God to bring me back to life."

Another boy asked, "Can you cure the sick?"

Russell laughed and said, "I can't even cure myself. Last week I had a toothache and I prayed to God to stop the pain. It didn't help. I finally had to go to a dentist. He stopped the pain when he gave me freezing in my gums."

The students laughed. One of the students spoke to another and said, "I think Russell can cure those who are ill. Anyone who has God as a friend and can call on God to bring his friend back to life can surely cure the sick."

It was soon after that, that rumors of Russell healing others began circulating around town. Many asked the clergymen of the Protestant churches and the Catholic Church if such a possibility was true. The clergymen weren't sure how to answer those queries. They added however that the boy was right about one thing. It is God who cures the ill, not a nine-year-year-old boy.

When the end of June came about, a traveling evangelist came into Nelson and rented the main auditorium of the Civic Center on Vernon Street. He was a man of about fifty years of age, sported a large mustache and dressed like a Texan with a broad brimmed hat and thin tape-like necktie. He had a Texan drawl. Over a thousand of the faithful came to hear him preach. Most of them were Doukobors. They were the Russian peasants who immigrated to Canada in the early part of the century and who lived on surrounding farms. When they sang hymns at public gatherings, they sang them in three-part harmony.

The evangelist had heard of Russell and co-opted Russell into appearing on stage with him for the purpose of reading from the scriptures. In actual fact, he really wanted Russell on the stage to add credibility to his own appearance in front of the large gathering of people who came to the auditorium to worship.

When Russell walked onto the stage, many of those in the crowd knelt onto their knees and began singing even louder. They believed that Russell really was Jesus and that he had returned to Earth again as a child.

The evangelist saw this and realized that there was a great opportunity for him to milk Russell's presence for all its worth.

He cried out in a loud voice, "My children. The Lord has sent us this young boy to minister among us and cure those of you who are ill."

The crowd called out in unison, "Halleluiah! Halleluiah!"

Russell was startled by this pronouncement by the evangelist. He didn't think he was going to be called upon to cure the sick. It was his understanding with the evangelist that he was only going to be called upon to read from the scriptures. The man who purported to serve God had betrayed him.

The crowd then began calling out in unison, "Jesus! Jesus! Jesus!"

Russell walked to the microphone and when all was quiet, he spoke softly. He said, "Despite what has been said of me, I am not Jesus. My name is Russell and I am an ordinary boy who has the gift of remembering everything I read, hear and see and the gift of being able to preach to others what I believe God wants them to hear."

There was a hush in the auditorium.

A voice rang out from the audience. "You raised the dead a month and a half ago. Surely you can cure those of us who are ill."

The evangelist responded loudly, "Of course he can!"

Russell spoke again, "I don't wish to contradict the evangelist but I must say this. "I called upon God to save my friend and it was God and not I, who saved him. We can all call upon God at any time to help us when we are in need. Sometimes God grants our requests but often he does not. Why he does not, I have no explanation to give you."

The evangelist was not one to lose an opportunity when he saw one, so he said, "I have an explanation. God listens to some people and not to others. He listened to this boy and when he did, his friend came back to life."

The crowd began chanting, "Halleluiah! Halleluiah!"

Russell was in a predicament. He knew he really couldn't cure anyone of their illness and if he tried to do it in the auditorium and failed, no one after that would ever take him seriously again. There was no one he could turn to for help. Then he began looking upward and the crowd became silent again.

He began, "Lord. We are all in need of help from you. Some of us will receive your help and others you may choose not to help at this time. We will not ask of you why you choose to ignore some of us but we will rely on your mercy and wisdom nevertheless and pray to you for your help."

The crowd shifted uneasily in their chairs.

Russell continued, "Lord, if there are any with us today whom you have chosen to ease their pain, please do it for them for they truly believe in you and seek your mercy."

Russell was smart enough to realize that the easing of pain is a lot easier to come about than asking God to make the blind suddenly be able to see and the lame suddenly be able to walk.

Then a voice rang out, "The pain in my back is gone! It's gone!"

While the crowd began singing out phrases like, "Praise to the Lord", more voices cried out, "The pain is gone!" and "I don't feel the pain anymore!" and "The pain has left me!"

It was at this time, that Russell decided he better leave the auditorium as quickly as he could. He knew if he stayed, he would be called upon to do miracles in God's name, miracles he might not be able to fulfill. As soon as he saw an exit door, he walked to it and then left the building and ran westward on Vernon Street as fast as he could lest others follow him and catch up to him.

Within hours, the 'miracles' that occurred in the auditorium of the Civic Center was on the lips of almost everyone in Nelson and the environs. They were now convinced that Jesus Christ had returned as a child and had blessed them by choosing to live in their community and raise their loved ones from the dead and save them from their pain and misery.

Within days, the story hit major newspapers across Canada and the United States. As a result of the stories, thousands of people from other towns and cities swarmed into Nelson, seeking the boy whom the townspeople called Jesus.

Russell knew that it wouldn't be long before they discovered where he lived, so he told the Hampstons that he was going to climb to the top of the mountain where the curious and the faithful could not follow him. While on the top of the mountain, he would seek God's guidance on what to do next.

Beatrice gave Russell a packsack with food. She then kissed him while William hugged him and in less than a minute, Russell was out of the house and heading towards the path that led upwards from Granite Road.

Within a minute, he was out of their sight and on his way up Granite Mountain; disappearing into the forest of evergreen trees that blanketed the mountain.

An hour after he arrived at his clearing at the summit of the mountain, he began putting more branches over his lean-to and after building a warm fire, he knelt down and looked up at the blue sky.

Lord." he began. "Please help me. I do not want to be thought of as Jesus, your son. I want to live my life as an ordinary person. I was born as an ordinary person and I want to die as an ordinary person. If you have given me powers that are similar to those you gave Jesus, your son, please take these powers from me. I will serve you in any other way you choose."

Later in the early evening, he stood up and faced the setting sun and began addressing God again. "I love the Hampstons. They have cared for me as their own. It is the first time in my life that I have been treated as a real son. Please, I beg of you. Don't force me to leave them to escape the exaltation from others that I don't deserve."

A few hours later he went to sleep beside the fire. Sometime in the middle of the night when the fire was reduced to red embers, he began to dream. He dreamed that he was on small hill close to a high stonewall in which three men were suspended on three crosses. He moved amongst the small crowd near the crosses and then moved towards the man in the middle whom he thought looked like the pictures of Jesus he had seen in paintings. As he looked up at the face of the man in the middle who in turn was looking upward, he thought he could hear the man's voice speaking to him.

He was puzzled because although he didn't see the man's lips move, he thought he heard his voice. The man on the middle cross then looked down at Russell and said, "I have sacrificed myself for you and yet you refuse to sacrifice yourself for me."

In his dream, Russell tried to speak but he couldn't.

The man on the cross continued to speak. "Has my sacrifice become meaningless? Do you not want to continue your service to Mankind in my name and that of our Father?

In his dream, Russell nodded his head in the affirmative.

The voice continued. "You have asked our Father to let you be an ordinary person. But our Father gave us the power to heal, which we could use to serve others. Do you really wish to throw away those powers he gave you?"

In his dream, Russell moved his head up and down to confirm that that was his wish.

"Then," said the voice, "you must continue your work in my name and that of our Father as others have and bear the pain as they and I did for the other gifts our father gave you did not come to you without a price."

After a minute had passed, the man on the cross spoke again. "You have asked our Father to take away the power of healing from you. He has heard you. It is up to you to convince those that believe in you that you do not have the power to heal or raise the dead. You must convince them that only our Father and I have that power."

"But," asked Russell, "How will I do that? Everyone believes that I have the power to heal."

The man spoke to Russell sadly, "Their belief with be the burden you will have to carry with you for the rest of your life. You must convince those who believe in you that only our Father and I have the power to raise the dead and heal the sick. He has left you with your gifts of remembering everything you read, hear and see and the gift of persuasion. You must teach those that are willing to listen to you that they must seek their healing by offering their prayers to my mother, Mary, our Father or me and tell them that it is their prayers alone that will heal them."

Russell added, "How long must I do this?"

The voice replied, "As my life was cut short, so will yours. You must serve our Father in whatever time you have left. When you are finished with his work, as my Father has rewarded me, so will he reward you."

"When will I die?" asked Russell, his lips trembling when asking that question.

The voice replied in a firm voice, "As I did not seek the answer to that question, neither should you." The voice continued, "As my death was not an easy one for me, so will your death not be an easy one for you. But rejoice when the moment of your death is nigh, for if you have served our Father and me faithfully and honestly and believe in us, our Father and I will be with you then and forever after in paradise."

Russell trembled in his dream. The voice continued again, "You must keep this meeting between us forever secret in your heart for none will believe you should you decided to discuss with others as to what I have said to you."

Suddenly, there was a bright flash of light and a loud roaring noise in Russell's ears. The image of the man began to fade along with the crosses and the hill he was standing on in his dream.

Russell sat up with a start. It was pouring rain and suddenly there was another flash of lightening and in less than a second, he heard the roar of thunder ringing in his ears again.

Russell was puzzled and asked himself a rhetorical question. *'How can I serve God if I no longer have the power to heal? Will anyone listen to me anymore when it becomes obvious to them that I am no miracle boy but rather just an ordinary nine-year-old boy?'*

Then he asked himself another rhetorical question. *'Is being just an ordinary boy going to be such a bad thing?'*

Luke, chapter 4, 5-6: And the devil took him up, and showed him all the kingdoms of the world in a moment of time, and said to him, "To you I will give all this authority and their glory; for it has been delivered to me, and I give it to whom I will.

John, chapter 9, 25: Whether he is a sinner, I do not know; one thing I know, that though I was blind, now I see.

Chapter Four

By nine in the morning, the rain had subsided and the morning sun began to dissipate the fog which had earlier covered the top of the mountain. By one in the afternoon, the sky was blue, the grass was dry, and a warm breeze was blowing through the cedars and into the clearing.

Suddenly Russell heard a noise in the area of the cedars east of him. He turned in the direction of the noise and saw a man coming into the clearing. It was the evangelist.

"Hello Russell. I am so pleased to meet you in such a beautiful setting."

Russell wasn't pleased at this chance meeting at all. The last person he wanted to see was this evangelist who had earlier betrayed him.

"You betrayed me." Russell said angrily. "You told the people in the Civic Center that I could cure them of their illnesses. I never told you that I could."

"My son," replied the evangelist in a smooth voice. "You cured some of them in that auditorium. They cried out that they felt no more pain."

Russell responded angrily, "I told them then and I am telling you now, that it was their faith in God that cured them, not I."

The evangelist paused to think and then said, "I think you have misunderstood your role in the service of God. He wants you to offer your prayers to him on behalf of others in need and I and my organization can help you achieve that righteous goal."

Russell remembered his dream the night before and then said, "If I am to offer my services to God, it will be to teach others to pray directly to God for help and to understand that not all of their prayers will be answered. I will teach them that they can do no wrong by at least praying to God for help to resolve some of their own problems."

The evangelist then replied, "If you come with me and let me lead you onto the right path, you will become a very rich man. Thousands of people donate money to our organization for us to make it possible for many people to attend our evangelistic meetings and as a member of our leadership team in our organization; you will reap the same rewards that I do. You will be chauffeured about, live in a luxurious home of your own and be powerful, for many will fear you just as they will love you. In the end, the world will be yours."

Russell immediately retorted, "Whatever gifts that have been given to me by God are not to be abused by me so that I can become rich, powerful and feared and loved at the same time. Jesus was not a rich man and yet he accomplished much by preaching in the manner in which he did."

"And look how he ended up." laughed the evangelist. "Nailed to a cross, abandoned by his God."

"It is true that Jesus in his final hour asked God why he had forsaken him but do you really think that God abandoned him? If he had, would Jesus have been resurrected again?"

The evangelist pondered that question and then asked Russell, "Is it your wish then to die as Jesus did?"

"No one in his right mind would choose to die a horrible death like he did but if it is God's intention that I must die a horrible death, who am I to question such a determination by God?"

"So you don't wish to become rich and powerful while preaching about God?"

Russell replied immediately to that question. His answer was short and to the point. "Not at the expense of my soul."

With no expectation of changing Russell's mind, the evangelist turned and without another word, walked through the cedars and out of Russell's life forever.

By six that afternoon, Russell returned home and Beatrice hugged him and said, "I am glad that you stayed on the mountain overnight. There were hundreds of people swarming all over our property looking for you. We told them that you were visiting relatives a hundred miles away. They finally gave up searching for you and left."

Russell spent the next two weeks with his adopted 'parents' and at Larry's home and he was extremely happy during those two weeks. During that time, he learned how the evangelist had learned where Russell had been when he was on the mountaintop. Unfortunately, Larry had inadvertently let it slip when the evangelist asked him as to where Russell had been. Russell forgave his friend for that mistake.

It was in the middle of July that the minister of the Anglican Church where he attended *Bible* study visited him at the Hampston farm.

"Russell." he began. "You have created quite a quandary for the church leaders in Nelson."

Russell replied, "It was not my intention to do so, Reverend."

"I know, my son. We're not faulting you for anything that you have done. In fact, the ministers and the bishop of both the protestant and Catholic Churches have nothing but admiration for you."

"Then why are you here, Reverend?"

The minister paused and then said, "We would like you to join us for a meeting so that perhaps we can help you decide what your future in the service of our Lord can be."

"I'm not sure that I—"

The minister cut him off. "Trust me, my son. We have nothing but the best interests of you at heart. The meeting will not be an inquisition, I promise you."

Russell replied, "Let me think on it."

"You can call us when you are ready." And with that statement, the minister bade his farewell.

For the following week, Russell and Larry went on hikes in the mountains and forests together and not once did they talk about God, Jesus or the *Bible*. Russell enjoyed himself as most children of his age do during warm summer months. They loved it in the forests and fields and spent much of their time in them, exploring them.

During the last week of August, Russell knew that he would have to meet the clergymen of Nelson eventually so he arranged to meet them on the following Wednesday, August 29th.

Just after lunch, the minister of the Anglican Church where he attended *Bible* study, picked him up from his home and drove him into Nelson. "Russell." he began. "It has been decided that there will only be three other clergymen meeting with you. We represent the Anglicans, the United Church, the Lutherans, and the Catholics." Russell wasn't too happy about meeting with the clergymen and the expression on his face made that obvious to the Anglican minister.

"Let me assure you, Russell that you will be treated with respect." The minister continued, "It's just that we would like to get to know you a bit better and see how we can help you in your quest to serve our Lord." They arrived at the vicarage of the Anglican Church and when they entered the minister's living room, the other three clergymen who were standing near a table talking to one another. They turned around and shook Russell's hand and thanked him for coming to see them. After some brief refreshments, they all sat down in a circle of chairs, which had been brought into the living room. The bishop began the interview. "Russell. We recognize the fact that you are an extremely remarkable boy. We also have no doubts that you are very conversant with the teachings of Jesus Christ, our Lord."

The Lutheran minister then said, "Further, we believe that you are truly a very devoted Christian."

The Anglican Church minister then asked, "Do you believe that Christ is returning to Earth to minister amongst the peoples of the world?"

Russell replied, "Of course!"

The Lutheran minister then asked, "Do you believe that you are Christ who has returned as a child?"

Russell knew that sooner of later that question would be put to him. He just didn't think it would be that soon into the meeting. He thought for a minute while the clergymen leaned forward to hear his answer. Then he replied in a soft voice.

"Let me ask you a rhetorical question. Did any of you believe when you were a nine-year-old boy; that someday you would minister to a congregation in your church?"

There was no reply. The answer was obvious. They did not.

Russell continued, "Do you believe that when Jesus was a twelve-year-old boy working with his father in carpentry, that he believed that one day he would be preaching to the Jews?"

Russell paused and before the clergymen could reply to his question, he said, "Just as I have asked you a question you cannot answer, you are asking me a question of which I too have no answer."

The Catholic bishop responded to Russell's reply, "Jesus preached to the priests of the temple when he was twelve. He had to have known that was going to happen before it happened, is that not so?"

Russell replied, "In Luke, chapter two, it says, and I will quote as best as I can."

The clergymen shifted uneasily. They had heard that this boy could memorize beyond what anyone else in Nelson could do. They opened their *Bibles* to Luke, chapter two.

Now his parents went to Jerusalem every year at the feast of the Passover. When he was twelve years old, they went up according to custom and when the feast was ended, as they were returning, the boy Jesus stayed behind in Jerusalem. His parents did not know it, but supposing him to be in the company, they went a day's journey, and they sought him among their kinsfolk and acquaintances and when they did not find him, they returned to Jerusalem, seeking him. After three days they found him in the temple, sitting among the teachers, listening to them and asking them questions and all who heard him were amazed at his understanding and his answers.

The clergymen sat there transfixed at what they had just witnessed.

Russell continued, "As you can see, Jesus didn't preach to the teachers when he was twelve years old and it is not my intention to preach to you."

There was silence in the room. Then Russell began again. "Do you believe that I am Christ who has returned to Earth to minister to the people of the world?"

The clergymen responded almost in unison. "No!"

Russell smiled as he looked at them and then said, "And neither do I think or believe that I am Christ who has made his reappearance before you but I am mindful of what John said in Revelations. He said, and I will quote literally from the *Holy Bible*."

He let the clergymen open their *Bibles* and turn the pages to Revelations. They read what he said by memory.

Remember then what you received and heard; keep that, and repent. If you will not awake, I will come like a thief, and you will not know at what hour I will come upon you. Behold, I stand at the door and knock; if any one hears my voice and opens the door, I will come in to him and eat with him, and he with me.

Russell realized that in quoting that part of the *Bible*, he was inadvertently implying that he was in actual fact, Jesus who had returned to Earth so he quickly added, "This is not to imply that I am the one you are really seeking. You are not witnessing another reappearance of Christ. As I have said it before, I am but an ordinary boy."

The bishop asked, "Do you believe that Christ will return to minister amongst us or those who follow us in the years to come?"

Russell immediately replied, "It was Paul who said that when Christ returns, he will not return as flesh and blood but rather in spirit. I am not sure if anyone now or in the future will see him in the form of a human being but if he doesn't appear to us in the flesh, I believe that those of us who live a life of goodness will have Jesus' spirit within us."

There was silence in the room. The clergymen shifted in their chairs uneasily. A child had not put this proposition to them quite this way before.

The Catholic bishop continued. "But Revelations and the Book of Mathew states that Jesus will one day, knock on our doors. What do you say about that?"

"I think that it means that the spirit of Jesus will enter our hearts, our minds or our souls or whatever, if we are kind to those in need, if we offer assistance to as many those in need that we can and if we obey the Commandments given to Moses by God and believe in God and Jesus. I believe that Jesus' spirit has been and always will be with Mankind after his spirit ascended into Heaven. We should not be looking for his reappearance in the flesh. His spirit has already arrived and has been within all of us since his ascension into Heaven. That's why I do not believe that I am really Jesus in the flesh making his reappearance on Earth."

The Lutheran minister then asked, "Have you ever had any visions?

Russell replied, "I don't know if I have had visions but I dream a lot."

The minister responded with a smile, "As do we all but have you ever dreamed about what your future is to be."

Russell wanted to tell them about the dream he had on the top of Granite Mountain but he remembered that he was to keep it secret, so he kept silent.

Russell continued, "I believe I have a calling to serve the Lord but how I am to serve him, I do not know."

One of the clergymen asked, "Russell. Do you believe in the existence of Heaven?"

Russell replied, "If you envision Heaven being a place where angels sit on clouds and play harps, no. I don't believe that is what Heaven is."

"What do you believe Heaven is?" asked another.

Russell replied, "In the beginning of Genesis, the *Bible* says that God created the Heaven and the Earth. Then it says that the Earth was void. There was no mention of Heaven being void. That would leave us to believe that Heaven and Earth were distinctively different and in different places."

The clergymen nodded in agreement.

Russell continued. "However, in verse twenty, it says, 'And God said, Let the waters bring forth abundantly the moving creature that hath life, and fowl that may fly above the Earth in the open firmament of Heaven.' The birds can only fly perhaps as high as fifteen thousand feet above the surface of the Earth so the literal translation of that verse would mean that Heaven is somewhere between the surface of the Earth and fifteen thousand feet above it. It is conceivable that may be where Heaven is. Further, in the book of Isaiah, chapter fifty-five, verse ten, Isaiah says, 'For as the rain cometh down, and the snow from Heaven, and returneth not thither...' Russell paused and then said, "Surely that could mean that the Heaven he speaks of is where the clouds form the snow particles that finally fall to Earth. I personally don't think that is where Heaven is.

One of the clergymen asked, "Where then, do you think Heaven is?"

"I don't think that Heaven is in any particular place. Rather, I think it is everywhere on Earth." Russell replied.

"Why do you believe that? asked another.

"When Jesus was saying farewell to his disciples, he said, 'And as ye go, preach, saying, the kingdom of Heaven is at hand.' I believe that he meant that the kingdom of Heaven is here on Earth and that it is at hand, that is, within the reach of those who are presently here on Earth and who believe in Jesus and God."

The Catholic priest asked, "Surely you're not saying that we can be in Heaven while we are still alive, are you?"

Russell replied, "I believe that there are people on Earth who are alive that are surely in Hell so why can't we be in Heaven on Earth while we are alive?"

"Because the *Bible* doesn't say that!" replied another quite loudly.

Russell replied, "I believe that Heaven is a place of perfection for those who embody the will and the spirit of God. If we are within God's graces, surely we are in Heaven."

The clergymen were silent, each with their own thoughts. Then Russell began again. "I believe that some day, which may well be beyond our lifetimes and the lifetimes of those who are our immediate descendants, there will be a day when those in God's presence will suffer no pain and little sadness and that our life on Earth will be extended until humans live well beyond a hundred years of age, when there will be enough food for everyone and no one will be in need and there will be peace on Earth. When that time comes on Earth, then our descendants will truly be in Heaven."

"Well," said one of the clergymen, "You have painted a rosy picture of what Heaven is like."

Russell laughed and said, "That concept certainly beats the one that suggests that those in Heaven will be floating on the clouds playing harps and at the same time, being bored beyond measure."

With that statement having been said, the clergymen stood up, walked to Russell and shook his hand and except for the Minister of the Anglican Church who hosted the meeting, the other three filed out of the living room and then left the vicarage.

The Anglican minister smiled and said, "I think you have left a good impression on them."

As he was driving Russell back to the Hampton farm, he said, "I hope that you will come to my church often. I would like to give you an opportunity to occasionally give sermons as my guest."

"I would like that a lot." Russell replied.

A few days before school began again, the Nelson News published an article about Russell and the meeting of the clergymen in the Anglican minister's vicarage.

The part of the article that interested Russell was the comment of one of the clergymen who said that he was speaking for the others.

We have had an opportunity to talk with Russell Hendrix, the nine-year-old boy who many have called, Jesus Boy. It is our collective opinion that Russell is an incredible human being with talents well beyond our own, which we perceive to be as gifts given to him by God. But we are also convinced in our own minds and it is our sincerest beliefs that Russell is not the reincarnation of Jesus Christ and Russell agrees with us on that point without any reservations.

Further, we are convinced that Russell does not have the ability to heal people of their illnesses or bring them back to life if they have died. Russell agrees with us on that point also.

We do however recognize that this boy has an incredible talent of being able to convince people that praying to God may on occasion, bring relief to those who are need of it.

His coming into Nelson has been like a warm breeze on a cold windy day. He has done much to bring home the message that God's son is our savior and Russell's presence amongst us is what continues to keep us warm. And for that, we are thankful that God has blessed our community by bringing Russell Hendrix into our lives. For this reason, we thank our Lord for this blessing he has bestowed on us."

This public statement didn't convince all the people in Nelson that Russell wasn't Jesus Christ returned to them as a child. After all, Russell had brought a boy back to life and removed pain from the bodies of others. As far as they were concerned, only Jesus before he died on Earth could have done that and only Jesus who would return as promised, could resurrect the dead and heal the sick. To them, Jesus was now amongst them in the form of a nine-year-old boy.

When Russell was invited to give a sermon at the Lutheran Church in September and part of it was published in the Nelson News the following day, it made the people in Nelson sit up and take notice that in their city there was a young boy who should be taken very seriously. In his sermon, he spoke about being blind to the needs of others. The excerpt from his sermon published in the *Nelson News* was;

In searching for the message that the former slave trader, John Newton was trying to portray in the hymn he wrote called Amazing Grace, his inspiration was found in the New Testament in John, chapter nine, verse twenty-six. It says, 'Whether I am a sinner, I do not know; one thing I know, that though I was blind, now I see.'

Many of us are blind to what is going on around us just as John Newton was blind to the suffering of slaves. If we are abusive and indifferent to the needs of our parents, we are blind to their feelings. If we ignore the plight of those who are bullied, then we are blind to those who experience fear. If we are blind to those who are victims of crime because we ignore them, then they suffer all the more. If we are blind to the dangers we heap upon our own bodies, then we are ungrateful for the gift of life that was given to us.

Alas, it is often that we finally see the light that was always there but because of our blindness, we were always in the dark but later, it was too late to see what was previously there to see.

How many times have we wished that we were kinder to our parents before they passed on? How many times do we wish that we came to the assistance of those in need when some tragedy befell them?

How many times do we wish that we had taken greater care of our own bodies before we suffered from the abuse we brought onto ourselves?

How easy it is for us to ignore the plight of the visually impaired by presuming that someone else cares for them. How easy it is to ignore the loneliness of a homeless person because we presume that they have chosen that way of life for themselves. How easy it is to ignore the teachings of the scriptures because we have our own interests at heart above all others.

But just as John Newton found his way back into the good graces of God, so can all of us. Just because a person commits a crime and is imprisoned, this does not mean that he has not later seen the errors of his ways and has been reformed. Just because we ignored the plight of others, this does not mean that we cannot have empathy for those whom we ignored. Just because we abuse our own bodies does not mean that we cannot take greater care of our bodies in the future.

Perhaps for the blind, they cannot see images and light again but this doesn't mean they cannot see. To see something is to understand something. The phrase, 'I see what you mean.' means that you understand what you are being told. It means that at long last, you fully comprehend what is going on around you. It also means that you now have empathy for the suffering endured by those less fortunate then yourself.

I, like many of my fellow human beings have been blind in the past but now I see. I have changed my ways because of my willingness to see what I had previously turned a blind eye to and refused to see.

The publishing of his sermon made a deep impression on those who read it but unfortunately, many of the citizens on that small city began to suspect that if Russell wasn't Jesus Christ who had returned, then he had to be one of his disciples who had returned. They knew that Jesus had given his disciples the power to heal and if he was one of his disciples, then Russell too had the power to heal. Attitudes towards him had changed somewhat since the article and his sermon had been published the week before. He reminded those students who nagged him about this new revelation from the clergy, that he never told anyone that he was Jesus or that he could cure anyone of their illnesses.

When Russell returned to school in January 1946, most of the students shunned him because they were disappointed that Russell wasn't Jesus Christ who had returned to be amongst them. A few months later however, those who were his real friends gradually approached him and renewed their friendship with him. Despite the public disclosure by the clergy that Russell was not, in their opinion, Jesus Christ, there were still many who believed that he was the expected one.

This kind of thinking was to cause serious problems for Russell years later.

Thessalonians, chapter 2/ 13: But we are bound to give thanks to God always for you, brethren beloved by the Lord, because God chose you from the beginning to be saved, through sanctification by the spirit and belief in the truth.

Chapter Five

Beatrice Hampston was well informed via the radio and newspapers what was going on during her lifetime. She had seen vast changes in the world since she was a child. She learned that in 1946, the American Army had made its first contact with the moon via radar, and the computer, *Eniac* could perform 1,000 times faster than humans. The DC 6 Douglas aircraft was built that could carry 70 passengers at 300 miles an hour. A civil war ravaged China. The Philippines was declared independent and twelve Nazi leaders were executed. The following year, a radical group of Doukobors near Nelson burned the homes of other Doukobors who wouldn't join their sect. In 1948, a leader of India, Mahatma Gandhi was assassinated. Russia banned all land transportation to Berlin hence the airlift to Berlin began. Babe Ruth, the famous baseball player and Orville Wright, one of two men who flew the Kitty Hawk died. Ninety percent of Canadian homes had radios but only fifty percent had phones. In 1949, NATO was created, Siam became Thailand, Apartheid began in South Africa, a two-stage rocket soared 250 miles at 5000 miles per hour straight up and the USSR tested its first atomic bomb. A DC-4 airliner made the first non-stop coast-to-coast flight across Canada in 8 hours and 32 minutes. In 1950, North Korea invaded South Korea and the Chinese invaded Tibet. Writers George Orwell and George Bernard Shaw both died that year. The world's first kidney transplant was performed, as was the first heart massage. By that year, a brick ranch home could be bought for just over $12,000 and a Havana cruise for eight days would cost only $150.

It was now 1950 and she wondered what this year was going to be like. She knew that the people in Nelson and everywhere else for that matter, the beginning of the fifties was a time of economic prosperity. Few people in Nelson were unemployed by 1950.

When Russell returned to the Trafalgar High School on Josephine Street in September 1950, he was in grade nine.

The Hampstons had a birthday party for Russell on November 10th and they invited Larry and his parents to celebrate Russell's fifteenth birthday. He told the five of them at his party that they were his best friends.

When addressing them, he said, "Friendship grows slowly like a beautiful flower. And once it blooms, it is something to behold. But when that bond between friends is separated because of death, like the beautiful flower that exists no more, it is a time to regret but never to forget."

They wondered if Russell was forecasting someone's death. They dared not ask him.

In that same month, Russell was invited to preach at the Ascension Lutheran Church on Silver King Road. His sermon was about 'faith'. The newspaper columnist again quoted excerpts from Russell's sermon.

"For a man who is lame and walks across uneven stones; his faith is his crutch. For a blind man who walks into an unfamiliar room; his faith is his eyes.

"Faith and hope are distinguishable. Without faith, there can be no hope. Without hope, there is a need for faith.

"To know that God exists, is truly faith. To think that God exists, is merely belief.

"If you look upon faith like one looks upon the light of day, remember that darkness follows the light of day and that is why your faith must be strong enough to be sustained throughout those moments of darkness."

In November, Russell was invited to give the homily in the Catholic Church on Ward Street on the Sunday before Christmas. He chose as his topic, 'The meaning of giving'. Again, he was quoted in the columnist's column.

"To give a poor man a bottle of Burgundy is akin to giving a pair of skates to a child who has no shoes.

"Sometimes a gift of kindness is like a Trojan horse. Its purpose is to get past the walls of your heart. But unlike the invaders of Troy, a Trojan horse and your heart can become one.

"It has been said that it is far better to give a gift than to receive it. This is an undeniable truth. What is equally enjoyable is that moment when you get to express your gratitude."

"There is no greater gift you can bestow upon other human beings than your willingness to share your life with them."

Being in grade nine was fun for Russell. The publishing of his quotations in the *Nelson News* gradually increased the respect of his fellow students and more of them gathered around him during the recesses, the noon hours and after school than they had done so previously.

They sought his advice on every imaginable subject they could think of and he tried to answer as many of their questions that he was able to.

Often he was invited to their homes for supper at the requests of their parents for they too wanted to meet their children's unusual friend. Russell realized that despite having many casual friends, there is a need in humans to have a connection with one another. As humans, he knew that everyone needs love, touch, contact and support. Humans want to know that their needs are going to be met and that there is at least one person in their lives who is able and willing to help them meet those needs. Love is a deep and tender feeling of affection for or attachment or devotion to a person or persons. It is also a feeling of brotherhood and good will toward other people. The attraction that Russell and Larry had for one another was not physical but instead, it was feelings of devotion and respect on Larry's part and a close friendship on Russell's part. That being as it was, they became almost inseparable.

Larry knew that everyone, to one degree or another is devoted to something or someone. He knew that most religions use the term 'love' to express the devotion the followers have to their deity, living guru or religious teacher. Larry thought of Russell as his religious teacher but as the years progressed, he began to seriously consider the possibility that Russell may very well be Jesus in the flesh whom God had returned to Earth.

After all, didn't Russell bring him back to life? But more importantly, who else but Jesus would know the intimate details of how he died almost two thousand years ago?

What was troubling Larry however was; how does he broach this subject with his best friend? He realized that to do that, he would have to do it like porcupines make love; very carefully. He wouldn't outright ask him if he was Jesus. He would simply wait for some sign, either from God or Russell himself that would convince him that Russell was the expected one. But looking for a sign that leads one in the right direction is not unlike driving on a highway. First, you have to begin your journey. He decided to deal with that question that had been constantly on his mind, during the Christmas holidays in 1950.

Russell and Larry often wandered about the mountains for days at a time. Larry knew that they would never be lost because of Russell's photographic memory; he always knew how to backtrack the exact way they came. It was for this reason that Bernice and William and Larry's parents gave their permission for the boys to wander on their own on the mountains behind their homes for three days at a time without adults accompanying them.

On December 20th, the boys decided to climb Granite Mountain again notwithstanding that they would have to trek through the deep snow that covered the mountain. This experience; hiking through mountains covered in snow would be a first for them. They each carried with them, a small pup tent, a sleeping bag, a tarp, two pairs of heavy socks, mitts, warm clothing including long john underwear, heavy windproof jackets with a hood, snow boots, a flask for water, a flashlight, a compass, a map of the area, a knife, matches and enough food to last them for three days. The weight they each carried on their backs was thirty pounds. They were to return no later than the evening of December 23rd. Larry spent the night at Russell's home so that they could leave from his home early the next morning.

They left Russell's home at six in the morning and began the long climb up Granite Mountain. As they trekked through the deep snow, they wondered if three days was sufficient time to go further than merely climb to the top of Granite Mountain. By two in the afternoon, the trees became less dense but the snow was deeper however. By four in the afternoon, they had reached the summit.

By six in the evening, their pup tents were erected and they had a warm fire going and were eating some of what they brought with them. As they looked westward at the setting sun, Larry began wondering how he could learn if Russell really was Jesus whom everyone was expecting to return to Earth as their savior.

Larry knew that Russell had a photographic memory and it was for this reason that Russell could literally quote the scriptures but if Russell was really Jesus in the flesh who had returned, then he would know more of the details of his life when he was on Earth almost two thousand years ago; details that couldn't be found in the scriptures. However, he was aware that when Russell spoke of Jesus, it was always in the third person as if he was telling a story about another person and not about himself. He also believed in his heart that Russell would not lie to him and tell him tales of Jesus' life that really didn't happen.

Larry remembered hearing stories of people who claimed that they existed in previous lives. If they had lived in the past, then perhaps Russell had lived in Jesus' time also and had the soul of Jesus within him and was remembering what had happened to him in the first century but despite that, Russell may not know that he was the Jesus who had lived and died twenty centuries ago.

"Russell," he began. "I have always been fascinated by the stories you have told of Jesus. Could you tell me some more?"

"What would you like to know?" Russell asked.

"Well, I remember reading in the scriptures that before he was crucified in Jerusalem, Jesus had enemies elsewhere who made attempts on his life. Is that so?"

Russell replied, "That's true. When he lived in the city of Nazareth, several attempts on his life were made during some of the great feasts that were held there."

"Why?"

"Because at those times, he would attend many feasts since by attending the feasts, he had a ready-made audience that he could preach too. He also suspected that he was the Son of God and this infuriated the people when they heard him make such a proclamation during those feasts."

"But he was the Son of God so why didn't they believe him?

Russell thought for a moment and then replied, "Man somehow always wants to believe that he is his own divinity but realizes that is not what Man is. The people of Nazareth were well aware that Jesus was only a son of a carpenter and a carpenter in his own right. What they were not going to accept was that if they couldn't proclaim that they were the Sons of God, then why should a simple carpenter get away with making that kind of claim? This is what infuriated them."

Larry paused for a moment before he asked the next question. "How did they try to kill him?"

Russell continued with his explanation. "The city of Nazareth is surrounded by hills. A short distance from the city on one of the hills is a huge rock in which one side of it is about eighty feet high. From the top, there is a drop of three hundred feet on the other side of the rock to the Plains of Estraelon. A crowd of people half carried and half dragged Jesus to the top of the cliff and were about to throw him off the cliff when he managed to slip from their grasp and run away."

Larry asked, "Did he ever return to Nazareth?"

"Jesus had brought about several miracles when he was in Nazareth but it seemed to Jesus at that time that the people in that town didn't really believe that a carpenter's son was the Son of God and as far as they were concerned, he was unwelcome there. Jesus being aware of that fact decided that he would look elsewhere to teach and seek out those who would be more responsive to his message."

Russell paused and then said, "There were at that time, two hundred and forty towns and villages in the province of Galilee. Some of them would have thousands of people living in them and as such, there would be more than one house of instruction that Jesus could preach in. That being as it was, Jesus concluded that there where better fields to plow beyond the immediate environs of Nazareth. Of course, it was his dream to be able to preach in the houses of instruction in Jerusalem."

"Houses of instruction?

Russell replied, "That's what they were called then. It was only later that they were called synagogues, which is the Greek word for 'gathering'.

Larry smiled and said, "I guess there were many more houses of instruction in Jerusalem than there were in each of the towns of Galilee."

Russell laughed and said, "There were four-hundred and eighty such buildings in the city of Jerusalem alone during Jesus' time. These buildings throughout the land were for the purpose of teaching the law, the words of the prophets and other sacred writings of the Old Testament. It was in some of these buildings that Jesus taught those who chose to listen to him."

Larry asked, "Would the people in those towns permit Jesus to just walk in such a building and begin to preach to them?"

"All the houses of instruction that Jesus would go to were operating on the basis that any person of learning was welcome and any visiting rabbi who wanted to preach to them was invited to do so by those inside. This was ideal for Jesus because no matter where he went, he was well-known as a teacher and a rabbi and it gave him immense opportunities to teach and preach too many people. In other words, everywhere he went, there were ready-made venues for him to pass on his message to them."

Larry was confused. *'That was never taught in school or at Bible class so how did Russell know about those details in Jesus' life? Was he there then, if not as Jesus but rather as another person?'*

The next morning, the two boys got up at around six and by seven, they had eaten and were packed and ready to move on to their next destination, wherever that would be.

They headed down the mountain on the eastern side and the next mountain was approximately a mile from them. A strong winter wind was blowing the snow over the summit of the mountain ahead of them and into the valley to the right of them. They became concerned for it appeared that a snowstorm was heading their way.

When they got to the foot of the second mountain, they decided that rather than try climbing up that mountain while facing the onslaught of snow being blown down it, they would hike along the gully which would lead them to the valley. When the boys arrived at the valley, they were dismayed. The snow was two feet deep. Their progress was slow and tiring. By four in the afternoon, they had only crossed a mile of it.

They knew that they would have to bivouac in the trees to their left of the valley since spending the night on the valley floor would be dangerous if the icy wind blew across it. They bivouacked at the base of the trees.

After they had eaten, it was beginning to get dark so they climbed into their sleeping bags in their pup tents and began talking to each other. This was made possible by the fact that the openings of the two tents were facing each other.

Larry had more questions to ask with respect to Jesus. He began, "Russell. "Where there other times when Jesus had to run for his life?"

Russell smiled and replied, "One day when Jesus was in Jerusalem, he visited the old temple which at that time was known as Solomon's Porch. There was a feast going on at that time. It was the last great feast before the Passover. It had been instituted by a man called Judas Machabeus to celebrate the purification of the temple after it had been profaned by the Syrians. The feast lasted eight days and it was on one of those days that Jesus happened to be at the feast.

Many recognized him as a preacher and one of them who distrusted Jesus approached him and asked, 'How long are you going to keep us in suspense? Are you the Christ we are expecting?' Jesus knew that by asking him that question, the man was attempting to trap him into saying that he was the Messiah that the prophets had earlier said would come and free them from the Romans."

"How did he get out of that trap?

"He didn't." replied Russell. "He told his inquisitor, and I quote, 'I have told you that I am the Son of God.' In other words, he was saying that he was the expected Messiah."

"How did the crowd react to that?"

"To say that the people in the crowd that had gathered around him were angry is an understatement. They were furious. You have to remember that they were celebrating the Feast of Dedication after the Syrians had sacked Jerusalem and destroyed the Temple. No one came to the Temple's rescue at that time and now with the Romans occupying Jerusalem, they prayed that a Messiah with a host of angels would come down from heaven and destroy the Romans and free the people of Judea. Since they hadn't been freed by anyone, including the expected Messiah, they wondered why this man in their midst was claiming to be that Messiah."

"I can see why they were angry."

Russell continued. "For centuries, the people of Judea were hoping for a Messiah to protect them from those who had conquered them but as time passed them by, they began to hope for a liberator who was merely a mortal and not the Messiah. When no one came to rescue them and they were still under the heel of their Roman masters, they had given up any hope of being freed so when Jesus came along and told them that he was their Messiah, they not only didn't believe him, they mocked him and scorned him for having the temerity to make such a claim."

"What did they do then?"

"Jesus saw some of them picking up stones so he immediately called out to them and reminded them that God had sent him to be amongst them in human form. He then asked them, 'My Father has made it possible for me to do many deeds of mercy while I have been amongst you in Judea therefore which of my deeds do you choose to stone me?' Naturally, once a mob gets incensed, there is no stopping it. They weren't listening to his words anymore. They began picking up stones and throwing them at him."

"Did he escape?"

"Yes, he did." replied Russell with a big smile on his face.

Larry asked, "Why are you smiling?"

I believe that had he not escaped the stoning, all of the stones in the courtyard would have been piled on him and I believe that some members of the mob were so angry, they would have dismantled the rest of the temple to pile that on top of him if calmer minds hadn't prevailed."

Larry was confused. If Russell in his past life had simply been a member of the crowd in Nazareth who wanted to fling Jesus off the cliff, what were the chances that the same member of that crowd was also at the Feast of Dedication in Jerusalem? He would have the rest of the night to think of another question for Russell to answer. Maybe he would learn the truth about Russell after he answered the third question.

When the two boys woke up the next morning, they were pleased at what they saw. The day was clear and the rising sun reflected its light off the rugged mountain peaks in the distance. They decided not to climb over them but instead they chose to hike along the gully that separated the peaks from the mountain they had spent the night on.

By two in the afternoon, they had reached what appeared to be an open field heading down the mountain. It was covered with snow but the snow wasn't as deep as what they had trekked through the previous day. Further, it was more packed so walking on it was much easier.

It was six in the evening when they decided to camp where they had stopped at the top of the third mountain. They looked far below them at a beautiful valley to the north of them. The setting sun had turned the trees that were up close and also in the distance, a reddish hue and the snow was in turn, pink, purple and dark blue based on the distances the snow was from them.

There was enough time for them to put up their pup tents and build a fire. After they had eaten and climbed into their pup tents and buried their bodies in their sleeping bags for warmth, Larry began his third and final inquisition of his friend again. He didn't intend to ask Russell any further questions with respect to the life of Jesus after his final question. He would have to form his opinion as to Russell's role in the first century; if he was alive two thousand years ago and he would do that after hearing Russell's response to the last question. He hoped that after hearing Russell's answer, he could arrive at an opinion as to whether Russell really had the soul of Jesus Christ or the soul of someone else who was there when Jesus Christ was around in the first century or alternatively, simply the soul of Russell Hendrix, a boy of the twentieth Century who had God-given remarkable gifts.

Listening to Russell telling him about two of the times that people tried to kill Jesus didn't really assist him in his search for the answers he was desperately seeking. Russell could have been Jesus or a participant in the two mobs that were trying to kill Jesus. He knew that in presenting Russell with the next scenario, it would have to be one in which anyone in the two mob scenes couldn't possible be privy too. That would be stretching a coincident too far. Ten minutes later, he found a scenario in his mind that would surely bring forth the answer he was looking for.

"Russell." he began. "Was there a woman who washed Jesus' feet with her tears?"

"Of course." Russell replied. "Her name was Mary."

"Was it Mary Magdalene?"

"No. It was a woman from Bethany simply called Mary. This incident took place in Galilee, the province that was directly north of Judea. Jesus was invited to a banquet of one of the Pharisees called Simon. The woman was not invited, but she was one of townspeople who had crowded around the walls inside the courtyard to see the Pharisee and his guests. That kind of an occasion would have been much more public then than it is today."

Larry asked, "What happened then?"

"During the meal, the guests were reclining on pillows on the couches in the dining area, supported by their left arms and eating with their right hands."

Larry was puzzled and asked, "How do you know that they were eating with their right hands? Couldn't some of them be eating with their left hands?"

Russell laughed and replied with a question. "When you relieve yourself, which hand do you use to wipe yourself?"

Larry smiled. Now he knew why people from the Middle East and elsewhere who eat from a communal bowl of food always use their right hands to pick up their food.

Russell continued. "Access to the dining area was simple enough so Mary, with an alabaster flask in her hand, approached the men reclining on their pillows. Even though she had let her long hair drape over her face, Simon recognized her as one of the town's prostitutes. Her appearance in his home annoyed Simon because it was not the custom then to permit women in the dining area when men were eating; especially a woman who was a known prostitute. This incident also embarrassed him because he had invited Jesus as his special guest and was concerned as to what Jesus might think of him for permitting a prostitute to approach them when they were eating."

Larry mused to himself, *'Well, this rules out someone being there who was previously in the two mobs Russell spoke about.'*

Then he asked, "Did she go directly to Jesus?"

"Yes, she did." You see, she knew who Jesus was and knew that he had been invited to dine with Simon. Before Simon could intercede, she approach Jesus' feet."

"Why did she do that?"

Russell thought for a moment and then said, "It was the custom in those days, as it is also the custom nowadays, that when people entered one's home in those days with their sandals on, it was a sign of rudeness by tracking in dirt from the street. Once inside the house, the guest would be led to a couch and after being seated on it, a servant would come into the room and approach the guest and wash his feet. Remember that in those days, no one wore socks. Then the host or a male servant would pour some fragrant oil over the hair or beard of the guest."

"Well, "said Larry, if that was the custom then, why would there be a need for Mary to wash Jesus' feet?

"For some reason, which I don't understand, Simon didn't conduct that particular ceremonial procedure when Jesus arrived. Perhaps Jesus was late and the others had already begun eating. In any case, as soon as Jesus arrived, Simon waved him over to a vacant couch and invited him to eat."

Larry asked, "What was in the flask that Mary carried with her?"

"Well, it certainly wasn't Nard."

"What is Nard?"

"Nard was an extremely important sweet-smelling ointment packed in alabaster boxes from the Himalayas. One pound of it was worth as much as a year's wages. It would be opened only on special occasions such as for a burial of a friend."

"What was in the flask then?"

"I don't know."

Larry suddenly sat up with a start. He asked himself, "*How did Russell know that Nard wasn't in the flask if he didn't know what was in it in the first place? Could it simply be a simple deduction that he arrived at, that deduction being, how could such a woman afford to carry a flask of Nard with her? Further, if she washed Jesus' feet with her tears, she wouldn't need to open the flask. But if that is so, then why did she bring the flask with her in the first place? Is it because she had no other place to put it and had to carry it with her at all times?*'

Then he asked, "What did Mary do then."

"Well since she saw Jesus enter the dining area and walk directly to the couch Simon had directed him to, she decided that to seek Jesus' blessings, she would wash his feet. By doing so, she violated the social convention by touching the feet of a man and by letting down her hair in public."

"This must have made Simon even more agitated."

"Agitated isn't strong enough word to express his anger at that particular moment." said Russell as he laughed. Then he continued,

"Prostitution in the Holy Land at that time in history was tolerated but certainly not sanctioned and inviting a prostitute into one's home would elicit severe criticism from one's friends, especially if the owner of the house was a Pharisee. Worse yet, if the prostitute were to touch the feet of Jesus, the sinner's touch would make Jesus unclean and therefore challenge the Pharisees' honor as well as the honor of Jesus."

"What happened then?"

As she got onto her knees and leaned over Jesus' feet, she began to shed tears of gratitude that he hadn't pulled his feet away from her. Her tears fell onto his feet so she wiped his feet with her disheveled hair that was drooped over her face."

"What was the Pharisee doing at this moment?"

"He screamed at her to get away from Jesus but Jesus rebuked him."

"What did he say to him?" asked Larry.

"Jesus said to his host, 'Simon, I have a word for your hearing only.' The two men talked alone. Jesus asked him a question. 'If a creditor has two debtors and one owes five hundred pieces of silver and the other only owes fifty pieces of silver and neither can repay their debts and the creditor forgives them both, which one of the two men loves the creditor more?' What Jesus was telling Simon was that the woman had sinned more than Simon had, therefore she had the greater debt and that being so, she was more grateful to Jesus than Simon was, especially since Simon didn't even give Jesus the courtesy of seeing that Jesus' feet were washed by him or one of his servants. Simon kept his peace after that and let Mary continue with her service to Jesus such as breaking the flask she carried with her and pouring the sweet-smelling contents on Jesus' feet as a sign of love for the man she believed was deserving of it. She had seen him before and in doing what she was now doing at the feet of Jesus was unburdening her heart to him."

Larry was completely overjoyed at what he had heard. If Russell didn't have the soul of Jesus Christ in him, then how did he know all these facts about what occurred on that very special day in Jesus' life?

He had to be Jesus. He went to sleep with this new revelation in his mind. Now he wondered as to how he was going to deal with it?

The sun rose early in the morning and the boys ate their breakfasts and after packing their gear and placing their knapsacks on their backs, they began their long hike home.

They had to trudge their way through the deep snow at the top of the mountain and then climb down it and over another mountain.

They spent another night on the top of another mountain and expected to arrive at the foot of Granite Mountain by the afternoon of the following day.

On the final day of their journey, the two boys trekked through the snow over the hills and valleys.

Since both of them had flashlights, they decided they would walk through the forests in the dark if they had to. They didn't want to be overdue, as their families would be alarmed if they didn't return on the day they promised they would.

As they walked through the forest and fields, the sun kept sinking further over the horizon. This alarmed them because they knew that even with a compass they could get lost. However, their fears were allayed when they stumbled onto a road leading towards Nelson. They were surprised however that they were northeast of the city and not west of it as they had originally planned. It wasn't until seven in the evening when they eventually reached the western reaches of Nelson.

After making calls to their homes, Russell and Larry began the two and three-mile walks to their homes on Granite Road.

The moon was out so they didn't need their flashlights as they walked westward on Granite Road. Russell arrived home at nine and Larry arrived at his home twenty minutes later.

When Larry got into bed, he began thinking about what Russell had told him about what he knew about Jesus. Larry still wasn't absolutely sure that Russell had previously been Jesus Christ. He asked himself a rhetorical question, '*Was Russell really Jesus Christ who had returned in the Twentieth Century as a child or was he someone who had been a witness at the time Jesus Christ had preached in the Holy Land?*' He ruled out of his mind, members of a mob and bystanders outside the home of Simon. Then it suddenly dawned on him. Jesus Christ would have told his disciples about his near-death experiences and what occurred in the Pharisee's home. Perhaps Russell has the soul of one of Jesus' disciples. This would explain how Russell knows so much about the life of Jesus Christ without having lived that life himself.

Russell on the other hand went to bed with no concerns or questions on his mind at all. He was at peace. What he didn't know was that within six months, he was going to have a terrible experience that no one should be subjected too, especially a fifteen-year-old boy.

2 Timothy, chapter 4: 1-2: I charge you in the presence of God and of Christ Jesus who is to judge the living and the dead, and by his appearing and his kingdom: preach the word, be urgent in season and out of season, convince, rebuke, and exhort, be unfailing in patience and in teaching.

1 Peter, chapter 2; 21-23...if when you do right and suffer for it you take it patiently, you have God's approval. For to this you have been called, because Christ also suffered for you, leaving you an example that you should follow in his steps. He committed no sin; no guile was found on his lips. When he was reviled, he did not revile in return; when he suffered, he did not threaten; but he trusted to him who judges justly.

1 Corinthians, chapter 15; 12: Now if Christ is preached as raised from the dead, how can some of you say that there is no resurrection of the dead?

Chapter Six

William Hampston began thinking about the years gone by and wondered just how many years he had left in his life. As each year passed in his life, he became more amazed at what was happening in the world. The year 1951 arrived without too much fanfare. By the end of 1950, a Pan American flight took only 9 hours and 16 minutes to fly from New York City to London, England. One could fly from San Francisco to New York City for as little as $88.00. People swore that they saw flying saucers in Israel, Hong Kong and Italy. The first kidney transplant was performed, as was the first heart massage. A brick ranch home with 2 bedrooms and 2 baths could be purchased for as little as $12,000 a three-piece suit could be purchased from

Sears for as little as $50.00. A Havana cruise for eight days could be had for $150.00. The Korean war had begun and the American forces landed at Inchon that led to the recapture of Seoul. In the larger cities, people were considering building bomb shelters, many performers in the United States were blacklisted as Communists. Otis created the self-opening doors on their elevators, Minute Rice and electronic beepers along with Sugar Pops and Sony tape recorders made their first appearance that year.

Previously, Russell had given eleven sermons in the churches in Nelson and in January 1951, he was invited to give his twelfth sermon at the Anglican Church on Ward Street on the second Sunday of the month. He could speak on any topic he wished. The sermon he gave was *God Hears Your Prayers*. The church was packed; which wasn't normal at that time of the year but it was Russell who was giving the sermon and although some were still dubious about a child giving sermons in place of clergy nevertheless, they came so the church was filled.

The *Nelson News* again set aside a column for excerpts of his sermon. In the column, he was quoted in part as saying during his sermon,

"When many pray together, no matter in what language or ritual for the health and wellbeing of others, it is a sign to those in need that there is a brotherhood of sympathy in Mankind.

"To pray at the moment of death, for life or salvation or both, is the one moment when repentance is most sincere. Those prayers are probably the most common form of prayers in all languages.

"Do not pray for riches or power for it is no better than a form of begging shamelessly. Instead, pray for the health and a soul of others, for it is no less than giving graciously.

"It is a fact of life that God does not answer all of our prayers. We must leave it to God to decide what prayers are in our best interests and the best interests of those we love."

At the bottom of the column, the author of the article wrote, Some came to scoff and instead, remained to pray.

In that same month, Russell was invited to preach again at the Ascension Lutheran Church on Silver King Road. Russell also was invited to give the homily in the Catholic Church on Ward Street on the last Sunday of January. The newspaper columnist again quoted excerpts from Russell's sermon.

"It is commonly said that pride is not a virtue and where it goes, shame is sure to follow. But if you have done a good deed for someone else or accomplished a difficult task given to you, then you should be able to rightly enjoy consuming the tonic of wholesome pride in yourself."

Russell enjoyed being in grade ten. The publishing of his quotations in the *Nelson News* increased the respect of his fellow students and more of them gathered before him in the school gym during the noon hours and after school to hear him preach than they had done so previously.

They sought his advice on every possible subject they could think of and he tried to answer as many of their questions that he was able to. By the middle of spring, he was at the zenith of his popularity in Nelson and like all human beings, he enjoyed it.

One early afternoon in the last week in June, he went swimming at Gyro Park, the park that overlooks downtown Nelson. Later in the afternoon when he was bicycling home on Granite Road while still in his white swimming trunks and white T- shirt, a car suddenly stopped in front of him and two men jumped out of the car and pulled him off his bicycle and threw his bicycle off the road and into the ditch. Then a third man jumped out of the car and went to the rear of the car and opened the trunk. He recognized them as the Ballards. He had seen them in Nelson and heard stories about them. All three of the men then threw Russell into the trunk and closed the lid down. It didn't close properly so they got some wire from the trunk to tie the lid of the trunk down as much as they could. Russell could see outside through the sliver of the opening at the rear of the trunk.

Within seconds, the men climbed back into the car and then the car was speeding down the road. Russell began screaming for help. A few minutes later, the car stopped and one of the men opened the trunk. He hit Russell on the head with a small hammer and knocked him out. Then the man partially secured the trunk again and the three men drove away.

The car stopped at an old farmhouse. The men pulled the unconscious boy out of the trunk and carried him into the house. The Ballard farmhouse was a two-story structure and painted white although it certainly needed a new paint job. Martha Ballard, the wife and mother respectively of the three who kidnapped Russell wanted to put curtains on the windows but her husband was too cheap to buy her the material to make the curtains. The roof was made of corrugated steel but it leaked because it hadn't been repaired in many years. The barn held six cows which the brothers milked every day.

Within an hour, Russell came too. He had been tied to a chair. Blood was dripping from the wound at the side of his head onto the floor. No attempt was made to stem the flow of blood. He was frightened because he knew that they were the men were the threesomes whom most Nelsonites considered not only unsavory but also crazy to boot. They were loners, for they hardly ever talked with anyone including the storekeepers.

He stared at the three men standing in front of him. One of the men was in his sixties. He had a full beard and his beard, mustache and hair were grayish white, dirty and in complete disarray. He was Harry Ballard, the father of the two other men. He was considered a blundering thief and had spent some time in the jail in Nelson. People always crossed the street when they saw him approaching as he always looked like a wild man who screamed profanities at them.

Donny Ballard, the oldest, was a bully when he was in school and later in the workplace until he was expelled from one and fired from the others. He was known to have tortured animals when he was younger.

Jerry Ballard was the youngest son. He wasn't necessarily mean unless he followed the directions of Donny or his father. Then he would get extremely mean and nasty if for no other reason but to impress his older brother and his father. He had a low IQ and this was presumed to be because his mother drank a lot when she was carrying him and he suffered as a result from fetal alcohol syndrome.

The only one in the family that was the recipient of any respect and pity was Martha because she was more or less stuck with her brood and overbearing husband. Many of the people in Nelson wanted to help her but her husband always kept them away from the farm. As a result, she suffered alone.

Russell asked the obvious question, "Why?"

The youngest of the men, Jerry, who Russell figured was in his early thirties, replied, "Our mother is dying and we want you to make her well again."

Russell replied, "I can't do that. I don't have the power to do that."

The dying woman's husband responded with, "You are the kid they call Jesus Boy. I read about you. You cure the sick and raise the dead."

"That's not true." exclaimed Russell who was now in a state of panic. "You have that all wrong. I cannot—."

He was cut off mid sentence by the old man. "My wife is dying and you are going to heal her."

Russell replied, "I will do everything I can for her. I will pray to God to save her."

"If she dies," said Donny who was the older son who was in his late thirties, "you better pray to God for your life because you will be joining my mother in death if she dies."

They carried Russell in his chair into the bedroom where the dying woman lay. She too was in her sixties and had white hair. She looked up at Russell tied in the chair and asked weakly, "Who is this boy?"

One of her sons replied, "Mother, he is Jesus Boy who has come to cure you from your illness and save you from death."

"Then why," asked the woman, "is he tied to the chair?"

Her husband replied in a gravely voice, "When he prays my dear, he swings his arms about and we don't want him accidentally hitting you."

Russell wanted to tell her that he was kidnapped but he knew it wouldn't help and it would just bring misery to the dying woman.

He then closed his eyes and began, "Oh Lord. I beseech you to spare this woman the agony that she is enduring."

Russell went on like this for an hour and the woman closed her eyes while she listened to the voice of the child beside her. As he prayed aloud, asking God to take her into his bosom, she began to smile.

Unfortunately, praying for her to get well wasn't working and during the second hour, she died peaceably in her bed. When it was obvious to the three men that their loved one had died, they dragged Russell's chair out of the room and placed him in the centre of the kitchen.

The husband of the deceased woman said, "Walter, get the bow and arrows. This boy is going to die."

There was nothing Russell could think of that he could say that would change their minds. He knew that he was going to die. His early death was forecasted by the image of Jesus on the cross in his dream. *At least*, said Russell to himself, '*I will die after having done God' work.*'

The old man whispered something to his younger son and the son ran out of the kitchen and returned a few minutes later with a large leather bag. The father asked, "You got what I asked for?" The son replied, "Yes. I got them, Pa."

They untied Russell from the chair and rebound his feet and hands and carried him back to the car and after opening the trunk of the car; they threw him inside and taped his mouth shut. When that was done, the old man snarled. "You make a sound of any kind, you won't just die, you will die horribly. Do you understand me?"

Russell nodded his head affirmatively. He understood although he was worried. Jesus had told him earlier that his life would be short and his death would not be a good one.

The three men climbed into the car and the car was driven onto a dirt road. In less than a minute, it was on Granite Road heading east towards Nelson in the early moonlit night.

Russell had managed to peer out of the small opening of the partially closed trunk lid and after a while, he saw the entrance to the Hampston farm as the car approached it and passed by it. William was standing on the driveway, obviously waiting for him to come home from wherever he was.

Russell began to cry; not because he was going to die but because he knew that the couple would spend the remainder of their lives wondering what wrong they may have done to him that would make him choose to leave them without even bidding them goodbye.

When the car reached the outskirts of Nelson, the father of the other two in the car spoke to the son who was driving the car. "Turn left on Government Road and then onto Railroad Street."

Russell could feel the turning of the car as the driver maneuvered the steering wheel while making the turns.

"Work your way onto Front Street. There isn't much traffic in that part of town." said the old man.

The vehicle moved east on Front Street and finally onto Nelson Avenue. As the vehicle was moving east on Nelson Avenue, a car began following it with its lights blinding Russell. Suddenly the car Russell was in, stopped, and the car following it, rammed into the rear of it. Russell was propelled towards the point of impact and knocked unconscious.

When he came too, he had difficulty seeing anything through the small opening of the trunk lid because of his blood dripping from a wound on his forehead running onto his eyes. He could however see that the car he was in had just crossed the lake on the small tow ferry and was heading east on Highway 3A.

Fifteen minutes later, the car turned left off of the highway and was being driven on Greenwood Road past the small hamlet of Willow Point. The moon was bright so the driver didn't put on his lights as he feared that people in the farmhouses nearby would be aware that a car was being driven on the road. After a while he heard the driver say, "There is a fork in the road, Pa. Which road do I take?"

"The one on the left." replied the old man. Then he continued.

"There is an abandoned farm at the end of the road. We will kill him there."

On hearing this, Russell began shaking nervously. He knew that soon, his life would be coming to an end.

The road to the left was much narrower than the one they exited from so the driver slowed down lest he run off the road. About ten minutes later, the car stopped and the men exited the car and within seconds, the trunk was opened.

The car's headlights were turned on and Russell could see that the car had stopped at a wide gate. One of the sons was trying to get it open further but it wouldn't budge. There was just enough room for them to slide past the gate if they went through the opening one at a time. The old man meanwhile turned off the headlights of the car.

All three of the men had flashlights and one of them carried a kerosene lamp with him also. After they dragged Russell out of the trunk of the car, they walked him towards the barn that was approximately a hundred yards away to their left.

The full moon was still lighting up the area. Russell could see to his left, a small shed by the fence and on the other side of the fence, the remains of a house that had previously burned to the ground. Russell could see from the reflection of the moon that the roof of the barn was made of corrugated sheet metal. To his right, was a field and beyond that, the forest that climbed up the mountain. The barn door was already open when they arrived at the barn and the three men pushed Russell inside

Russell concluded that it had been a horse barn because it had four stalls on both sides of the barn where horses had been previously kept.

There were square pillars on each side of the stalls with six heavy crossbeams six and a half feet above the floor of the barn that were supported by the pillars. The barn stank of old horse manure that was dried up and still lying on the floor.

One of the men placed the kerosene lantern in the middle of the floor. It lit up the immediate area where they all stood.

"Tie him to this cross beam!" yelled the father as he pointed to one over the entrance to the second stall from the entrance of the barn. Russell knew that there was no point in resisting. The three men were strong enough to counter any resistance he might have to offer. One of the men grabbed a piece of rope out of the large leather bag they brought with them and looped it twice around one end of the cross-beam while his father, who was standing behind Russell, held him fast. The son who seized Russell's left wrist, tied one of the two ends of the rope around his wrist. The other son went through the same procedure with Russell's right wrist.

The three men then stood back and looked at their victim. The father then said to one of his sons, "Tie his feet together and loop both ends around the pillars."

When this task was completed, he joined the other two as they stared at their victim. The father then said crisply, "Remove his T-shirt."

One of his sons pulled out a hunting knife from the scabbard on his belt and began cutting away the T-shirt. When it was lying on the floor in pieces, he asked, "What about his swimming trunks?"

The father screamed, "Cut them off also!"

They stared at the naked boy as blood from his wound on his forehead and left temple began dripping down onto his shoulders and down his body in small streaks.

The father then reached down to the leather bag at his feet. He opened it wide and pulled out a thick electrical cable. It had remnants of five small wires protruding a couple of inches from one end of it. The cable was three feet in length. He handed it to one of his sons and while Donny held it in his right hand, his father reached into the bag again and pulled out a roll of black electrical tape. He began wrapping the tape around his son's hand and the electric cable grasped in his hand. After cutting it from the roll, he then said, "This will prevent the whip from slipping from your grasp."

The old man then faced Russell and said angrily, "You led us to believe that you were the reincarnation of Christ. My wife begged me to bring you to our house so that you could save her from her cancer but when I asked you to come, you refused."

Russell tried to think back in his memory any sign that he might have met the man before. He couldn't remember exactly when but he remembered faintly that during the previous year, someone spoke to him about his wife suffering from breast cancer. But he had always told people that he could not cure them from their illnesses.

Russell replied, "I have never told anyone that I was Christ and I always denied that I could really cure anyone of their illnesses. I cannot—."

One of the sons interjected, "I was in the Civic Centre when you called on God to stop the pain of the people in the auditorium and you stopped their pain."

The other son yelled, "And don't deny that you raised the dead boy and brought him back to life. You are Jesus and you have been reincarnated as such and if you are not, you at least have his powers."

The old man snarled, "I begged you to save my wife and you refused to come to my home. And even when I finally brought you to my home, you asked God to let my wife die."

Russell replied, "I asked God to let her die in peace."

One of the sons reached into the bag and brought out four large spikes and a hammer. Then after showing them to Russell, he smiled and said, "Since you have chosen to live like Jesus, then you can die like Jesus. And just as he was whipped, so shall you suffer in the same manner."

Russell closed his eyes. He knew that there was nothing that he could say that would change their minds. They intended for him to die horribly. He began thinking of his dream on the top of Granite Mountain. He remembered the message of the man in the centre cross, '*You must continue my work as others have and bear the pain as I have for these gifts do not come to you without a price.*'

Russell was frightened. He was now to bear the pain that Christ did. That was the price for the gifts that God gave him.

What he and his tormenters didn't know at that moment was that in the hayloft above them, were two teenage girls from Willow Point; Silvia, a seventeen-year-old girl and her sister, Maria, who was a year younger. They were overnight camping in the barn. They didn't go to the same school as Russell but they had heard of him. They had been sleeping in the hayloft when Russell and the three men entered the barn but awoke when the men began talking. They peered down through a large crack in the planking in the floor and saw and heard everything. They were petrified and realized that the only way out of the barn was down the ladder and past the three men. They whispered to each other and agreed that it was safer to stay where they were and remain absolutely still and quiet.

Russell closed his eyes and began to pray. "Lord. I have served you as best as I can. Please—."

He heard the swishing of the makeshift whip as it flew through the air and then suddenly, he felt a searing pain across the width of his abdomen.

Maria suddenly exclaimed "Ohh!" as this was far too much for her mind to grasp. Her older sister whispered, "Maria, be quiet! Don't make a sound."

"What's that?" asked the son standing next to his father.

"Stop the whipping!" cried out the father to the son with the whip.

The three men cocked their ears trying to listen. All they heard was the wind blowing through the openings of the barn.

"Search the barn!" The younger son began searching the stalls while the older son climbed up the ladder to the hayloft. He began tramping through the hay and as he approached the girls who were unseen but only five feet from him, his father called out, "Do you see anything up there?"

"No. There's nothing up here."

"Come on down and let's continue our task." replied the father.

In less than a minute, the whipping began again.

The pain on Russell's chest, belly and his sides increased with every stroke of the whip. His tormentor alternatively swung the whip from his right and after he struck another blow, he would bring his right arm across his chest, and then swing the whip from his left. The marks on Russell's body sloped downwards at each stroke. The ends of the whip began tearing away his skin until it much of it was shredded. On occasion, the ends of the wires cut into his veins and small arteries, sending rivulets of blood coursing down his torso and legs to the floor. As the torture continued, he moaned at every stroke but he never spoke a word.

His tormentor stopped after fifteen minutes and said, "I'm getting tired."

He looked at his victim. Blood was running from the open wounds. A few of the wounds were welts but most were open wounds. The lacerations brought about by every stroke tore into the boy's underlying skeletal muscles and produced quivering ribbons of bleeding flesh.

He pointed to his brother and said, "You take over for a while."

After the whip was secured to the other man's right wrist, his father said, "Go into the stall and do the same thing to his back."

The son obeyed his father and then began whipping Russell's back and sides as furiously as his brother had whipped the boy earlier.

The father of the tormentor cried out to Russell. "Where is your God now?"

Russell ignored him. Answering the old man would be pointless.

Later, the old man told them to take a break. His sons had been alternatively whipping Russell for an hour, now they stared at their handiwork.

Russell's blood covered most of his body from his forehead to his feet. The tearing of his flesh was from his shoulders to his hips. He was breathing heavily and shivering and it was the first time since the whipping began, he spoke, "I'm cold." One of the men smirked and said, "Put on your T-shirt then." The two other men laughed uproariously. Russell was cold because pain and blood loss was gradually setting the stage for circulatory shock from the beating he was getting. His blood was rushing to his inner organs and gradually leaving the surface of his body, causing the surface of his body to feel the chill of the night with greater intensity.

Half an hour later, they began their torment of him again. His ribs at his sides were beginning to fracture because of the continuous onslaught of the heavy cable resulting from both the frontal and rear attacks. This made his breathing all the more difficult.

The girls peering down onto the scene were horrified but they knew that there was nothing they could do to save the boy. After a few more minutes of staring and listening to the horror beneath them, they turned over and lay on their backs, closed their eyes and put their fingers in their ears. Watching and listening to Russell being whipped to death was far more than they could bear any longer.

At one in the morning, the old man called a halt to the whipping. He said, "Let's rest for a while. You two go to sleep in one of the stalls and I will keep watch." Later at four, one of the sons relieved his father.

Meanwhile, Russell continued to suffer from the pain encompassing his torso and from the difficulty he was experiencing in breathing. To make matters worse, insects drawn to him because of the kerosene lantern being placed near him, began biting at his open wounds.

When the moonlight began slipping through the cracks of the barn and through the main entrance of the barn, the son who had relieved his father woke him and his brother up and told them, "It's time."

The three of them then stood in front of the semi-conscious bloodied form hanging from the cross beam.

The old man spoke to his sons. "Now you can secure the boy to one of the supporting posts of the stall."

They moved Russell's inert body to the post on his right and after securing his feet to it (one beside the other) and his wrists to the cross beams on both stalls on both sides of him, the old man motioned to one of his sons to bring the leather bag to him. This was done and the bag was dropped at his feet.

The old man reached into the leather bag and brought out the hammer and one of the four eight-inch spikes they brought with them. He brought the spike to Russell's face and snarled, "You wanted to live like Jesus; now you will die like Jesus." Then he yelled to his sons. "Hold him secure!"

The two men wrapped their arms around Russell's legs and the post and their father knelt down at Russell's feet and placed the point of the spike onto the middle of Russell's right foot. He raised the hammer up high and paused and then swung it down hard on the head of the spike."

Russell let out a piercing scream. The girls above them who had been asleep after the whipping had stopped, were jolted out of their sleep after the first blow drove the spike into Russell's foot. By the time the second strike of the hammer against the head of the spike had been made, the point of the spike had been driven in between the first and second metatarsal bones, several inches from the end of his toes and through tendons and flesh and through the sole of his foot. The same was done likewise with the second foot. The impact of the hammer against the nail head the third time drove the spike a couple of inches into the wooden pillar just as it had when he drove the first spike into Russell's other foot.

Russell's body sank downwards to the point where his knees were bent. He then began gradually slipping into unconsciousness.

The old man turned to one of his sons and said, "Fetch the ladder. You will need it to drive the spikes into his wrists."

The old man then ordered his sons to pull the boy upwards so that his wrists reached the cross beam. They then tied the boy's wrists against the crossbeam. In doing so, his body was not entirely erect; something that Russell feared. This meant that his knees would protrude outward thereby forcing him to pull himself upwards via his wrists in order to not suffocate.

With the ladder propped where the cross beams met and being directly in line with the pillar, the old man said to his oldest son. "Do your thing, son."

The oldest son climbed up two rungs of the ladder and after being handed the hammer and another spike, he leaned towards his left and then after placing the spike against Russell's left wrist, he began driving the spike into the soft flesh. The nail penetrated Russell's wrist without striking the metatarsal bones. The point of the nail was driven through the muscles, blood vessels and nerves of his wrist and finally four inches into the cross beam.

The sudden pain brought Russell back to full consciousness again and he screamed from the shock of the new source of pain. As he writhed in agony, the youngest son, on the instructions of his father, climbed up two rungs of the ladder and repeated the same torturous procedure with the boy's right wrist. Russell screamed again. This time his screaming was prolonged even longer than before.

The three men then removed the ladder and replaced it back where they got it; the top of it leaning against the opening of the ceiling above them. Then they returned to the pillar to stare at Russell and as he moaned and writhed; the old man said to Russell with a sarcastic voice, "It looks like God has abandoned you just as you abandoned my wife."

Russell stared at the three men. He realized by now that the old man and his two sons were mentally ill and had no idea of the gravity of what they were doing to another human being. Knowing this, he said softly and haltingly to them, "I forgive you—for you don't know any better. I have asked God—to forgive you also."

"We don't need your forgiveness or his!" screamed the old man. "You should be seeking our forgiveness but since you have chosen not too, you will just have to die like Jesus did—slowly and very painfully."

Russell was suffering from excruciating pain but unknown to him; his body wasn't reacting the way an ordinary person would react; such as screaming his lungs out. People who suffer pain have a strategy to cope with pain. Many turn to religion. Russell was very religious and those with strongly held religious beliefs are better able to cope with pain. Further, he knew that he was destined to suffer as Christ did so as foretold when Russell was on the top of Granite Mountain so he accepted his fate and as a result, some of the traumatic effects of the pain he was subjected to were to some degree lessened, albeit very little.

The three men then walked towards the opposite stalls and sat down on the floor with their backs leaning against the posts. When the light from the full moon shone through the opening of the barn they had entered through and onto Russell, his body took on a light bluish-grey colour. They stared at the semi-conscious form in front of them, his body reflecting the bluish-grey light from the moon. Soon, all they could see was his body and nothing else. As their eyes became fixed on the form in front of them, the moonlight reflecting off the form in front of them, gave it an eerie look.

The men stared at their young victim for an hour, watching and listening to him writhing and moaning in agony.

They watched with fascination as Russell kept pulling himself up so that his legs would be straight. They didn't realize that if he didn't do this, he would suffocate to death. All they were interested in was watching a human being suffer just as Christ did. They wanted Russell to suffer as Christ did.

The major pathophysiologic effect of Russell's crucifixion, beyond the intense pain, brought about a marked interference with his normal respiration, particularly the process of exhaling. The weight of his body, pulling down on his outstretched arms and shoulders, fixed his intercostal muscles and diaphragm in an inhalation state and thereby hinder passive exhalation. Accordingly, his exhalation, which would be primarily brought about by his diaphragm moving upwards toward his lungs, became very shallow. This form of respiration was not sufficient for too long and soon abnormally high concentrations of carbon dioxide accumulated in Russell's blood. The onset of violent involuntary muscle contractions due to fatigue and the excess carbon dioxide in his lungs; hindered his respiration even further.

The only way Russell could bring himself any form of relief from the inability to exhale was to lift his body upwards by pushing up on his feet and by flexing his elbows and adducting his shoulders. However, this maneuver placed the entire weight of his body on his feet and wrists and produced searing pain in those extremities because of the nails tearing at the flesh and nerves in his feet and wrists even more. Furthermore, flexion of his elbows causing rotation of his wrists about the iron nails brought about fiery pain along his damaged median nerves. Lifting his body also was painful because in doing so, he scraped his scourged back against the rough wooden pillar. Muscle cramps and the pins and needles sensation of his outstretched and uplifted arms added to his discomfort. As a result, each respiratory effort became painful and tiring and was leading him towards eventual asphyxia, which in turn would bring about unconsciousness and finally, death.

The three men could see from the expression on Russell's face that he was suffering in extreme agony. They were enjoying their revenge to its fullest. Even they knew that revenge can be a balm that eases the loss of a loved one. They knew that their revenge against Russell wouldn't completely relieve them from the anguish of having lost their wife and mother respectively, but it least Russell's suffering eased their own pain to some degree. Their only regret however was that their revenge couldn't be pursued after Russell's death.

Hours later, as the light from the early morning began to light up the inside of the barn, Russell began to hallucinate. He found himself dreaming that he was again on Golgotha, the hill beyond the walls of Jerusalem where Christ and the other two men died. This time, however, he wasn't one of the crowd staring at the condemned men; he was one of the condemned men hanging on the cross next to Christ.

Russell turned his head to his right with tears in his eyes and faced Christ. "Lord." he began, "Is this the moment you told me about when I was on the top of the mountain?"

The man in the centre cross turned his head to face Russell.

Then Russell began hearing a voice from the man although he couldn't see his lips move. "Your work is not finished. You have more work to do to serve our Father."

Russell replied, "But I am dying beside you. How can I serve our Father when I am dying while nailed to this cross?"

"Have you already forgotten what you have been preaching all this while?"

Russell hadn't prayed to God to save himself so he said, "But Jesus, our Father didn't save you from death on the cross. Why would he save one such as me who is far less worthy of his intervention than you were?"

"My work on Earth was finished. Your work is not." the form beside him replied.

Russell looked upwards and began to pray as loud as he could. "Father. My service to you is not finished yet. Please spare me this death and let me return to those in need of my service in your name. I will accept any death willingly you choose for me after I have fulfilled my ministry. "

Suddenly an old man in the crowd near the foot of the three crosses approached Russell's cross on the hill and while standing at the foot of the cross, he sneered, "You were given an opportunity to save my wife and you failed. Why should I take you off the cross now when you can no longer help her?"

Russell's eyes opened wide and he suddenly realized that he was still in the barn and talking to the old man who had a sneer on his face and who was now standing a few feet from him.

The old man then continued, "You have asked for a death of my own choosing. I am going to give you that death."

He then said to his youngest son. "Bring me the bow and arrows from the car. "The younger son ran out of the barn and down the dirt pathway leading to their car. Within minutes, he had returned and handed a bow and three arrows to his father.

"My sons." he began. "The time has arrived for us to kill this runt who presumes to be the Son of God and yet refused to save your mother from death."

He handed the bow and one arrow to his younger son. "Now you remember how I taught you to shoot arrows so I don't expect you to miss."

The old man then pointed to the stall immediately across from the post Russell was secured to. "Go to the back of the stall and shoot this little bastard in his chest."

The old man and his other son got out of the way and each stood at the entrance to the stalls on either side of the stall the younger son was standing in.

Russell closed his eyes tightly. There was some comfort in being shot in the chest with an arrow, He would die quickly and his suffering would finally come to a quick and merciful end.

The arrow flew out of the stall and with a slight thudding noise; the force of the bow had driven the arrow four inches into Russell's left thigh. Russell's scream was long and piercing.

The old man hollered out, "You damn fool! I said his chest, not his thigh."

The old man grabbed the bow out of his son's hand and handed it to his older son. As he handed him the second arrow, he said angrily. "Do you know what part of his body is his chest?"

"Yes, Pa." replied the older son as he walked to the back of the stall.

"Then shoot him in his damn chest, damn you!" the old man screamed.

The second arrow flew by the two other men and struck Russell in the lower left part of his belly. Russell again screamed in agony.

"Damn you, you bloody fool! His chest isn't where his belly is."

The old man was furious. Then he walked up to Russell and pounded on his sternum, and then said, "That is where his heart is. These arrows are sharp enough to go through his sternum and into his heart. That's where you should have shot him, you bloody fools."

With that said the old man walked to the back of the stall and fired the third arrow at the screaming boy.

The twanging of the bowstring was superseded by the whistling noise of the third arrow as it flew across the open space towards their victim.

"Well, I'll be damned!" yelled out the old man as he walked out of the stall towards Russell. "I missed the sternum by four inches."

The arrow had gone into Russell's upper right lung.

Russell was gasping for air as his right lung collapsed. His screaming had now been reduced to loud groans and gasps for air. Within a minute, he was semiconscious again.

"Well, Pa." said the younger of the two men, "We can pull out the arrows and shoot him again. This time we are sure to hit the right spot."

The old man growled at his son and said, "How many times have I told you that these kinds of arrows are the kind that the arrowheads remain behind when you pull out the shaft. You want to shoot arrows with no arrowheads?"

"No, Pa." whined the younger son.

"I guess we should have brought more arrows, eh?" the older son hinted.

The old man retorted. "If you had shot the arrows correctly, we wouldn't need more than three."

"But Pa." said the younger son, "You missed his heart also."

The old man looked at his son and made a growling noise. Then he walked up to Russell's limp form and said, "Well, the little bastard is still alive but I doubt that he will be alive much longer. Let's pack up our things and get to our car."

"Pa," one of his sons asked, "Aren't we going to wait until he dies?

"No, we aren't. The kid will be dead in an hour. We don't have an hour to spare. We got to get across that tow ferry before people in Nelson start walking the streets. We don't want anyone seeing us in Nelson this early in the morning."

"Why Pa?" asked one of his sons.

"Because, you stupid idiot, your mother died last night. Don't you think that people will begin to wonder why it is that we were in downtown Nelson and hadn't reported your mother's death to the hospital?

"Can't we say that she died this morning?"

"Yeah, sure." said the old man. "And we can then explain why her body shows signs of decay so soon after her death."

As the old man herded his sons out of the barn, he looked back at the limp form hanging on the makeshift cross inside the barn. He noticed that the sun was shining through the opening above the main door of the barn onto Russell's face. He began to wonder why God played such a dirty trick on him by having him sire two idiot sons instead of bright ones possessing similar brains of the dying kid in the barn.

Within minutes, they climbed into their car and were speeding down the narrow dusty road towards the main highway. They knew that they had to get back to their own home before anyone suspected that they had been anywhere other than at their home all night.

The two girls in the loft climbed down the ladder to the main floor of the barn and they stood at the pillar where Russell has been crucified.

The oldest of the girls said to her younger sister, "Run down the road to the nearest farm house and get some help." The younger girl ran out of the barn and in ten minutes, she reached the nearest farmhouse, which was almost a mile away on the left side of the road.

The oldest girl said to the unconscious form hanging limp on the makeshift cross, "I don't know how to get you off the pillar but my sister has run for help at the nearest farm house. Please don't die. They won't be long."

The girl then knelt down at the feet of Russell and prayed to God that he wouldn't suffer any longer.

Russell managed to get enough strength to speak again after pulling himself upwards. He said, "Please. Wrap the ropes around the post and my legs, both above and below my knees tightly. I have to remain in a standing position in order to breathe."

Half an hour later, the noise of two vehicles could be heard, followed by voices. In less than a minute, three men entered the barn. One was carrying a bolt cutter. The expressions on their faces showed that they were in complete shock and disbelief at what they were seeing.

There before them was a young naked boy nailed to a makeshift cross, his body covered in blood and three arrows sticking out of him. On the floor of the barn at the base of the pillar the boy was crucified on and the stall he had been whipped in; were two pools of blood. The blood oozed from his body, not so much from the wounds in his wrists or feet or even from the arrows protruding from his body but instead from the many lacerations on his torso, front, sides and back.

One of the men said to Russell. "It won't be long, son. We'll free you from this post in a moment."

Fortunately for the boy, the nails hadn't been driven to the point where the heads touched the surface of his feet and wrists. The bolt cutter nipped the heads off each nail.

Within five minutes, the men pulled Russell's hands and feet free from the shafts of the beheaded nails and he was then laid down onto a blanket previously laid on the floor by one of the other men. Russell was totally unconscious by this time. While the men arranged for a make-shift litter to be made, the girl held Russell's head in her arms with her tears dropping on his face. A few minutes later, the three men lifted the prone body off the floor and onto the make-shift litter and then they carried him out of the barn and onto a pickup just outside of the gate. After laying him on a number of blankets placed in the back of the pickup, everyone including Silvia got into the two vehicles and they drove to Willow Point where they would wait for the ambulance coming from Nelson.

Fifteen minutes later, the ambulance arrived and Russell was put in it and taken to the Kootenay Lake District Hospital on View Street in Nelson. The men then dropped off the older sister at her home in Willow Point and went back to the neighboring farmhouse where the younger sister was waiting to be picked up.

When the ambulance arrived at the hospital, Russell was wheeled into the emergency department. The doctors and staff looked in horror when they saw the naked 15-year-old, all bloodied and some of the young nurses felt faint when they looked at the punctures in his wrists and feet and the three arrows protruding from his body.

He was immediately taken to the operating room where surgery could be undertaken to remove the arrows from him. Until his face was cleaned of the blood that had run down his face from the two wounds in his head, no one had recognized him. As the blood was being wiped off of his face, one of the nurses explained, "Oh my God. It's Russell Hendrix." Then she addressed her comments to the unconscious boy on the operating table, "You poor boy. What have they done to you?"

The others looked at the face of Russell, which by now appeared relaxed and as if he had died in peace. They flinched in shock.

The anesthetist called out. "Ok. Let's get him prepped for the operation."

Meanwhile, a reporter for CKLN radio station got the phone number of the girl's home in Willow Point and the girls gave him the information he was seeking with respect to what they had heard and seen.

This information was immediately passed onto the police and it took approximately half an hour for them to come to the realization that it was the Ballard brothers and their father who had brutalized the boy. Three squad cars carrying nine officers headed west on Granite road to arrest them.

When they were nearing the Ballard farm, they saw a dark blue Ford leaving the farm and heading west. They chased after it and seeing three men in it, they concluded that it was their quarry. The chase lasted half an hour and after they had passed Castlegar, the car slid out of control and went head first into a small rock cliff close to the side of the road and crashed into a nearby ditch.

The car immediately burst into flames. As the officers watched the three men trapped inside the unapproachable flames, screaming and writhing in pain, one of the officers said to another. "Let em burn. This will give them some idea of what Hell is going to be like when they get there."

Later, it was confirmed that the three men who died in the fire so hideously were also the three men who had tortured Russell. No one in Nelson who later learned of their deaths offered a tear for their demise although the women who knew Mrs. Ballard grieved over her death. They knew that she too had been a victim of her husband and her two sons. She was buried in a local cemetery. The ashes of her husband and sons were shoveled up and placed in a large paper bag that was then placed in a small cardboard container and later buried in a small cemetery near Castlegar with no gravestone or plaque to designate who they were as all they got was a number for the three of them. To this day, there is no record of what the number designates. The names were mysteriously inked over in the record book at the Cemetery office and the number plate over the grave later vanished. A new grave was later dug on the same spot for a burial of someone else.

At two in the afternoon, CKLN began telling the Nelsonites what had happened to Russell. They put out a plea to all adults to come to the hospital to donate blood as he was in urgent need of it. The announcer said that Russell had lost almost a third of his blood and would die if he weren't given a transfusion to replace what he had lost. His blood type was made known but most people who heard the announcement and were willing to donate their blood didn't know what their own blood type was so they showed up at the hospital anyway to do whatever they could do for the boy.

The announcer also asked the people of Nelson to stand outside the hospital and pray for Russell's recovery.

Within half an hour, over two hundred people were lined up to donate blood. In the second hour, over five hundred people were lined up for two blocks on View Street. Within the next hour after that, another seven hundred were standing on the street praying for Russell's recovery and even when it began to rain; it didn't deter them from staying.

At five in the afternoon despite most of his missing blood having been replaced and the arrowheads having been removed, he died on the operating table.

The chief surgeon stated that Russell's death was probably hastened by his state of exhaustion and by the severity of the whipping he received, with its resultant blood loss and pre-shock state.

Russell was wheeled into one of the rooms near the operating room and his wrists and feet were bandaged up and a sheet was placed over his body.

Within an hour of his death, the radio station CKLN was making an announcement every ten minutes until midnight telling its listeners that Russell had died on the operating table.

The Anglican minister asked to see the Administrator of the hospital. "Gerald." The minister said as he was led into the administrator's office. "I have just heard the sad news."

"Reverend. We too are heartbroken that we couldn't save the boy."

The minister continued, "I could see from where I was standing on View Street that over a thousand are lined up donate their blood or pray for Russell's soul. I have a suggestion you may wish to consider."

"Yes?"

"Why not let all of those outside have the opportunity to see the boy lying in his bed facing them. Knowing that some of them donated their blood in their attempts to save the boy or prayed for his soul will ease their pain at their loss when they look at him lying so peacefully on the bed."

"This is most unusual request." replied the administrator.

"Of course it is." replied the minister. "This is an unusual event."

The administrator said he think about it. He did and agreed with the suggestion.

The bed Russell's body was in was moved along side the window facing the hall so that anyone walking by the window in the room would see him lying in the bed. His bandaged wrists and feet were on the outside of the sheet so that the public would realize what a terrible thing had been done to their favorite son. The heart monitor was moved to the head of the bed and left on with a green flat line showing on the screen and a soft non-pulsing tone emanating from the machine. The nurses felt that the public should see the monitor to convince them that their favorite son really was gone from them.

Fifteen minutes later, the men and women began filing past Russell's room. Some made signs of the cross as they stared at Russell's face. Many were crying. By midnight, everyone had passed by his body.

The hospital staff had notified William and Beatrice when Russell had been brought in and they remained in his room when the people were filing past. Unbeknown to them, it was the same room that Larry had been in years earlier.

While still sitting in the chairs in Russell's room at one o'clock in the morning, they heard a soft beeping noise from the heart monitor.

They looked up and saw the small green line on the screen fluctuating. They stared at it, then at Russell's face. He still appeared to be dead to them. They both frowned when looking at the machine because they had got used to the original non-pulsating tone but the beeping noise interfered with their private thoughts.

"Maybe," said Beatrice, "we should tell someone that the machine is making some kind of beeping noise."

"I'll look for a nurse." replied William as he stood up.

He found a lone nurse at the nurse's station on the phone.

"Nurse. There is something—."

The nurse interjected, "I will be with you in a moment, Sir."

She continued talking on the phone for another minute.

After the minute had passed, she was still talking on the phone when William impatiently said, "The machine in Russell's room is making a beeping noise. Could you come into Russell's room and turn the machine off?"

Only a second had passed before his words sunk in. The nurse dropped the phone on the desk and exclaimed, "Oh my God!"

She ran down the hall and stared at the monitor. Then she went to Russell and opened one of his eyes. In an instant, she ran back to the nurses' station and the Hampstons could hear her speaking into the phone. "I got to hang up."

A second later she dialed a number and spoke again. "Get the doctor up here right away. "I think the boy is alive." There was a pause. Then she said as if answering a question, "Because his pupils are no longer fixed and dilated."

In less than a minute, seven nurses and the doctor were on the floor. The doctor entered the room and pulled out a small penlight from his breast pocket and shone the light into Russell's left eye. He then looked at the monitor. He pulled the sheet back and put his stethoscope to Russell's chest.

"The boy is definitely alive." He then began pressing on Russell's chest just below his sternum while he kept looking at the heart monitor. William and Beatrice meanwhile stood next to the wall with their hands clasped in prayer.

The nurses outside the room were talking to each other excitedly. One of the nurses exclaimed to another, "This is the second time this hospital has been blessed with a miracle." She looked at her watch. It was ten after one in the morning.

At eight in the morning, the radio station was on the air again. The announcer said. "This is CLKN and it is eight in the morning. Nelson has been blessed with a second raising of the dead. Russell Hendrix is alive! Yes folks. Russell Hendrix is alive. He was discovered breathing at around one in the morning. The hospital has confirmed that he is unconscious but he is currently breathing on his own. It was your collective prayers that did it folks. Russell Hendrix is alive!"

This message was repeated every ten minutes for the rest of the morning.

It was Sunday morning. The sun was out and by ten o'clock; thousands of people were standing in front of the hospital. Many were singing while others prayed. Most were by now convinced that Nelson was blessed with the second coming of Christ. They believed that without a doubt, Jesus had returned as a child and had been living amongst them all along. Some even chastised others for having doubted that Russell was in fact Jesus as a child who had come to save them, just as he promised he would.

At eleven, the churches were packed. They wanted to hear their clergymen explain to them this miracle that had come to Nelson.

The Anglican minister said to his congregation, "There can be no doubt in anyone's mind that Nelson is indeed blessed with a miracle. I have been asked to tell you whether or not Russell Hendrix is Jesus Christ. I must confess that at this moment, I am confused. I want to believe that Jesus has returned to us but I am not sure."

The other clergymen said more or less the same in their churches. They too weren't sure.

The hospital was footing the bill for the care of Russell and the churches agreed to foot the bills for the doctors. Donations to the churches were plentiful for the doctor's bills.

Meanwhile, a specialist in the treatment of deep incisions was brought in from Vancouver to try to salvage as much flesh and skin as could be salvaged from Russell's torso so that the scars would be minimal if at all possible.

The first task of the nurses was to clean the wounds. Because the hospital thought Russell had died, they originally thought it pointless to work on his wounds. The manure dust in the abandoned barn had settled on Russell's wounds and infection had formed in many of the cuts. The specialist cleaned and then sutured the minor wounds. Those wounds would eventually leave hairline scars.

The gaping irregular wounds on the other hand were left open, as the damage was so extensive, the edges were ragged. They would have to heal from the inside out. The nurses periodically cleaned them so that infection wouldn't form. Eventually healthy tissue formed and the wounds would later be surgically sutured. Mercifully, all this while, Russell was spared the pain as he was unconscious and in a deep coma.

The two questions on everyone's minds were, 'Will he come out of the coma? If not, who will take his place?'

2 Maccabees, chapter 3: 29-30: While he lay prostrate, speechless because of the divine intervention and deprived of any hope of recovery, they praised the Lord who had acted marvelously for his own place.

Chapter Seven

At two in the afternoon, all the clergymen in Nelson met at the vicarage of the Catholic Church. Bishop Johnson said to the gathering. "My brothers. We are faced with a dilemma. Our people want to know if Russell Hendrix is really Christ, our Lord who has come back to us as a child."

One of the ministers added. "I too want to know if we are experiencing a reappearance of Christ."

"Did he not come back to Mankind on the third day after he was crucified?" asked the third.

"And did he not speak with his disciples later?" asked another. Then he added, "The question before us is whether or not Jesus is expected back on Earth again. I suggest we look to Revelation."

The clergymen opened their *Bibles* and began searching through Revelation. One of them pointed out a passage. It read;

> Then I looked, and lo, on Mount Zion stood the Lamb, and with him a hundred and forty-four thousand who had his name and his Father's name written on their foreheads.

Now, Brothers." said the same man who suggested that they look to Revelation for their answer. "We all know that it was John in Revelation that spoke of this and we know that the Lamb he speaks of is the Son of God, Jesus, our lord and savior. And he said this long after Jesus ascended into Heaven."

The other men nodded in their agreement with him. The same man quoted again from Revelation.

> …..they will make war on the Lamb, and the Lamb will conquer them, for he is Lord of lords and King of kings…..

"We have all known that Jesus Christ is the king of kings." said another.

One of them then remarked with a smile. "If Jesus is to return to Earth at the head of a hundred and forty-four thousand, and do this from the top of Mount Zion, then this rules out Russell Hendrix. He came into Nelson as an orphan boy and alone at that. Christ our Lord is expected to arrive for his reappearance on the small mount in the centre of Jerusalem. Nelson is not Jerusalem and Russell is not Christ, our Lord. He is hardly what we expected, now is he?"

The clergymen again nodded in agreement. The bishop suggested that they reflect on their problem for an hour and look into their *Bibles* to see if there was another explanation.

Fifty minutes later, the bishop exclaimed, "I believe that I have found our answer!"

The others looked up and one of them asked, "Where?"

"Hebrews, Chapter nine, verses twenty-seven and eight.

The clergymen flipped the pages of their *Bibles* to that part of the Holy Book and stared at the passages.

> And just as it is appointed for men to die once, and after that comes judgment, so Christ, having been offered once to bear the sins of many, will appear a second time, not to deal with sin but to save those who are eagerly waiting for him.

"Surely my brothers," continued the bishop, "this is a clear indication that Russell's appearance is not, I repeat, not the second coming of Christ. That part of the *Bible* clearly implies that the second coming will come on judgment day. That day, my dear brothers, is not yet upon us."

The Lutheran clergyman smiled and said, "I certainly hope not. I'm not sure I am ready for judgment day."

The Catholic bishop said with a frown on his face, "Didn't Jesus return a second time three days after he was crucified?"

The Lutheran responded, "That was his first reappearance."

The priest responded, "No, brother. His first appearance was on the day of his birth. When he reappeared three days after his resurrection; that was his second appearance."

"That appears to conflict with the scripture we just read." said the Anglican priest. Then he asked, "When is judgment day supposed to be upon us then?"

The bishop said in reply, "All I know is that it is to be some day in the future. Admittedly, past disasters have often been treated by those who experienced them as a series of world judgments but I believe that these past judgments have been culminating into one final judgment which I strongly suspect is far into the future of humankind."

The Anglican minister had been looking through his *Bible* and then he said to the others, "I refer you to Mathew, chapter twelve, verse, thirty-six. He quoted it, *'I tell you, on the day of judgment, men will render account for every careless word they utter.'* My brothers. He refers to the day of judgment. That means to me that there will only be one day of judgment and that day is sometime in the future and not now."

The others nodded their heads in agreement.

There was further discussion amongst them but their collective thinking was as one—Russell Hendrix was not Jesus Christ making his reappearance onto Earth.

One of them asked the others, "Do we need to make a joint announcement to this effect considering we made it last year and Russell Hendrix has already admitted that he was not Christ returning to us as a child?"

The bishop responded, "I am afraid we will have too."

Another added, "When we had made our original public announcement, the boy had not been whipped and crucified and died as a direct result of his torment just as Christ did. And to make matters worse, he hadn't come back to life again, just as Christ did."

Another piped in, "And on a Sunday, would you believe it?"

"I am afraid, my brothers, we will have to make another announcement and make it a joint one as before."

"The Anglican minister said, "Let's make it next Sunday morning in our churches and then publish it in the afternoon with CKLN and our local newspaper."

They agreed to meet on Wednesday to write the final draft.

Meanwhile, Russell was still unconscious. William had driven home to milk his cows and when he returned, Russell's doctor said to him as he entered Russell's room, "I am afraid that Russell is in a coma. I have no idea as to whether or not he will ever come out of it or remain in a coma for the rest of his life. He lost a lot of blood and that may have resulted in him being brain dead."

Beatrice began to cry and William placed his arm around her shoulder to comfort her.

The crowd outside had dwindled considerably after a doctor went outside and announced that Russell was still alive but in a coma.

Larry visited Russell every day after school and spent most of the evenings in his hospital room until his father picked him up and brought him home. When he was with Russell, he read him stories from books.

When Wednesday afternoon arrived, the clergymen met at the bishop's vicarage again and they began working together to write their joint announcement. They spent three hours writing and rewriting and when it was finished, they made copies of it for themselves and agreed to read the announcements in their churches at exactly eleven thirty on the next Sunday morning.

That Sunday, the churches were filled to overflowing. Loud speakers were set outside so that those who couldn't get into their churches could hear the sermons and the announcements being said inside the churches. The parishioners and others, who attended those churches, knew that a special announcement would be made that day with respect to the miracle of Russell's resurrection. When it was eleven thirty, the clergymen in each of their churches began reading their collective announcement.

The clergy of the Christian churches in Nelson have recently had several meetings together to draft this joint public announcement with respect to Russell Hendrix, the fifteen-year-old boy that so many of us have grown to love and respect.

It was a terrible thing that happened to Russell and God has seen fit to keep him alive so that he may continue to serve our Lord and Savior, Jesus Christ and God in the way that he has done so in the past.

It is extremely coincidental that just as Jesus was brutally whipped and crucified, so was Russell. Admittedly, they both died and came back to life. But that coincidence, in our respectful opinion, does not mean that Russell is Jesus Christ who has returned to Earth and come to us again as a child.

It must be remembered that many Christian martyrs where whipped and crucified and they weren't our Lord Jesus anymore than Russell is.

We continue to acknowledge however that Russell is a very devoted Christian who has suffered dearly for his service to our Lord and Savior, Jesus Christ just as thousands of martyrs before him suffered and as such, he should be treated with the greatest respect that can be bestowed upon a fellow human being whose presence amongst us is truly a gift from God.

It is our sincerest hope that Russell will get well again and that he will join us as soon as possible so that he can continue to serve our Lord Jesus and God in the way that so many have done so before him.

We beseech our Lord Jesus and God to spare Russell Hendrix from any more pain and suffering and make him well enough to walk amongst us again and preach to us as he has done so in the past.

During the weeks that followed, there were discussions everywhere as to whether or not Russell really was Jesus Christ who had returned to Earth as a child during his reappearance. Their positions and opinions were swaying like trees in the wind. Sometimes they believed he was Jesus and other times they weren't sure and other times they were convinced that he wasn't Jesus.

One thing that they had no doubts about however was, as their clergymen stated, Russell was deserving of their highest respect.

Letters from all over the world were placed in boxes that were piled high in his room. Larry would open them and staple them to the envelopes and sort them as per each country.

A form letter that was signed by him was sent to each person whose letter had a return address. The churches chipped in to pay for the printing and mailing of the letters going out. Each letter said,

> I am Larry Anderson, the best friend of Russell Hendrix. He is still in a coma and I know that he would thank you personally if he could do so for your thoughtful message.
>
> His doctor does not know if he will ever come out of his coma but if he does, be assured that Russell will pray for all who wrote him and also pray for their families and friends.
>
> We in Nelson feel so blessed having him in our small city but Russell has always believed that God is in every city, town and village and in all of us, wherever we are and he further believes, as we in Nelson do, that we can all pray to God to help us ease our pain and suffering.
>
> I know that I speak for Russell and the people of our fair city when I say that we hope that God blesses you, your family and your friends.

One evening, Larry was reading out loud from the book, *The Robe*. Over a period of a week, he had been reading it to his unconscious friend. He was now reciting from the last page of the book while the Hampstons sat nearby listening to him.

Caligula drew himself up erectly.

"Tribune Marcellus Gallio." he announced. "It is our decree that you be taken immediately to the Palace Archery Field and put to death for high treason."

Suddenly Larry and the Hampstons heard a weak voice coming from Russell's bed. As they looked at Russell, he opened his eyes and looked at Larry and smiled. Then he said, "He was to suffer from the same fate I did; being shot with arrows."

There was great rejoicing in the room. William ran out into the hallway and screamed, "He's back! He's back!"

The nurses and doctors ran to the room and stared at what was to them, another miracle.

The next day, the newspaper's headline in large letters was, HE'S BACK.

Although the churches weren't as filled like before, but many people attended them nevertheless that following Sunday. The minister of the Anglican church more or less summed up the feelings of everyone in Nelson when he said in his sermon.

"We have prayed and waited and God has answered our prayers. Russell Hendrix has returned to us. It is our sincerest hope that some day soon, Russell will walk among us again and preach the good word to us."

That day came sooner than expected. By the end of August, Russell's ribs were healed and there were only fourteen deep scars on his torso that could still be seen if he took off his shirt. The scars where the nails protruded into his wrists were visible also and would remain so.

It was agreed by the principal of the junior high school and the Hampstons that Russell would arrive at the school two days after the school year began in September and further that the principle would make an announcement on the first day of school as to what the students should not be saying when speaking to Russell.

On the first day of school, the principal turned on the microphone in his office that would carry his voice through the public address system into all the classrooms. He said, "As you are all aware, Russell

Hendrix is well again and he will be returning to our school in two days time."

A great cheer could be heard throughout the school. When the din subsided, the principal began again. "He has suffered a terrible ordeal and it follows that he doesn't want to relive it by telling anyone what it was like to suffer as he did on that horrible day in June. For this reason, I am asking you to refrain from asking him to tell you about that event in his life."

The students could understand that and were nodding their heads in agreement. The principal continued. "As you are well aware, the clergy of our city have pronounced that in their opinion, Russell is not, I repeat, not Jesus Christ who has come to us from heaven. He is an ordinary boy. Let me correct myself, he is a remarkable boy whom God has seen fit to bless us by sending Russell into our community, as many of you will agree."

There was more nodding of heads in agreement.

He continued. "Russell has asked that he be treated no differently than any other student in this school. To treat him differently would in effect, make him stand out and that is the last thing he wants to do—stand out as someone special. I sincerely hope that you will follow my advice."

The principal turned off the mike and wondered to himself. *'Do students really follow the advice of their principals and teachers?'* He doubted it. He didn't when he was a student.

Two days later, Russell and Larry were approaching the school while being driven north on Josephine Street by Larry's father. When they were half a block south of the southwest corner of the school property, Russell said that he would prefer to walk the rest of the way. He and Larry got out of the car and together they headed towards the school. By the time they got to the long centre pathway that led directly towards the front doors of the school, a hundred students were bunched up at the entrance to the pathway.

Many voices rang out, "Hi Russell." and "Glad you are back."

Many of the students approached him and shook his hands and patted him on his shoulders. No one asked him what it was like to be whipped, crucified and shot with arrows. Many however wanted to know what it was like to die and then come back to life again but none dare ask him. The principal was wrong. His students did listen to him and they did heed his advice.

For the next three months, he was treated as someone very special. There was simply no getting around it. He was very special. He had lived and died as Jesus did and came back to life just as Jesus did. His incredible memory was legend around town. He remembered what everyone he had previously spoken to had said to him and when they said it. His words of wisdom were repeated everywhere.

Then in the first week in December, that was to all change for the worse.

1 Timothy, chapter 5: 13: .... they learn to be idlers, gadding about from house to house, and not only idlers but gossips and busybodies, saying what they should not.

Luke, chapter 2: 46: After three days they found him in the temple, sitting among the teachers, listening to them and asking them questions.

Chapter Eight

Gossip and rumors differ in that the former is a form of hurtful talk between friends, neighbors and even strangers about another person which is usually done behind the victim's back. Often it is slanderous and done with indifference with respect to destroying someone's reputation. The latter is simply a repeating of a piece of information that hasn't really been verified because the person telling it doesn't know if it is true. It can be as innocuous as repeating a story about someone moving out of town. Gossip that is passed around town is like the collection plate being passed to you in your church. There is no way of avoiding it.

Some of those in Nelson who originally heard the gossip merely said, "It ain't so." and "Unbelievable." and "I don't believe it." They believed that the originator of the gossip was someone who wanted to get back at the victim of the gossip for some imagined wrong committed against them. The victim of the gossip was none other that Russell Hendrix.

It was alleged that he had asked for a large sum of money from a dying person before Russell would pray for that person. The money wasn't paid and Russell didn't pray for the dying person. Shortly after that, the person died. It was a terrible allegation that was untrue but since no one knew where the story began, it was impossible to determine the validity of the allegation.

It appeared to Russell that there were only six people who had heard the gossip who were unquestionably convinced in their own minds that Russell was incapable of doing such a dastardly deed.

They were; William and Beatrice, Larry and his parents and the minister in the Anglican Church. Others simply weren't sure. However, most of the people who spoke of this were convinced that Russell had betrayed them all by conducting himself in such a repulsive manner.

This became obvious to him when people on the street would cross the street rather than pass him on the same sidewalk. Those who were on the same sidewalk would either scowl at him or tell him to his face how horrible he was. He was being greeted by the people in Nelson the same way old man Ballard had been greeted. The students at the school were even crueler.

Even when he sat in a pew in church on Sundays, people in the pew moved to another pew and he ended up sitting alone.

He gave up trying to explain to them that he was innocent since it didn't do him any good. No one cared or alternatively they said, "I don't want to get involved" or words to that effect.

On weekends, he chose to be alone so he would wander around the countryside so that the only communication he would have with anyone would be God. He needed time to re-think what his mission in life was going to be.

On December 16th, the second Sunday before Christmas, Russell had a meeting with his minister about this problem.

"I don't know what I can do to solve this problem, Reverend," said Russell sadly.

The minister replied, "I wish I could think of a way in which I could help you but stopping a gossip from crashing through all barriers of decency is like trying to stop a runaway train. Sometimes in the attempt, you get run over yourself."

"Are you saying that you won't help me?"

"Of course not! Let me speak with the other clergymen and see if we can make a joint public announcement that will put an end to this once and for all."

The other clergymen met and between them, they created a joint response to the allegations against Russell and it was agreed that it would be presented to their congregations on the 21st of December, four days before Christmas. CKLN agreed to read it over the air ten times that day in both the afternoon and evening. The local newspaper agreed to publish it on December 24th. The announcement said;

> We are fast approaching that great moment in our lives when all Christians can celebrate the birth of our Lord, Jesus Christ. But there is a shroud over Nelson that that has befallen us. It is an evil shroud that brings blackness to the hearts of many.
>
> There has been an evil unsubstantiated story going around Nelson that Russell Hendrix refused to pray for a dying man unless he was paid a large sum of money first. There is absolutely no evidence of such an accusation being true. Further, no one even knows where the story began or who the so-called dying man was.
>
> Whoever initiated this horrible story and those who carry it onto others, is each doing a sinful act? Ask yourselves, "What do they profit by the advancement of this story?"
>
> The initiator may have done his or her deed for some kind of revenge for some imagined wrong committed to him or her by Russell. Those who move the story along are motivated by some need to shock others—a form of self-created entertainment if you will.
>
> In Jeremiah, chapter 13, verse 25, it says, "This is thy lot, the portion of thy measures from me, saith the LORD; because thou hast forgotten me, and trusted in falsehood."
>
> Russell is not our Lord but you trusted in him nevertheless and now you have forgotten his deeds and now some of you trust only in a falsehood. Those who trust in falsehoods have no foundation in which to build their beliefs.

You should seek forgiveness from our Lord but you do not need to seek it from Russell. He does not seek it from those who have perpetuated this falsehood because he believes that all persons have goodness in their hearts and he holds no malice against anyone in his.

Why is it that those who on the surface appear to be most virtuous in the eyes of their neighbors and yet at the same time, their hearts are filled with evil?

Those of you who either initiated or have alternatively, moved this horrible story along and then have entered God's house to pray, are guilty of hypocrisy. Was it not in Mathew 7, verse 5 in which he said, "You hypocrite, first cast out the beam in thine own eyes; then shall you see clearly to cast out the mote in your brother's eye?"

We say to you. If you seek forgiveness from God for your deeds, do not be hypocritical and continue acting out those deeds.

Treat Russell Hendrix with the deep respect he unquestionably deserves.

May the blessings of our Lord be upon this message and those who heed it.

By the time Christmas Day had arrived, there were very few who hadn't either heard or read the message. Things would improve for Russell in that aspect now that the gossiping had more or less vanished like the mist from the heat of the early morning sun.

Christmas at the Hampston homestead was a joyous occasion. Larry and his parents shared the Hampstons' Christmas dinner with them and there was singing throughout the evening. The hit tune, *I'm Dreaming of a White Christmas* sung by Bing Crosby, had full meaning to everyone as snow flakes fell over the city of Nelson and the countryside, creating a soft blanket of snow over everything.

For many people around the world, the year of 1952 would be an interesting one. Irish Coffee and White Rose Redi-Tea would appear for the first time as would aluminum-faced homes and 3-D movies. Elvis Presley would onto the scene as a singer, Scrabble would become a fad and the state of Ohio would finally be admitted to the United States as one of its states. The Salk vaccine would be used for the first time to vaccinate millions of children to protect them from polio and the first open-heart surgery would be performed that year.

When Russell showed up at his school, he was greeted warmly by the students. A number of them asked him for his forgiveness for treating him so badly. His response was a simple, "No need to apologize." By the time February arrived, many of the students began asking him again for his advice on religion and information about events in history. They also asked him to intercede on their behalf when there were problems between them and other students. He enjoyed the role he was playing. He felt that he was serving a useful purpose in life.

One day in February 1952, a number of students were sitting around him in the gymnasium at school and they began asking him questions about the *Bible* again.

One asked, "It says in the *Bible* that God made the Heaven and Earth in seven days. That doesn't seem possible. Can you explain that to us?

Another responded, "God can do anything he wants in as many days as he chooses."

The group looked at Russell for his opinion. He began, "Does it not seem strange to you that it takes a month for a tree to bud and yet God created Heaven and Earth in only one day? The question you must ask yourself is, 'What did the writers of the Old Testament mean when they spoke of one day? Was it really twenty-four hours or was it between one billion and a hundred billion years?"

A student piped in, "If it was a hundred billion years, why didn't they say that?"

"Perhaps," said Russell in reply, "they couldn't really fathom what a hundred billion years was. For example, when you were four years old, did you know what a hundred billion of anything was?

Another student responded jokingly, "He still doesn't know what a hundred billion of anything is."

Russell said, "If you placed one hundred billion one-dollar bills side by side, its length from one end to the other would be six thousand miles. Those one-dollar bills would stretch from Nelson to the shores of China."

The students shook their heads in amazement at his explanation.

Russell continued, "What we as students in this school have learned since we were born, are thousands of times more than those who wrote the Old Testament had learned when they were alive. They didn't know as much as a grade six student in our modern era does. The writers of the Old Testament began writing it four hundred years ago and in the sixteenth century, King James instructed many of his learned subjects to rewrite the *Bible*, the book we call the King James Version. They simply chose to accept the original text and stick with the word 'days' rather than use 'eons' for example, a word that wasn't in their vocabulary then."

A student asked, "Is there anything you can't answer with respect to the Holy *Bible*?"

"Of course." replied Russell. Then he continued, "I refer you to Chapter four of Genesis, verse fourteen. Cain says to God, 'Behold, you have driven me out this day from the face of the Earth; and from your face shall I be hid; and I shall be a fugitive and a vagabond in the Earth; and it shall come to pass that everyone that finds me shall slay me.' Now ask yourselves this question. If Cain was the son of Adam and Eve who were supposed to be the first two humans on Earth, and Cain killed his brother Abel, then who was he talking about when he expressed his concern that everyone that finds him would kill him?"

None had an answer. Then Russell continued, "You have to ask yourself if Adam and Eve really were the first two humans on Earth. It is conceivable that they were two of very many human beings on Earth at that time but were the first to be spoken of."

A student responded, "But the *Bible* says that they were the first on Earth."

Russell smiled and said, "The *Bible* also says, and I quote from verse seventeen of that same chapter. 'And Cain knew his wife; and she conceived, and bare Enoch: and he built a city, and called the name of the city, after the name of his son, Enoch.' This means that he impregnated a woman and she gave birth to their son and he built a city he named after his son. Who was the woman? It wasn't his mother Eve because Cain had been ordered to move away from his parents and find another place to live. He couldn't build a city all by himself so that means there were many people in the same area on Earth when Adam and Eve came onto the scene."

Russell realized that he had a responsibility to not tell his friends that the *Bible* wasn't to be totally believed. With this thought in mind, he said to them, "Millions of people believe the *Bible* is the infallible Word of God. To them, the Scriptures are inerrant. But to others, the *Bible* is merely a collection of ancient, uninspired writings that may have some historical, poetic and inspirational value. Most Christians however do not really believe that the humans who penned the books of the *Bible* were always accurate in everything they wrote down. Other people are convinced that the *Bible* is inspired in that the writers did put down some of God's ideas, but maybe some of the writers of the *Bible* put some of their own uninspired ideas in it also. For example, God may have inspired them but left them to express those ideas as they saw best and like all human beings, they were not infallible.

The students were satisfied with Russell's answer even though some were confused as to whether his answer was closer to the truth than that of the teachings of the *Bible*.

Three years earlier, the United States Supreme Court had ruled that religious instruction in public schools violated the American Constitution. This finally became an issue in 1952 that was some concern to the citizens of Nelson and school, church and civil authorities in Nelson. Subsequently, a meeting was held in the auditorium of Trafalgar Junior High School. All the teachers and clergymen including a rabbi were present. Russell was also invited because it was believed, and correctly so, that he really held the pulse of the students. The superintendent of schools chaired the meeting.

The superintendent was a man in his late fifties who had been a principal for twelve years before he got his appointment. He had often joked that he began getting his white hair after he got the appointment because he had to deal with teachers instead of students.

After he introduced the others on the stage who were the clergymen, the school principals and Russell, he began his opening address.

"As you are all aware, the United States Supreme Court had previously ruled that schools in the United States cannot teach religion in the schools anymore. We have to decide whether or not, we should continue to teach religion in our schools."

"A principal angrily interjected before the Superintendent could continue. "We are not bound by that court!"

"That's true," replied the superintendent, "but I have received many letters from the parents of students in the various schools who have sought answers to this issue.

One of the principals asked, "Does this mean that we are to cancel prayers at the beginning of the school day?"

The rabbi said, "I for one do not believe that the prayer should be the Lord's Prayer. That is a Christian prayer and not all of the students are Christians. It should be remembered that Christianity is not the only religion in the world. There are Jews, and Muslims and those who are Buddhists who pray differently than Christians do."

"The majority are Christians." responded another principal.

The rabbi continued, "In our country, do we consider what is best for ourselves by the majority or do we consider the wishes of all?"

"In this city, the majority rules!" retorted one of the principals.

Russell asked, "Wasn't it Gladstone in his House of Commons speech in 1870 who said, and I quote; 'The oppression of the majority is detestable and odious.'

Russell again had his audience in wonder as to his ability to recite word for word from any textbook he had previously read.

Russell then replied to the statement of the principal, "Perhaps the abuse of Jews in Canada is not done in the same manner that had befallen them under the Nazis during the Holocaust but how many Jews are invited into our Christian homes? How many Jews are permitted to stay overnight in our hotels? How many Jewish students are expected to recite the Lord's Prayer in class when they are not Christians themselves? Are these not forms of oppression?"

The superintendent then said, "Students shall have the right to pray individually and quietly in their classrooms or in groups or to discuss their own religious views with their peers or anyone else so long as they are not disruptive and that goes for those of the Jewish faith and any other faith."

When put to a vote, all agreed. The rabbi placed his hand over Russell's and smiled; it was his form of gratitude.

A principal asked, "Are we still to ask our students to recite the Lord's Prayer at the beginning of the school day?"

"Yes." replied the superintendent, "But no one has to recite it aloud. Those who are not of the Christian faith may pray in any manner they so choose."

That decision that was arrived at without a vote seemed to please the principals.

One of the principals then asked the superintendent, "Are we permitted to teach creationism as per the biblical text or are we to only teach the evolutionary theory?

The superintendent replied, "Schools should not refuse to teach the evolutionary theory simply to avoid giving some offense to religion nor should they circumvent my decision by reaching religious faith as science. Put another way, our schools shouldn't teach as scientific fact or theory any religious doctrine, including 'creationism'. Of course, any genuinely scientific evidence for or against any explanation of life should be taught. Just as teachers should neither advance nor inhibit any religious doctrine, they should not also ridicule, for example, a student's religious explanation for life on Earth."

Again the conferees agree.

A teacher asked, "If in a sex education class, a student remarks that abortion should be illegal because God has prohibited it, how should we reply to that question?"

One of the clergy responded, "A teacher should not silence the remark, ridicule it, rule it out of bounds or endorse it, any more than a teacher may silence a student's religiously-based comment in which he is against abortion. Abortion is illegal in this country and it cannot be condoned or brought about."

There was some grumbling in the auditorium.

Another teacher asked, "Not even when there has been a rape?"

The superintendent said quickly, "We are not here today to discuss abortion. Let's stick to the purpose of our meeting; religion in school."

One of the teachers in Russell's school said, "Russell Hendrix preaches religion in our gymnasium in our school, in fact he also preaches elsewhere on school property. Is he then not to preach religion on school property?"

The superintendent looked at Russell and then spoke into his microphone. "Let Russell give us his opinion on that issue."

Russell thought for a moment and then after leaning towards his microphone, he began to speak.

"Students should have the right to speak to others and attempt to persuade their peers about religious topics just as they do with regard to political topics. But school officials should intercede to stop student religious speech if it turns into religious harassment aimed at a student or a small group of students. At no time during my talks with my fellow students have I spoken about anything other than loving our neighbors, praying to God, and literally quoting from the *Bible* and interpreting it."

"Is that all you preach?" asked a principal?

Russell responded, "I also preach to them about civic virtues, including honesty, good citizenship, sportsmanship, courage, respect for the rights and freedoms of others, respect for persons and their property, civility, the dual virtues of moral conviction and tolerance and hard work. The mere fact that most, if not all, religions also teach these values does not make it improper for me to refer to the *Bible* to reinforce these attributes that are ideal in every student."

A teacher then asked, "Did you not say to some students recently that the biblical term, 'a day' found in Genesis is not a twenty-four-hour day?"

"Yes I did." replied Russell.

"Then you are preaching evolutionary theories while quoting from the *Bible*, are you not?"

Russell responded, "The U.S. Supreme Court of the United States has repeatedly said, 'It might well be said that one's education is not complete without a study of comparative religion, or the history of religion and its relationship to the advancement of civilization.' I agree with that view."

Russell continued. "We cannot escape the undisputable fact that world did not begin a little more than five thousand years ago as per the creationist's view anymore than we can escape the gravitational pull of our planet."

The clergymen shuffled uneasily with this statement by Russell.

Russell could see the expressions of concern on their faces so he added, "As I personally see it, not everything in the *Bible* is to be taken at face value. For example, Moses passed a law that anyone that worked on the Sabbath was to be stoned to death. That punishment for that reason hasn't been applied in a very long time. Times change and so must our beliefs."

"Are you saying that you don't believe in the teachings of the *Bible?*" asked another?"

"Do you?" asked Russell.

"Of course. I believe in them all literally."

Russell smiled and asked his antagonist, "Do you believe that the beginning of Earth took place about five thousand years ago?"

"Naturally." replied the clergyman. "The *Bible* doesn't state that but looking back through the pages of Genesis, one can make that assumption."

One of the teachers suddenly asked the Superintendent, "Aren't we getting off topic here. I thought that we were here to discuss whether or not religion can be taught in our schools."

The superintendent replied, "That's true but now the issue has been changed to whether or not Russell can preach in our schools considering that he is more of an evolutionist rather than a creationist."

Russell thanked the superintendent and then continued, "In the *Bible*, it says in Genesis and I will quote; 'In the beginning God created the Heaven and the Earth. And the Earth was without form, and void; and darkness was upon the face of the deep. And the Spirit of God moved upon the face of the waters. And God said, 'Let there be light: and there was light. And God saw the light, that it was good: and God divided the light from the darkness. And God called the light Day, and the darkness he called Night. And the evening and the morning were the first day.'

He paused and then continued, "The words; 'and darkness was upon the deep and God moved upon the face of the waters' refers to the depth of our oceans. In verse three, it says; 'And God said, Let there be light: and there was light.' This means that after he created the oceans on Earth, he created the sun. Does that make any sense? In verse four, it says in Genesis; 'And God saw the light, that it was good: and God divided the light from the darkness."

Russell continued, "Now from this, we can surmise that was the moment when our planet began spinning on its axis. But here is the conundrum. Earth began its existence about four and a half billion years ago. When Earth began spinning on its axis, there was no water on Earth. Earth only consisted of molten magma. Therefore God could not have caused the spinning of Earth after the water was on the surface of Earth. It was spinning long before that."

The minister didn't respond.

Russell then said, "I don't accept all of the words of the *Bible* literally. I do however take many of the passages of the *Bible* as being most appropriate as a guide to living a proper life. That is what I am attempting to tell my fellow students."

There was silence in the gymnasium. Then the superintendent spoke, "As I see it, Russell Hendrix does not harass other students while he teaches them in the manner in which he does and although his views sometimes conflict with those who prefer to accept all the words of the *Bible* in their literal form, this does not mean that he is wrong in giving his views of how the *Bible* should be interpreted. For this reason, he may continue to preach on our school property if the students ask that of him."

With that, he closed the meeting. As Russell was leaving the gymnasium, the minister of the Lutheran church approached Russell and asked, "Could we meet next week? I want to discuss with you a sermon you might wish to give to my congregation the following Sunday."

Russell smiled and said that would be fine.

The two met at the minister's office on the Tuesday and after a brief chitchat, the minister got right to the topic of the proposed sermon; Love. The sermon would be given the following Sunday.

On Sunday, the 14th of February, Valentines Day, Russell preached to the Lutheran congregation. It was later read on the air and printed in the local newspaper. He said in part;

> There are seven kinds of love. There is the love of one's parents, the love of a sibling, the love of one's own child, the love of one's spouse, the love of a sweetheart, the love of a friend and the love of a pet. Each kind of love is distinct from the other and yet none is necessarily more intense than the other.
>
> Love is a gift that is bestowed on each and every human being and that gift is the highest form of pleasure one can obtain.
>
> Many will sacrifice much to obtain and retain it. One may sacrifice a crown whereas another will sacrifice his or her freedom and another still, will risk life itself to obtain and retain it.
>
> It is fascinating indeed to think that when God made it possible for human beings to perpetuate the species, he included love as an important ingredient.
>
> To love another fully and to be loved in kind is to have reached the environs of Heaven itself.

When those words were published, other clergymen began inviting Russell to preach in their churches again. Things were now looking better for him. He was now very popular with both the students in his school and the adults in the community for they believed in his mission as a young preacher of the good word.

What he didn't know at that time was that he was soon going to face a far greater problem that may become insurmountable to him and as such, destroy his own reputation and his mission on Earth.

Psalms, chapter 109, 3-5: They beset me with words of hate, and attack me without cause. In return for my love they accuse me, even as I make prayer for them. So they reward me evil for good, and hatred for my love.

John, chapter 8, 7: And as they continued to ask him, he stood up and said to them, "Let him who is without sin among you be the first to throw a stone at her."

Chapter Nine

Russell had learned at school that puberty is the period of time when sexual characteristics develop and sexual organs mature. He knew that there is also a significant growth spurt and the timing of that 'spurt' can vary from person to person. Along with sexual maturation and development, a wide range of emotional changes also take place. Some boys go through this period very easily and for others it can be more difficult. With boys, it usually begins when they are fourteen.

Russell was different than most other boys his age. He was already sixteen but he had entered puberty at an earlier age. Even though the structure of his body was changing, he was still looking younger than he really was. However, his emotions had changed when he was younger. How he thought and felt about himself, his friends, and the whole world, seem different to him as he matured. As he progressed into puberty, he began to make important decisions for himself, take on more responsibilities and become more independent. The fact that he chose to run away from an abusive uncle and was prepared to live on his own at the age of nine is evidence of his maturing at an earlier age.

As a sixteen-year-old, he had also been developing a gradual sexual interest in girls his own age. Of course, he had this interest earlier in his life but now his interest was more obvious to him than it was when he was younger. The apple in his eye was a beautiful sixteen-year-old brunette girl with brown eyes that seemed to Russell as always being focused on him. That could be because she sat just behind him in the row to his right in his classroom.

One day, he spoke to Larry. "You know that brunette with the cute face that always attends my group sessions in the gym."

"You mean, Theresa Davis?"

"Yeah. That's the one."

"What about her?"

"I think I'm in love with her."

Larry said in a joking manner, "I thought you loved all the girls in our school."

"I do, but I love Theresa more."

"Have you told her this?"

"No. I want you to tell her for me."

Larry spoke angrily. "There is a lot I will do for you but I will not procure your girls for you?"

Russell replied in a whine-like voice "I don't want you to procure girls for me. I want you to ask her if she will go out with me."

Larry smiled and asked rhetorically, "Am I to understand that the boy who isn't afraid to ask the clergy in our city questions he knows they can't answer, is afraid to ask a girl if she will go out with him?"

Before Russell could reply, Larry continued, "Am I to also understand that the boy who said to two others that he would let them hit him as many times as they wanted to, to stop their fighting is too afraid to ask a girl if she will go out with him?"

Again Russell tried to get a word in edgewise but Larry cut him off again by raising his voice with the next rhetorical question. "Am I too understand that a boy who while being crucified and didn't beg for mercy, IS TOO AFRAID TO ASK A GIRL IF SHE WILL GO OUT WITH HIM?"

"Alright already. I will ask her myself."

Larry smiled and asked, "Can I come along? I don't want to miss this great moment in your life...PLEASE?

Russell replied, "Next thing you will want is to be present when I kiss her."

"Oh, yes, please. Can I watch?"

It was a week before Russell got up enough courage to approach Theresa. When the two of them were alone, he asked, "Theresa. Would you like...?"

She interjected, "Yes."

"Yes, what?" he asked.

"You know." She said in a cooing tone of voice.

"I know what?"

Theresa replied, "You were going to ask me if I would go out with you and I said, yes."

Russell exclaimed, "That's great! Are you free tonight?"

She was and he took her to a movie at the Civic Centre. Thus began a very warm relationship between the two of them.

A couple of evenings later, Russell was talking to William after supper and he asked, "Is it okay to have sex with a girl you have only gone out with for a couple of evenings?

"That depends on two things." he replied. Then he continued, "Both your ages and whether or not she wants to have sex with you."

Russell said, "Well, we're both sixteen..."

William interjected, "Hey, wait a minute. You're far too young to be having sex with the girl."

"She's sixteen also."

"That's not young?" asked William in a sarcastic voice. "Beatrice and I didn't have sex until after we were married."

Russell smiled and jokingly responded with, "But that was a very, very long time ago. Things have changed since then."

"Not that way." replied William. Then he asked, "Are you aware of the consequences?"

"What consequences?"

"People make mistakes and mistakes make people. Do you understand what I am saying to you?"

Russell did. He fully understood. What he wanted was some encouragement from William; encouragement he obviously wasn't getting.

"But William," Russell replied, "I have self-control. Nothing will happen."

William responded, "I knew a man who said he only wanted two children. He said he had self-control and that he wouldn't have any more children even though he would continue to have intercourse with his wife."

"And?"

"He had five more children. All unexpected! So much for self-control."

Russell didn't intend to have five children. He didn't even intend to have one. He just wanted to make love to the girl.

William smiled and said, "Would you like me to tell you how to avoid making a girl pregnant?"

"Oh, yes. Yes please!" Russell replied excitedly.

"Eat a Macintosh apple. It is the best method of birth control on the planet?"

"Uhh?"

William continued, "You don't eat it just before sex, you don't eat during sex and you don't eat it right after sex."

Russell was puzzled. "How will that work?"

"You eat it instead of sex." Then William laughed uproariously. Bernice came into the room to see what the commotion was and asked, "What are you two talking about?"

Russell replied, "Its man-to-man talk."

Beatrice smiled as she looked directly at her husband and then said, "Oh. That's nice. Russell finally recognizes you as a man."

"Get out, woman!" laughed William. "Let us men talk amongst ourselves."

As Beatrice walked out of the living room and into the kitchen, they could hear her muttering to herself. "They sound like two of my hens cackling in the henhouse."

William began the conversation again. "Russell, I understand why you want to have sex with a beautiful girl but you are not ready for it. Trust me."

Russell replied, "My body has been ready for it for quite a while." "I didn't mean you aren't ready for sex in a physical way, rather I mean in an emotional way. When one truly participates in a sexual act with another human being, the act is one that should include love and devotion to the person who shares the sexual act with another and with those two emotional feelings added to the physical act, then and only then is anyone truly intimate with that other person."

Just as Russell began to open his mouth to respond to William's homily, William continued, "You cannot express these emotional feelings with a harlot. Sex with her would be purely physical. That form of sexual relationship with another human being is no different than indulging in self-gratification."

Russell was quick to say that Theresa wasn't a harlot although he knew that he didn't really know her well enough to arrive at that conclusion.

It was a month before Russell got the courage to ask Theresa to have intercourse with her. She readily agreed, much to Russell's surprise. They found a place a mile from her home in a secluded spot in the forest where no one could see them. On June 4th, his moment he had dreamed of was finally realized.

When they were finished, Theresa told Russell that she loved him and he responded in kind. It was however the only time that they were that physically intimate with one another.

Russell had learned that love and sex are not the same thing. He realized that love is an emotion or a feeling and that there is no one definition of love because the word 'love' meant many different things to many different people. He also realized that sex, on the other hand, is a biological event and even though there are different forms of sex, most sexual acts have certain things in common and may or may not include penetration.

One thing that was constantly on his mind was the fact that when two people are sexually intimate and in love at the same time, their intimacy both at love and in sex are intensified. This certainly applied to Russell and Theresa when they had the indulged in their one and only sex act together.

Meanwhile, many people in Nelson were pestering Russell to cure them of their ills and a few even asked him to raise their deceased loved ones from the dead. He continued to tell them that he could not cure them of their ills and he made it clear to them that he certainly couldn't bring their deceased loved ones back to life again.

He remembered how he had suffered at the hands of the three crazy men who believed he could do these things so he took great pains not to ignore those who were now seeking his help. He generally would say to those who asked him for help, "I am not Jesus Christ who has returned to Earth. I cannot raise the dead or even cure the ill. What I can do is pray for you and your loved ones and ask God to ease the pain you and your loved ones are going through. I can even teach you how to pray to God. Please don't ask me to do for you what I cannot do."

Despite his statement to those seeking help that he couldn't help them other than pray for them, many still believed that he could raise the dead and cure the sick. Their pestering continued, unabated. Some days he would be approached on the street ten or more times. People would even call on him at the Hampston farm, seeking his help. Some even offered him money which of course he refused outright. Unfortunately, some even cursed him because he would not go to their homes and pray for their sick family members.

There were times when he wanted to be completely alone so he would bicycle on his mountain bike through the fields and forest paths. Other times, he would go on long walks along old roads. It gave him an opportunity to concentrate without being disturbed by anyone, not even by his best friend. For the most part however, he was completely immersed in bible classes on Wednesday evenings, his school studies for the rest of the week and on Sundays; he spent the mornings in the various churches.

It was getting to the point that the only time he could be alone with his best friend Larry were Saturdays and Sunday afternoons. He was having less time to spend with Theresa resulting in him seeing her only on occasional Saturdays. This constant seeking of help by friends and strangers was cutting into his free time. However, when he graduated into grade eleven at the end of June, this gave him more time to be with Theresa and Larry.

One day in July, Theresa phoned him and asked him if he would like to have supper with her family. He agreed to bicycle over to her home on the following Saturday afternoon which was on July 12th.

Theresa had previously told him something of her father and mother. Her parents were the owners of a large home and her father made millions in his investment business. Her mother was a former teller in a bank and that is how they met. They only had one child; Theresa. Because Theresa's mother had suffered from ovarian cancer, she couldn't have another child.

Russell had to pedal his new bicycle (his original one was never found after he was kidnapped) along Granite Road and into Nelson and then through the city to the ferry that took him across the lake to Highway 3 and then eastward for five miles along the highway to Theresa's home.

When Russell arrived at her home around three-thirty in the afternoon, he was surprised at what he saw. He had no idea that her family owned a large estate. The house was three stories in height with a peaked roof and was not unlike large English-styled manors found in England. The grounds were five acres in size and beautifully kept with fountains and rows upon rows of roses along the pathways meandering through the estate.

Part of a beautiful forest was in the estate. The front of the property had a large iron fence and entrance to the estate was through an electric-controlled gate.

When he pushed the button and then yelled out his name into the two-way speaker system, the gate opened and he bicycled to the main entrance to the house. Theresa was waiting for him at the door.

"Hi, Russell. I'm glad you could come."

"Thanks for inviting me." he replied as he hugged her.

Theresa took him onto the rear patio where her parents were waiting for them. After the introductions and some small talk, they moved into the house and into the large living room. At both ends of the room, were large floor-to-ceiling windows, which looked out at the gardens in both the front and back of the property.

Theresa's father said, "Thank you for coming to visit us, Russell. Theresa has often spoken well of you."

He was in his sixties, was tall, and had a receding forehead and brown hair. He also had a friendly face. Theresa's mother was in her late fifties, she had long red hair, with streaks of white in it and she too had a friendly face.

Theresa's father motioned Larry and their daughter to sit in the two matching leather chairs across the coffee table that separated them from her parents.

For about an hour, they spoke of many things including his devotion to the readings of the *Bible* and his work as a young preacher. When a maid approached them and said that dinner was ready, Theresa led Russell into the large dining room. Never in his life had he ever sat at a table with such a splendid table setting.

Theresa's mother remarked to Russell that they only put the silverware with the gold-plated handles on the table when they have a special guest for dinner.

"I appreciate it very much that you think of me as a special guest." He replied.

Theresa's father added, "Any friend of our daughter is a special guest to us."

Russell was glad that that was the reason and not because they thought he was Jesus.

After supper, Theresa joined her mother in another room and her father invited Russell to join him in a small study. When they sat down on the two leather chairs, Theresa's father began the conversation.

"I want to ask you a rhetorical question."

"Yes?" asked Russell in a quizzical tone of voice.

"If a man does something wrong, he is expected to make it right, is this not so?"

"Of course." replied Russell.

Theresa's father continued. "A fellow student—a boy in her school, has made Theresa pregnant."

Russell could feel the sweat suddenly streaming down his forehead. He shifted uneasily.

"How far along is she?" he asked.

"Four and a half months." was the response.

Russell felt relieved. He had sexual intercourse with her on June 4th. That meant that someone got into her ahead of him sometime in February.

Her father continued. "Now obviously, they are too young to marry so this means that they should wait until at least when Theresa and the young man are eighteen."

"At least until they are eighteen." replied Russell. Then he asked, "Is she going to return to school in September?"

"No." replied her father. "We will be sending her to live in Toronto with her aunt until the baby is delivered. Then after a couple of months, she will return to us."

"With her baby?" asked Russell.

"Of course! We want her to keep the baby. We will look after the baby while Theresa continues going to school."

Theresa's father paused for a few moments, lit up his pipe, sucked on his pipe stem and the after exhaling the smoke, looked Russell directly in his eyes and asked, "Are you going to be faithful to her while you wait until you are both eighteen years of age?"

Russell sat up with a start and responded loudly, "I'm not the father of her baby!"

Theresa's father got up without a word and walked to his desk where he then pressed a button on his desk and a moment later, Theresa and her mother entered the room. They sat on the nearby chesterfield. Her father looked at Theresa and asked, "Who is the father of your child?"

"Russell is, daddy."

Immediately Russell denied it. He reminded Theresa that the only time they had sexual intercourse was on June 4th. He added, "That would mean that someone else had intercourse with you sometime in February. I didn't even know you then, let alone having sex with you in February."

Theresa's mother's friendly face turned into a scowl. She exclaimed angrily, "You had sexual intercourse with my daughter, you, a boy who proclaims that he is a follower of Jesus and his teachings? How dare you!"

Russell tried to interject but was cut off by Theresa's father. "Yelling and screaming is not going to help, my dear. Let me deal with this."

Russell looked at Theresa in pleading eyes and begged, "Theresa. Tell them that we only had sex that one time and that we didn't have sex at any other time."

Theresa knew that if she admitted to that, it meant that she had sex with someone else earlier. This she was not prepared to do.

"Russell." she began softly. "Don't you remember us having sexual intercourse at your friend's place last February.

"You mean, Larry's place?"

She paused before responding. She had never met Larry before. She didn't even know where he lived. Then she said, "No. One of your other friend's home."

Russell asked, "What was his name?"

"I don't know. I just know that we went to his house and you had sexual intercourse with me in his house."

"Where was his house?"

"I can't remember."

Russell could see that her lying was obvious. He turned to Theresa's parents and said, "Anyone can make mistakes but anyone who persists on making the same ones over and over again until they enlarge the first one to the point of absurdity, is a fool."

Theresa's mother asked, "Are you saying that you didn't make her pregnant?"

"Not if she is over four months pregnant!" replied Russell impatiently.

The mother continued, "I don't want you ever seeing my daughter again."

Russell responded by first looking at Theresa and then at her mother, then he said, "You have my assurance that not only will I not go out with her again, I would be less than honest if I didn't say that I can no longer generate enough interest in her to go out with her EVER again."

He then decided to add a comment, which was more or less directed to Thesesa even though he didn't look at her while speaking.

"One should be wary when getting too close to someone you hardly know. That person may be trying to establish where in your back to stick the knife."

He then looked at Theresa's mother and said, "Thank you for the fine supper you gave me. I have to leave now as I have a long way to bicycle home."

Theresa's father said, "I will drive you home if you like."

"Thank you all the same, Sir, but I prefer to leave you and your family as quickly as I can. As Shakespeare said it so aptly, 'Parting is such sweet sorrow' however in this instance, my parting is sweet, my sorrow is because I can't leave you and your family fast enough."

Russell then went into the foyer, picked up his jacket and opened the front door and as he did, he heard Theresa's mother yell out to her, "HARLOT!"

Russell climbed onto his bike and began pedaling towards the front gate. By the time he got there, the gate was already being remotely opened for him. As he pedaled his bike in the rain, his thoughts turned to Theresa. He realized that the way he treated her was shameful. He should have remained behind. He wasn't sure if that would help but it was better than leaving with the acidic comments he said to her family.

It took him two hours for him to reach the Hampston farm. Meanwhile, Theresa had enough of her mother's chastisement and grabbed her favorite skipping rope and a paint can and ran out of the house and into the forest nearby, heading towards her own private clearing where she could sit on the can and contemplate about what she should do about her problem.

The following day, Beatrice asked Russell to come into the kitchen.

"Russell. Did you ever know a girl called Theresa Davis?"

Russell replied, "Yes. What about her?"

Beatrice continued, "I just heard on CKLN that she hanged herself yesterday in a forest near her home."

Russell's face suddenly went white. He turned and walked back to the barn. He began looking for a private spot where he could suffer alone.

Russell knew that guilt was a paramount source of sorrow and he blamed himself for her death. He knew that his final remarks to her parents were really directed to her. At the time he said them, he was angry with Theresa for betraying him and lying to her parents about him. Despite that, he would never forgive himself for what he said. He hadn't looked at the situation from where Theresa had stood. She didn't want to appear to her parents as a slut who cavorts with just any boy who wanted to get into her. She wanted them to believe that her first and only experience in making love to another human being would be with the one person who had the respect of all others including her parents. She wanted them to believe that Russell was her only choice. Unfortunately for her, Russell denounced her instead. Russell realized that a person has to feel compassion, not just interpret it. In this sense, he had failed her miserably. He began realizing that there is no pain that is greater to bear than accepting the responsibility of bringing about a friend's death through indifference to the friend's plea for help.

Theresa's funeral was held three days later. Her family was Catholic but because the bishop told her parents that their daughter couldn't be buried in hallowed ground since she had killed herself, they decided to hold their daughter's funeral in the Anglican Church.

The church was packed. Many of the people who attended didn't just come because they knew or loved Theresa. The death of a loved one brings sadness to family and friends who attend the funeral but the suicide of a stranger brings about a less acceptable reason for attending the funeral; curiosity. Many may not have known Theresa but they recognized Russell when he entered the church.

The whispering of those in the church, like the rustling of leaves when a wind passes through a forest, followed him as he, William and Bernice walked towards the front rows of pews.

The minister of the church, without consulting Theresa's parents had reserved a place for them, two rows behind Theresa's parents.

They hadn't been seated in their pew more than a minute when Theresa's mother turned around to see if one of her friends had entered the church. When she saw Russell who was sitting a few feet from her, she immediately stood up and faced him directly.

Russell's adrenalin began coursing through his body as he looked at the scowl on the woman's face.

Her screaming voice could be heard as far as the back of the church. "WHO INVITED THAT HENDRIX BOY TO OUR ONLY CHILD'S FUNERAL?"

There was complete silence in the church. No one wanted to miss anything that was being said at this point.

The minister approached her and tried to calm her down. She responded with another tirade, "I WANT THAT BOY OUT OF HERE! MY DAUGHTER KILLED HERSELF CARRYING THAT BOY'S BABY!"

The minister looked at Russell pleadingly. He got the message. He and his surrogate parents immediately left their pew and walked down the aisle towards the rear of the church. As they were walking down the aisle with every eye on him, his embarrassment was no less than had he been a pedophile being paraded in front of his victim's parents.

When they were outside, William said to Russell, "When we get home, we are going to have to talk."

On the way home, not a word was said by either of them. Russell sweated profusely. He figured that William and Bernice were going to ask him to leave their home.

Once they were in the house, Bernice stayed in the kitchen while William led Russell into the living room. If there was going to be a form of chastisement. Bernice figured that it should be done by William rather than the both of them.

When Russell and William were seated, William said, "Russell. I thought that our talk a while ago about having sex with a girl at this time in your lives was not appropriate, got through to you."

Russell replied, "I know William and what you said made a lot of sense. I guess things got out of hand."

"Out of hand, you say!" retorted William angrily.

Russell searched for another answer. Then he found it and spoke again. "There comes a time in the sex act when trying to hold back is as futile as trying not to pee when your bladder is about to burst."

He explained to William that the baby was not his but he admitted to having sexual intercourse with her in June. He added that she was impregnated in February at a time when he hadn't even gone out with her. William thanked Russell for his honesty and suggested that it would be best all around if he didn't go into Nelson for the rest of the summer as he would probably be considered persona non grata by everyone in the city.

He was right. Within a day, everyone was talking about the Hendrix boy and how he abandoned his baby's mother and as a result, he drove her to suicide.

He knew of course in his own heart that he wasn't the baby's father and that he hadn't abandoned her in that sense but nevertheless, he still felt a sense of guilt over her death.

Larry and his parents also believed in Russell's innocence and that relieved him of some of the anguish that he was undergoing at this time. But he also suffered from another emotion; fear. He knew that he was going to have to return to school in September and face the anger of his fellow students.

He wondered to himself, '*Which of my accusers in school is so pure in heart that he or she will cast the first stone?*'

2 Timothy, chapter 4, 16-17 At my first defense no one took my part; all deserted me. May it not be charged against them! But the Lord stood by me and gave me strength....

Sirach, chapter 16, 17: Before a man are life and death, and whichever he chooses will be given to him.

Chapter Ten

Russell felt betrayed. No one from the city came to the farmhouse to give him support, not even the ministers of the churches. It was if all of the people who he had preached too believed that he was a sinner unworthy of forgiveness and incapable of redemption.

Aside from William and Bernice, his other really close friends were Larry and his parents. Larry believed Russell when he denied making Theresa pregnant. By now, he suspected that Russell really was Jesus who had come back to save the world. He couldn't admit to himself that he knew this to be fact, but he didn't have any reason to believe that he wasn't Jesus. He realized that Russell had failings, just as he and every other kid in Nelson who were their ages had them. But he remembered Russell one day quoting from the fifteenth chapter of Romans, *'We who are strong ought to bear with the failings of the weak, and not to please ourselves; let each of us please his neighbor for his good, to edify him.'* The way in which Larry could please his friend was to be his friend and help him cope with his feelings of guilt.

For the next month, Russell and Larry were together much of the time. They were either sleeping at Russell's home or at Larry's home or they were hiking and camping together. By now they were very familiar with the areas surrounding Nelson. Both Larry's parents and

Russell's surrogate parents trusted the boys to be careful and always watch out for each other.

To Larry and Russell, friendship is one of seven kinds of love. They knew that the solidarity of friends, based solely on their personal and voluntary commitment to each other, is unfettered by any selfish concerns. Each gives what the other needs without thought to cost or reward simply because of the fact of their friendship. Russell and Larry recognized the importance of friendship and the significance of their friendship and what it meant to them.

On several occasions, they climbed Granite Mountain to their private clearing where they would spend several days and nights. On one occasion when they were on the top of the mountain, they found a secluded spot about two hundred yards from the clearing in which Russell said of it, "If I am ever to be buried after I die, this is where I would like to be buried."

The spot was a much smaller clearing than the one they camped in but in a sense, it was even more beautiful. It too was surrounded by cedars however it was covered in deeper grass than the one they camped in.

Somehow, the wind did not penetrate the cedars in the smaller clearing. In fact, once the sun passed overhead, the clearing was in deep shadows. It was as secluded as anywhere they had ever been.

On August 5th, Russell and Larry had borrowed a neighbor's canoe and spent the day canoeing up and down the southern lakeshore of Kootenay Lake just west of Nelson. It was their intention to spend two nights at the lake before returning home.

At about eleven at night, while they were looking at the stars above them, they heard a growling noise but they couldn't determine where it was coming from.

Larry got out of his sleeping bag and turned on his flashlight. Nine feet from him were two glowing eyes. Suddenly, an animal lunged at him. Larry struggled with the animal. It was a coyote. Russell grabbed his flashlight and quickly got out of his sleeping bag and grabbed the tail of the animal. The coyote let go of Larry's flashlight and turned and lunged at Russell's hand, the one that was holding his flashlight. He didn't pull his arm away fast enough and the animal's teeth sank into his lower right arm.

He dropped his flashlight to the ground and tried to pull the animal's jaw open with his left hand. Larry began beating the animal on its head with his flashlight and finally it let go of Russell's arm and ran into the nearby bushes, yelping all the way.

"Let me see your arm, Russell" said Larry with concern in his voice.

Russell rolled up his sleeve and showed his bare arm. They could see from the light of the flashlight that the animal's teeth didn't sink too deeply into the flesh of his arm however, there was some bleeding. Larry took his shirt off and cut some of it into strips. Then he tightly wrapped one of the strips around Russell's arm to stop the bleeding. The bleeding stopped as expected.

"Do you want to go back to my house?" ask Larry.

"Naw. It's okay." replied Russell as he began climbing back into his sleeping bag. He added, "We're going home tomorrow. If it needs attention, I will see to it there."

Two days later, the wound healed and Russell stop changing the bandages on it. Bernice expressed some concern nevertheless about the wound and suggested that Russell see a doctor but he assured her that the wound was healed and the pain was also gone.

For the next few days, after Russell helped William milk the cows, he would spend the rest of the day at Larry's home. For several hours, they were spraying Larry's family's apple orchard with DDT.

On August 9, Russell noticed a tingling feeling in his lower right arm. He was also feeling a bit restless and had a headache. He left Larry's farm just after lunch, complaining that he wasn't feeling too well.

The next morning, he began to feel considerable pain and twitching of the muscles in his arm. Beatrice put iodine in the wound but by evening, his arm still hurt. The next day, he bicycled into Nelson and went directly to the library at the Civic Centre. When he got there, he looked through the medical books trying to figure out what it was that he was suffering from. He found a book that described medical symptoms and eventually, his eyes focused on the part that referred to the symptoms of rabies. From what he read, he realized to his horror that the coyote had been rabid and he too now had rabies and it was at the final stage where nothing could save him. He would die horribly in days.

He also knew from reading the text that had he washed the wound immediately and then left it open so that the air could get at it, there was a chance that the bullet-shaped viruses would have died in the wound. He also realized that he should have gone to see the doctor right after he got home. If he had, he would have been given an antidote. As it was, he failed to do what he was supposed to do and he was going to pay for his foolishness with his life.

He knew that his dying would not only be agonizing for him, it would also be traumatic for William and Bernice and anyone else in his hospital room to watch him suffering through the throes of an agonizing death. He would have to be tied to the bed otherwise in his agony; he would try to attack people near him while screaming in pain at the top of his voice. He didn't want them to remember him in this way. It would haunt them for the rest of their lives. He knew what he had to do. He would climb to the clearing on the top of Granite Mountain and die alone.

The virus had already infected the nerves of Russell's spinal cord, and it had traveled up the axons via retrograde transport mechanisms to his brain. The affinity of the rabies virus for neurons and their close proximity throughout the central nervous system provided an ideal environment for the virus to spread throughout his entire body.

By the time Russell arrived home, he began to feel a loss of feeling in his right arm and his headache was getting worse. He hugged William and Bernice tightly and said, "I am going up the mountain today." William was puzzled, as Russell had never hugged the two of them in the past just prior to going up the mountain.

"Are you alright?" asked Bernice who was concerned about this sudden behavior. "Yeah, I am fine." Russell replied. "I have a bit of a headache but I will take some aspirins with me." He then went into his room and wrote two notes, put them in a small paper bag and put the bag in his pocket.

After having done that, he put the small lunch Bernice made for him into his knapsack and then he slung the knapsack over his shoulder. He then went to the barn and placed a small length of chain in a leather bag and after choosing one of the locks and its key that was on a table in the barn, he placed them also in the bag. Then he walked out of the barn, up to the highway and then directly into the forest leading upwards to the top of the mountain.

On the way up, Russell felt depressed because of his impending death, but he remembered what Saint Paul had said in Romans, chapter eight; *'But if Christ is in you, although your bodies are dead because of sin, your spirits are alive because of righteousness.'* Although Russell knew he would soon die on the top of the mountain, he believed that his spirit would live forever for he had done his best to live his life in righteousness and in the service of God.

His climb was difficult as he was gradually losing some of his muscle functions. His legs had begun getting wobbly. His throat was sore and he was constantly thirsty.

When he stopped at a small stream to drink some water, he swallowed some and began gagging on it, spitting it out. He was also experiencing a feeling of strangulation, caused by the spasmodic contractions of his diaphragm and larynx.

By the time he got to the top of the mountain, a thick secretion of mucus had been collecting in his mouth and throat, resulting in him desperately spitting and attempting to cough the mucus out of his throat.

He knew that as the day wore on, his suffering would be so fierce, that he might attempt to climb down the mountain and if he made it to the Hampston farm, William and Bernice would see Russell in the terrible condition that he was in. That is why he brought with him the chain and lock. He knew that if he chained his feet to the base of a tree, and locked the two ends together and threw the key beyond his reach, he would remain on the mountain and spare William and Bernice the terrible anguish they would otherwise experience.

After wrapping the chain around his ankles several times and wrapping it around the tree twice, he managed to lock the two ends together and having done that, he pulled out the paper bag from his pocket which held his two notes, placed the key in it, put it in the leather bag, secured the end of the bag shut and then threw it away from him as far as he could. It landed near the flat rock where he and Larry had built their campfires. Now he was truly going to suffer alone.

That night, as he lay on his back, looking at the stars above him, he prayed to God to spare him from the horrible painful death waiting for him. Soon after, he fell asleep.

Within minutes, he began to dream. In his dream, he was climbing up the mountain carrying the chain over both of his shoulders. A mob was following him and two men were whipping him across his back.

He cried out to them, "Why are you doing this to me?"

Suddenly a faceless form appeared in front of him in his dream. Only he could see it because everyone in his dream acted as if it wasn't there. The form spoke to Russell. "Did not Jesus tell you that one day you would suffer as he did?"

Russell replied, "And I did suffer as he did but why am I doomed to suffer again?"

The form spoke again, "Did not your Lord Jesus say to you that as his death was not an easy one, so will your death not be an easy one for you?"

Russell replied, "Yes, he did."

"Then, take heart," said the form, "for I shall, repeat what your Lord Jesus is saying to you." The form paused and then said, "Rejoice when the moment of your death is nigh, for you have served your father and I faithfully and honestly and believed in us, and for this reason, our father and I will be with you and you shall enjoy forevermore, the pleasures of life in Heaven."

As the form vanished before his eyes, Russell managed to utter more words from his parched lips, "I shall rejoice for I am ready to meet my Lord Jesus and our Father in Heaven."

The next morning, his conditioned worsened. He looked at the sky and saw storm clouds approaching from the west. He knew that if it rained, the rainwater would enter his mouth or nose and when it went down his throat, it would cause spasmodic contractions of his larynx and he would begin to choke to death. Never had he suffered from such fear before. By then, the virus had been completely circulating throughout his nervous system, resulting in him being almost paralyzed.

As the day wore on, he kept praying to God to accept him into Heaven. He also prayed for William, Bernice and Larry and his family and all those who were his friends. He even prayed for those friends in Nelson who had abandoned him.

By early evening, lightening and thunder were everywhere. At every flash and clap of thunder, they triggered spasms in his body. He was constantly twitching as his nervous system was out of control but the lightning and thunder increased his twitching limbs to the point of convulsions. Much of his limbs by now were becoming numb and independent movement was almost impossible. He was drooling and his toes and fingers began to turn inward just as they did when the dentist was drilling into his infected tooth.

His life as a living being was ending when the rain began to fall. Despite his efforts to keep the rain from going down his throat, it was impossible to prevent it from happening. He was choking and gasping for breath and in less than an hour, he became semi-conscious. It was then that he was to experience another dream.

In his dream, Larry appeared through a mist in the forest, followed by William and Bernice. As they approached him, he called out to them but they didn't answer him.

Suddenly his dream changed. He was hanging on a single cross. The three of them stood at the foot of the cross and looked up at him. Russell spoke and said to William and Bernice. "I have loved you as if you were my only parents. My spirit shall remain behind and always be with you here on Earth."

Then he turned to Larry and said, "Larry. You have been the best friend I have ever had. Follow in my footsteps and carry on the work I have done and you shall be rewarded by our Lord Jesus and our Father in Heaven. I shall always be with you also in spirit here on Earth."

Suddenly he began dreaming that he was conducting a symphony orchestra; something he always wanted to do. As the wind howled, the wind instruments and strings were being played and as the thunder roared, the tympani drums were being beaten, and as he screamed in pain, his voice were the horns in his orchestra. With the sound of his symphony orchestra ringing in his ears, his mind then focused on that great moment when he would meet his father again in Paradise.

In Russell's mind, he was still hanging on a cross. Slowly another image began to appear beside him. Russell called out, "Jesus!"

The image responded, "As I foretold, the time has come for you to meet our father."

"Has my service on Earth come to an end?" asked Russell.

The image replied, "Yes, my son. It has."

Russell struggled to speak despite the mucous clogging his throat. Then he asked, "Will I be able to serve our father again?"

"Yes, my son. You will."

Far above them, the storm clouds were gradually moving away and being replaced by clouds reflecting the sunset. Russell slowly became conscious again but at the same time, he believed he was still hanging on the cross. He managed to gather enough strength to speak to the form beside him. He said, "Please show me where I will be when I am with our father after I die." He smiled as he looked at the clouds high above him and then cried out in joy, "Yes! Yes! It's what I always believed it would be like."

Seconds later, as Russell was staring beyond the pink and orange clouds and into the blue sky above him, he began to think of his mother that he had lost years ago in a car accident when he was a small child. She was the one person that Russell had missed the most in his life. His mind began desperately searching through billions of his dying neurons and cells in his brain for an image of his mother.

As his mind raced through those neurons and cells in his brain that hadn't yet died, he finally found an image of his mother as he remembered her. In his mind, he saw himself being carried on his mother's back with him whispering in her ear as they looked at themselves in a mirror on a street. "Mommy! I love you so much." She smiled when she turned her head towards him and replied. "I love you too, Russell."

That was the last thing that Russell ever saw or ever heard as the image of him and his mother faded into black. He unclenched his hands so that he could grasp the outstretched hands of his mother he could no longer see. His eyes were open wide as his tears ran down his cheeks. From his partially cyanosed closed lips, there issued only his shallow rattling breath, the sound of the dying.

The memory of his mother was the last functioning thing that was in his dying brain when at exactly seven in the evening on August 14, 1951, Russell Hendrix, at the age of sixteen, died lying on his back on the rain-soaked grass with his arms stretched out in the attitude of crucifixion with his feet securely bound to a tree with a chain. He died the same way he came into the lives of everyone in Nelson—alone.

Later in the early evening, high above his lifeless body, a small bird flying overhead saw what Russell always enjoyed but would see no more. The clouds in the west were parting and a beautiful orange sunset was unfolding before the creature's eyes.

"Mister Cunningham! Mister Cunningham! Are you awake?"

The reporter opened his eyes and then sat up. "Yes, I'm awake. What time is it?"

"It's four thirty." replied Larry.

"Oh, God. Did I sleep all of this time?"

Larry responded cheerfully, "There is no need for you to fret, Mister Cunningham. I changed the tapes for you. All four of them."

"Thank God!" Cunningham exclaimed.

Then he thought for a few seconds and then said, "You know. I don't think I missed a thing you said."

"Oh, really?"

Cunningham continued. "Correct me if I am wrong. Russell Hendrix came into Nelson as an orphan and was adopted by an older couple. As the months went by, people in Nelson began to believe that he was Jesus Christ who had returned, especially when he brought back to life his best friend, Larry." Then he looked at Larry and asked, "Are you the Larry that was in my dream?"

Larry smiled and said, "It was I."

The reporter continued. "Russell was crucified and he too came back to life also. Am I right, so far?"

Larry smiled some more and said, "It looks like you didn't miss a thing."

"But," asked the reporter, "what happened to Russell after he died from rabies when he was on the top of the mountain?"

At that moment, a woman's voice came from the kitchen. "Supper will be ready in ten minutes. Would you two gentlemen like to freshen up first?"

When they entered the dining room, Larry's son, Albert was about to sit down when his father introduced the reporter to him."

Cunningham asked him, "Did you follow in your father's footsteps?"

Albert smiled and said, "I have chosen to be a farmer but I try to live like my dad would like me to live." Then he added, "Dad had a great teacher back in the late nineteen forties and early fifties. I guess my father's told you a little bit about his mentor, Russell Hendrix."

"Oh!" exclaimed Cunningham. "He told me more than just a little bit. I feel as if I already knew that remarkable boy."

"That's an advantage my father has over you and I. He actually knew the boy personally. We didn't."

Larry turned to the young reporter and said, "I will tell you more about Russell after supper."

Chronicles 35, 2: And he set the priests in their charges and encouraged them to the service of the house of the Lord.

John, chapter 3, 4: How can a man be born when he is old? Can he enter a second time into his mother's womb and be born?

Chapter Eleven

After supper, Larry took the young reporter outside to the patio and directed him to one of the four lawn chairs facing west. Ahead was the Henderson's apple orchard. Larry's son brought out four opened bottles of beer for the men and then went back into the house.

The two men sat in their chairs, looking at the red clouds above them in the early evening.

"You were going to tell me what happened to Russell after he died." said Cunningham.

Larry thought for a few minutes and then he began telling the young reporter the rest of his story.

"William phoned me in the early afternoon, the day after Russell went up the mountain. He said that he and Bernice were concerned that Russell hadn't returned. I went to their home and then began climbing up the mountain myself. When I got to the top at around noon, I found Russell lying on his back in the clearing."

Cunningham asked, "Was he dead?"

Larry looked at the reporter and said sadly. "Yes. He was dead. His body was in a rigid state of rigor mortis. It was the saddest time of my life to look at the face of my best friend in the clearing and knowing that he died alone on the top of the mountain."

The reporter said, "I guess you were confused when you saw that his feet were secured to the tree."

"Yes. At first, I was."

"Did you know that he had died of rabies at that instance?"

"No. I didn't." replied Larry. "That is I didn't know until I read his note to me which I found in the paper bag in the leather bag near the rock. It was then that I realized how much he sacrificed himself for the rest of us.

It made me cry when I looked back at his body, chained by his feet to the tree. I cried not only for myself since I knew that I could no longer share my life with Russell but I also cried for William and Bernice because after trying for so many years to have children, God gave them Russell, only to take him back after such a short time. I also cried for Russell because his life was cut short and he could no longer enjoy life to its fullest."

Larry paused for a moment and then tears began to run down his cheeks. He said softly, "Only a person who had a real appreciation of the feelings of his friends would choose to die such a horrible death alone with no one near to comfort him in his last hours of life."

Larry paused for a few minutes then he said, "Considering the agony he must have been suffering from in his last moments, I was surprised to see a smile on his face. It wasn't until several months later that I realized why he was smiling at the moment of his death. I had a dream that I was standing at the foot of a cross in which Russell was hanging and I overheard him talking to Jesus. He asked Jesus to show him what Heaven was like and judging from Russell's response, he saw what he believed Heaven was really like. He also asked Jesus to take him with him and I believe that he did. I think that is why he was smiling."

The reporter asked, "Do you believe that on that day he died, that your mind was in sync with his?"

"Yes, I do." replied Larry. "Although I didn't realize it at the time, I now believe that I had subconsciously picked up his thoughts and those thoughts came to the surface of my mind later in a dream."

What did you do after you discovered your friend's body in the clearing?" asked the reporter.

"Well, I knew that I couldn't carry his body back down the mountain because Russell's body was fixed in a specific position, with his arms outstretched as a result of cadaveric spasm...."

"Uhh?"

Larry responded to Cunningham's quizzical expression. "A body will undergo an instantaneous cadaveric spasm if immediately before a person dies, he or she has undergone a violent physical and or emotional experience. Russell's final moment of life would have been very traumatic considering that he died of rabies and for this reason; his body would have gone into an instantaneous cadaveric spasm at his exact moment of death. His arms were stretched outward and because his body was stiff because of it being in a state of rigor mortis, it would have been impossible for me to carry him down the mountain in that condition. Besides, he previously told me that he wanted to be buried on the top of the mountain so I left him up there and then headed back to the Hampston farm."

"Where you going to leave his body to rot on the surface of the clearing."

"Of course not!" replied Larry angrily. "The *Bible* says, '*When you find any who are dead, commit them to the grave and mark it, and I will give you the first place in my resurrection.*' I had nothing to dig his grave with. I knew however that because it was chilly on the mountain top, I had perhaps ten more hours to bury him before putrefaction took place so I had to go back down the mountain, get a shovel and climb back up the mountain, take Russell's body to the burial place he had chosen for himself and bury him there."

Larry paused for a minute and then continued. "When the Hampstons read Russell's note to them, they cried."

"What did his note to them say?"

"He loved them as parents and that he didn't want them to see him die so horribly from rabies and that is why he secured himself to the tree with a length of chain. Bernice couldn't stop crying and I could see that William had tears running down his cheeks also. They really loved Russell. He was the son they never had. William was really moved when Russell said in his note that his spirit would be with them forever.

The reporter then asked, "What happened then?"

"I phoned my parents and told them that Larry had died on the top of the mountain and that he had died from rabies. After my mother stopped crying; she and my dad loved him too; I told them that William had given me a shovel and asked me to bury Russell at the top of the mountain. Then I hung up the phone and began to walk out of the house with William towards his barn. When we got there, William showed me a brass bell in a cupboard. The bell was about ten inches in circumference. He told me that he had been an engineer for the Canadian National Railway for thirty years and when he retired, the bell, which was a replica of the larger ones on the steam engines, was given to him as a going-away present."

The reporter then said, "That must have been very heavy for you to carry while you climbed the mountain."

"It was, but Larry was my friend and for him, I would carry more than that up the mountain if I had to."

"Did you bury him in the clearing?"

"No. I buried him in the spot he chose that was several hundred yards away. I don't think he wanted anyone other than me to know where he was buried."

"What did you do with the bell?"

"I secured it onto a branch of a small tree. When the wind blew, the tree swayed and the clapper in the bell hit the bell slightly. I knew that as the tree grew, the bell would ring louder when the tree sways even more in the wind.

"Wouldn't anyone up there find the bell and Russell's grave if they heard the bell ringing?

"That was my original concern but when Russell and I were up there together and we found his gravesite, I headed towards the clearing while he remained behind. When he called out to me, I heard his voice but it seemed to be coming from the opposite side of the clearing. He was at his burial place on one side of the clearing but his voice was coming from another side. As I moved about the immediate area of the clearing, his voice seemed to be coming from another direction from the first time I heard it. I realized later when

I was hanging the bell, that no one but I would know exactly where his gravesite was."

"But why hang the bell near it?"

"You may remember that I said that the scriptures said that a marker must be left at the grave. The bell was the marker. When it rings, it's sort of a physical reminder that someone very special is resting on the top of the mountain where his spirit had waited for his entrance into Heaven."

"Did you just lay him in the grave?"

"No. William gave me a rubber tarp to wrap his body in so that it would more or less be a sort of waterproof shroud. Then I replaced the dirt and grass over him."

"Have you gone up there since?"

Larry smiled. "Many times until I moved to Vancouver to study for the ministry. His gravesite is overgrown with tall grass and the bell still rings when the wind blows through the area. You can't hear it down here but you can when you are at the top of the mountain."

The reporter asked, "But what is the point if no one hears the bell at the foot of the mountain?"

"If the people from Nelson want to hear it, they have to climb the mountain and go to the clearing at the top of the mountain."

The reporter was confused and it was obvious to Larry when he asked, "Why would anyone else go to the clearing? I thought that was a private location for you and Russell alone."

Larry replied, "Many of the people in Nelson learned that Russell was last known to be in that clearing before he disappeared from their lives so they visit the clearing for all-day hikes in the summer months. There is a wooden sign at the edge of the clearing. I arranged for it to be placed there."

"What does the sign say?"

Larry went inside his house and brought out a large picture of it. He then handed it to the reporter who then read the words.

It was at this location in August 1951 that Russell Hendrix, age 16 (also known as Jesus Boy) was last known to be. He was never seen again.

He came into Nelson like a warm breeze and while he remained with us, the citizens of our city, through his teachings, learned about faith, prayer and respect for others.

Russell thought of this place as a place where he could be alone with God. We, of the City of Nelson regard this beautiful clearing in the same way we regard the inside of a holy place. If while you are here, you are brushed by a warm breeze, perhaps Russell's spirit is with you also.

"How do the people of Nelson feel about Russell no longer being with them?" asked the reporter.

Larry thought for a while and then said, "Some think he moved on and is serving God in another city. I spoke to many of them after that and many of the people in Nelson felt ashamed for they believed that having closed the door on Jesus who had come back to save them, he returned to Heaven, disappointed in his failure in saving them. Others who were convinced that Russell wasn't Jesus but at the same time was a decent and remarkable boy, felt ashamed for having forced him to leave Nelson and wander elsewhere in search for a new home."

The reporter asked, "Do you think Russell knew that he would die of rabies after he was bitten and deliberately chose not to seek treatment so that he would fulfill his destiny given to him in his dream; the message being that he would die so horribly?"

Larry thought for a while and then said, "Perhaps he wanted to emulate Jesus' death and like Jesus, made no effort to save himself from his agonizing death that was soon to follow."

"But how could Jesus have saved himself?"

Larry smiled at the reporter and said, "Jesus knew the law of the land. He knew that he couldn't legally be tried before the morning sun had risen and yet he kept that knowledge to himself so that his death would invariably follow as predicted earlier in the scriptures."

"Do you really believe that Russell's spirit is with those who climb the mountain and enter the clearing?"

Larry smiled at the young man and said, "Of course. Let me tell you about his spirit." Larry paused for a moment and then began, "There hasn't been a night when I haven't had a dream in which Russell has played a role in it. And I often visited William and Bernice while I was in my teens and before they both died, they told me that he was in their dreams every night also."

Cunningham asked in a quizzical manner, "One thing that puzzles me is; how did you know about Russell's final moments when you weren't with him when he died?"

Larry replied, "You may recall that I said that Russell's spirit is with me all the time and in my dreams. Well, a week after I buried him, I began wondering how he died. That night, I had a dream about that very event. In my dream, I, Bernice and William were in the clearing right in front of him. We couldn't do anything in my dream to help him however. I guess God intended me to witness Russell's final hours on the top of the mountain just as I seen him being whipped, crucified and shot with arrows in another dream."

Cunningham asked, "Do you really believe that Russell brought you back to life and that when he died in the hospital, he too was resurrected"

Larry thought that about that question for a minute and then said, "When I was in Russell's hospital room a couple of days after he came back to life, I noticed the nurses changing the heart monitor for another one. "Perhaps the readings of my heart and that of Russell's heart in the original monitor were false. I just don't have a real answer for you."

Larry shifted his position in the chair and then looked at his watch. Then he said, "It's almost seven o'clock. At seven every evening since that fateful day when Russell died, a warm breeze strikes me, no matter where I am or what the weather is like outside. I believe that seven o'clock was the actual time in the evening when Russell died. In fact, it was thirty-seven years ago this evening that he died on top of Granite Mountain; the one that is right behind us."

"Come on, Reverend. You're fooling with me." responded the reporter, as he looked his own watch.

As the two men were looking at the sunset, Larry pointed to the far end of the orchard. Then he said, "You will know when Russell's spirit is approaching when you hear the wind brushing past the branches of the apple trees at the end of the orchard."

The young reporter was dubious. However if the breeze came as the old man predicted, he would accept the rest of Larry's story about Russell Hendrix as being fact and not a myth. Suddenly he heard the wind blowing against the leaves of the trees in the distance. As the rustling of the wind against the leaves branches got louder and closer, Cunningham's heart began to beat faster.

He looked at Larry and observed that Larry's eyes were closed and he had a big smile on his face. Cunningham closed his eyes as the branches of the four trees on the right of them began to wave in the wind furiously. Suddenly, he felt the warm breeze that Larry spoke of.

A few minutes later, the warm air vanished as quickly as it appeared and the cool air of the evening returned.

Cunningham opened his eyes again and turned to Larry and asked, "Is there some rational explanation for what we have just experienced?"

Larry replied, "Many people have experienced personal encounters with some unseen being who provided them with companionship, encouragement, guidance and hope; in other words, helping them to live beyond their sorrow with respect to the loss of a loved one. Studies have shown that as many as forty percent of widows and widowers have reported having felt the presence of a loved one who has passed on."

"Do you think that what we have just experienced is the spirit of Russell being in our immediate presence?"

"I would like to think so however many theories exist so there is no definitive explanation. There is a possible scientific explanation based on the concept that the stimulus between the two hemispheres of the brain suggests that the presence of a being can be artificially stimulated, and that people having this experience are able to solve problems beyond their normal abilities. Some psychologists believe it's an example of bicameralism."

"Bicameralism? What's that?" asked Cunningham.

"In psychology, bicameralism is a controversial hypothesis which argues that the human brain assumes a state known as a bicameral mind in which cognitive functions are divided between one part of the brain which appears to be speaking, and a second part which appears to listen and obey. Under stress, the usually dominant left hemisphere loses some hold over the mind, and logical thinking declines. The right brain, involved in imaginative thinking, intrudes so to speak."

Cunningham asked, "Is it the same as one's conscious?"

"Possibly."

"Have many others had this experience?"

"Apparently thousands have. For example, just to name one instance, Charles Lindbergh felt there was a presence inside the cabin of his plane. During his first solo, non-stop transatlantic flight in 1927, he was flying just above the ocean and he was desperately struggling to stay awake. Twenty-two hours into the trip, he became aware of vague forms aboard the Spirit of St. Louis. They offered him reassurance and discussed navigational problems with him. They stayed with him until he spotted the Irish coast and Paris was within reach. Mind you, it could have simply been his brain kicking in and what he was experiencing was hallucinations within his mind.

"What do you believe?

"Well, just as Jesus' spirit can be within all of us, does it not follow that the spirit of a loved one who has also passed on would also be in all of those who loved that person?" Larry paused for a moment and then continued, "Some believe it's a guardian angel. Others say it's the brain's way of coping under great duress. Whichever, the experiences are eerily similar: the sense of a presence that encourages; advises and even leads a person out of peril. With me, it soothes me like drinking alcohol does to some. Just as we have a biochemical response to stress through adrenaline, there is a mental process that definitely helps us to calm down.

"Does it come to people only when there is a need?"

"Perhaps but with me, it doesn't come to me just when I need it. Every day at seven in the evening when I experience Russell's spirit within me, my mind is in a complete state of rest and when the feeling of Russell's presence passes, I feel refreshed again as if I had just awakened from of a thorough sleep. I could say that this daily dose of warm air brushing past me is no different that a psychological pick-me-up."

That made sense to Cunningham because he was already feeling a sense of calmness within him. He asked, "Do you think Russell Hendrix will return again for another appearance?"

Larry replied, "Oh, he has already returned again."

"Uhh?"

Larry laughed and then he said. "Let me tell you why I think he has come back."

The young reporter stared at Larry, waiting in anticipation for the explanation.

Larry continued. "Sixteen years after Russell died; I was conducting the funeral of one of my parishioners in Vancouver. After the service, I was in one of the cars that was taking me to the cemetery and our car stopped at an intersection to let an ambulance go by. As I looked to my right, I saw a boy on the sidewalk who was about sixteen years of age. He was looking at me with a big smile. I swear that his face was identical to that of Russell Hendrix when he was sixteen. Same hair, same eyes, same features. The boy smiled at me as if he recognized me because his mouth opened as if he was surprised at seeing me. The stunned reporter asked, "Was it Russell Hendrix?"

"I hope so." replied Larry. "I believe that God in his mercy brought him back so that Russell could have his chance to live his life again, only this time, just as an ordinary boy who would grow into manhood and enjoy life to its fullest. It would be God's reward for Russell's past deeds."

The stunned reporter asked, "Reverend, Are you saying that he was actually reincarnated?"

Larry thought for a minute and then said; "There is no absolute scientific proof of reincarnation, and none against it. It is up to each of us to decide whether or not we believe in it."

The reporter asked, "But how would a person come back to life?"

Larry responded, "Reincarnation could conceivably be the souls of deceased persons moving from deceased bodies to other bodies being conceived.

"But," asked the reporter, "would they know that they lived in a previous life?"

Larry smiled and replied, "The memories of children's past lives are quite remarkable especially in western countries, where children have seldom been exposed to the concept of reincarnation. Often such memories can fade as some grow older, while others will be able to recall past incarnations all their lives. Thousands of cases have been documented by various researchers from around the world and some children are recorded as having described where they had lived and recognized family members by name, even when these families live in different areas of the continent. Many have successfully passed tests set by the identified family. What is remarkable here is that in most cases the children appear to have no incentive, financial or otherwise to make such claims."

Larry paused before he continued, then he spoke. "Let me give you an example. Back in the early nineteen hundreds, when India was still a colony of the British Empire; there was a boy of about five years of age living in a small village in India. One day, he and his parents went to visit some relatives in another small village that was several hundred miles away. This was the first time they had ever been in that village. When they arrived, their young son began talking with the elders in the village. He asked them questions about certain members of their families and about their own health. He appeared to know all of them and about what they had been doing in the village five years earlier."

Cunningham said, "This must have been a real shock to them"

"It was." replied Larry. "Although many of the people in India believe in reincarnation, experiencing something like this was rare indeed so a big thing was made about it. The governor in that area arranged for British scientists to interview the boy and the villagers. They finally came to the conclusion that in all likelihood, he was the reincarnation of an old man who had died five years earlier in that village. As the boy grew older, he remembered less and less of his previous life in the village until finally, all memory of his past life had left his conscious mind."

Cunningham asked, "Do you think that the boy on the sidewalk remembered you and your lives together?"

Larry replied, "I think any memory of what his life was like in his past life was for the most part gone but there was probably some remnants of his previous life left in his mind that made it possible for him to at least recognize some aspect of the structure of my face as a familiar one he had seen before but couldn't remember where. Of course that was many years ago and if he saw me now, he probably wouldn't recognize me at all because his current mind would be cluttered with events of his life as he is living it now and memories of his previous life would be pushed back into the recesses of his mind and lost to him forever."

Larry continued, "As you know, our sense of smell brings back memories of events that took place in our childhood years that we would normally be unable to recall as we got older. For example, if a favorite aunt used to hold you in her arms when you were a small child and she used a certain perfume that you found pleasant, your memories of your relationship with your aunt would come back even if you smelled that scent many years later and had forgotten all about her. However, as you approach middle age, it's possible that the scent of her perfume wouldn't bring the image of her face back to you." Larry paused and finally said with a smile, "In all likelihood, Russell's image will remain with me longer than my image would linger in his mind if his spirit really did return to Earth as another human being. However, as he would get older, his facial features would change and since I didn't see him after he died at the age of sixteen, there is no way that I can imagine what he would look like as an adult."

Cunningham turned his head and faced the setting sun. Suddenly, he heard Larry call out to his son. "Albert! Bring us out a couple more beers!" Then he turned and faced the young reporter and said, "I guess you have a few more questions you want to ask me."

"A few?" gasped Cunningham. "Does a public library only have a few books?" Cunningham then said, "The Catholic Church should make Russell a saint."

Larry smiled and said, "There was some very serious consideration by the Vatican in that respect"

"Really? What happened?"

"Forty-three years ago, I was spoken to by a Catholic priest. He was Father Stephen who was sent by the Vatican to talk to me and others about Russell. It was the plan of the Vatican to beatify Russell if at all possible?"

"Beatify? What is that?" asked Cunningham.

"It is the first step at being made a saint."

"You mean that the Vatican really considered making Russell Hendrix a saint?"

"Yes, they did. Father Stephen became a close friend of mine in Vancouver in the nineteen seventies. We served on an ecumenical committee together after he returned to Vancouver after completing a ten-year stint in the Holy See in Rome.

"The Holy See?"

"The Vatican." Larry paused and said, "I guess you are pretty new in the Religion Department of the newspaper, eh?"

Dave smiled back and replied, "Pretty new."

Larry continued. "When he returned to Vancouver in nineteen-seventy, he was Monsignor Stephen. Just before he died in nineteen-eighty, he was Bishop Nichols.

Larry excused himself, went back into his house, and then returned with another photograph. He showed it to Cunningham. It was a photograph of the bishop.

"Bishop Stephen told me in great detail as to what had happened when he was asked to investigate Russell's background, a necessary step when the Vatican is considering someone for beatification. Would you like to hear about it"?

"Yes!" replied the young reporter enthusiastically.

"Then lean back and close your eyes and I will try to tell you everything that Bishop Nichols told me. I want to point out however that there is a certain part of this tale that is off the record. After I have told you the tale, I will tell you the part that is off the record. I am only telling you this second aspect of the Russell Hendrix story so that you have a better understanding of the entire story."

Cunningham replied, "I understand and I agree that a certain portion of what you are telling me will be off the record."

The reporter having the ability to imagine himself as being anyone that was described to him and place himself in their setting, waited enthusiastically for the continuation of the story so he closed his eyes and within a minute, he was semi-conscious, waiting for his promenade into the past again. Larry began the continuation of his tale.

Father Stephen was sixty-three years of age in nineteen-sixty. His real name was Robert Nichols. When he was in his middle years, he was a detective in the Homicide Squad in the Vancouver Police Department but years later he was discouraged as seeing so much death so he resigned and chose to join the priesthood. When he graduated, he chose the name Stephen and was always referred to as Father Stephen. Years later, he had been given his own church and had built up a fair-sized active congregation in his small church that was located at the outskirts of Vancouver. When he was offered the opportunity to be raised to the rank of a monsignor, he begged off the promotion saying that he wished to remain in the Church as a simple priest.

One day, he received a written directive to drive to Vancouver and meet the archbishop of the Vancouver archdiocese. He was very nervous about meeting the archbishop because there had been a complaint filed against him by a parishioner, a complaint that his superiors had already dismissed out of hand.

Archbishop William Duke was often referred to as the 'Iron Duke' because he was a strict disciplinarian who didn't let anything slip by. Father Stephen had met the archbishop a few times and had spoken to him twice. By 1966, the 'Iron Duke' was eighty-seven years of age and didn't show any signs of slowing down.

When Father Stephen arrived at the Chancery Office, a much younger priest led him into the archbishop's study. The room was well furnished and had deep brown wooden paneling on the walls. This was his first visit to the archbishop's study.

"Come in, my son." The archbishop said as he saw Father Stephen being led into his office.

Father Stephen approached the archbishop and when the latter held out his hand, the priest took it in his and kissed the archbishop's Episcopal ring. That was the first time he had a chance to see the ring up close. The ring was 14-karat gold with a red octagonal-shaped amethyst in the centre. It was a rather ornate piece of jewelry with a chalice engraved on one side of the setting, a bishop's mitre engraved on the other. The priest knew that the bishop's ring was a sign of his authority. He was wearing a black cassock and around his waist was a purple sash; called the cincture and on his head was the purple skullcap; the zucchetto, the colour of the zucchetto that is worn by all bishops and archbishops.

"Sit down, my son."

Father Stephen sat down uneasily.

"Have you ever visited the Vatican in Rome?"

"Yes, I have, Your Grace. I did so in 1954"

"Were you impressed?"

The young priest smiled and said, "I have no words to describe it that would give it the exaltation it deserves."

"My sentiments also." replied the archbishop. Then after a pause, the archbishop asked, "Would you like to serve our Church in the Holy See?"

Father Stephen had to think before he answered that question. He was a happy priest in Vancouver with a fairly large congregation and was respected in religious and community circles in Vancouver. This was a lot to ask of him; to give up everything he had worked for. He would end up in Vatican City without a friend and he would be a nobody in a conclave of monsignors, bishops, archbishops and cardinals. But then, he remembered hearing about an archbishop in the United States who was a bishop when he was in the Vatican and when he returned to the United States ten years later, he was an archbishop.

"What would be my duties?" he asked.

"Father Stephen! replied the archbishop angrily. "You are to serve our Lord in any capacity the Church directs you to do. Does it matter what your duties are?"

"Of course not, Your Grace. If it is the will of the Church, I shall obey."

"That's the spirit, my son!" responded the archbishop with a smile. Then he said, "I know why I have been asked by the Holy See to send you there. Trust me. You will be pleased with your new challenge. You will leave for the Vatican at the end of the month." The archbishop then handed Father Stephen an envelope that included his airfare and sufficient money in Italian currency to subsist on for the first month that he was in Rome.

Father Stephen stood up, thanked the archbishop and after leaving the Chancery, he headed back to his own vicarage to prepare for the trip to Rome.

At the end of the month, he took the flight to Rome and after his plane arrived at the Rome Fiumicino Airport that is 20 miles from the center of Rome, a young priest met him at the airport and the two of them; after Father Stephen got his bags from the carousel, headed out of the airport and directly to a large black limousine bearing a Vatican flag on it. Both he and the young priest were dressed in black suits with grey shirts and their clerical collars and with their black platter hats on their heads.

"The flag gets us through the traffic without any difficulty." said the young priest as he smiled at his fellow passenger.

He then signaled the driver to take them directly to the Vatican. The young priest was right. The traffic police always stopped traffic so that the limousine could be passed through the busy intersections. It gave Father Stephen a feeling of power, power he really didn't have of course.

Father Stephen had been in Vatican City before and visited St. Peter's Basilica, the Sistine Chapel and the Vatican's art gallery but that was the extent of his visit. Now he would live in Vatican City and no doubt see it in its entirety, except of course the Popes' private apartments.

The particulars of the Vatican came to mind as he approached it. It is the smallest sovereign state in the world, measuring only 109 acres. It is ringed with centuries-old walls and entirely surrounded by the city of Rome. Within the walls, there is some open space, but for Swiss Guards out for a jog, the size of the Vatican gives a whole new meaning to the idea of running 'cross country.' But it is a separate nation, formed in 1929 in a treaty with the Italian government.

He also knew that the Vatican has its own television and radio station and issues its own postage stamps and coinage. Vatican City is in the centre of Rome on the right bank of the Tiber River and is situated on one of Rome's famous hills; the Vatican hill. Less than a thousand people live within the confines of the walls surrounding this miniature nation within a nation. Another three thousand laypersons, who work there, live outside of the Vatican.

The medieval palaces, for the most part, later redesigned inside more towards the Renaissance, form an irregular mass of three-story and six-story buildings and are built on long, plain lines and broken by additions and alterations. The pontiff's residence is on the north side of the colonnade and the papal offices occupy that part of the complex near the south colonnade, and the rest is given over to the Vatican library and museums, being among the most important in the world.

There are driveways throughout the complex and the magnificent gardens are surrounded by a small forest of trees and a walk through the walkways in the gardens is restricted to those who work at the Vatican. The Pope's apartment faces St. Peter's Square so that those in the Square can see him when he greets them from his balcony.

The Vatican is the seat of the central government of the Roman Catholic Church. Because of the papacy's vast interest in temporal as well as spiritual affairs, an elaborate bureaucracy has been developed over the course of centuries. The pontiff has full legal, executive, and judicial powers. Executive power over the area is in the hands of a commission of cardinals appointed by the pontiff. The College of Cardinals is the pontiff's chief advisory body. The pontiff governs with the College of Cardinals. He may act as he chooses without their consent, but in practice, he relies on the cardinals for advice as well as for the administration of the church government. The whole administrative body surrounding the pope and responsible to him is called the Curia Romana.

The papal court for a long time had all the characteristics of a royal court, such as elaborate rituals and uniforms, and complex rules of precedence until 1958 when the rituals were simplified by Pope John XXIII.

It was in this serene setting and during Pope John XXIII's rein that Father Stephen was to find himself living and working in, or so he thought so at the time.

The driver took them to a building inside the Vatican after a cursory glance by security and then he was taken to his living quarters that consisted of a very small box-like room with a single bed, a dresser, a chair and table, a set of shelves and suit rack. He got out of his ordinary street clothes and put on his black cassock and placed his platter's hat back on his head.

The young priest, who picked him up at the airport, knocked on his door and then took Father Stephen to another building in the Vatican where he was to meet Cardinal Bellini who was to be his immediate superior.

They walked down a long hallway with a high well-lit rib-vaulted ceiling with frescos painted all over the ceiling. As they approached a large doorway leading into the offices of the cardinal, Father Stephen observed the lettering above the doorway. It read, AVVOCATO DEL DIAVOLO. He recognized the words right away. This was the office of the 'Devil's Advocate'. He concluded that this meant that he was going to be an investigator for the Holy See. His job would be to investigate the backgrounds of all persons who were nominated for sainthood.

When he stepped into the office of the cardinal, he noticed that the young priest who had been with him up to now was no longer with him. The Cardinal's office was quite large and the ceiling quite high; typical of old buildings in Italy. It was sparsely furnished but his desk was a large ornate table, that was piled high with documents. There were three chairs in front of it. The walls were covered with tapestries except where there were bookshelves.

The cardinal appeared to Father Stephen as being around seventy years of age and he had white hair and he was fairly tall. He was wearing his black cassock with red buttons down the centre, a wide scarlet cincture around his waist and his scarlet red zucchetto on his head. The sunlight from the window reflected a greenish sparkle off of the cardinal's emerald cardinalatial ring.

"Let me welcome you to the Holy See, Father Stephen. I am Cardinal Bellini."

Father Stephen knelt slightly with one knee and kissed the cardinal's ring that had been bestowed upon him by the pontiff during the Mass of the Rings when he received his appointment to the College of Cardinals. Father Stephen knew of course that cardinal's rings are large, modernistic gold rectangles bearing something representing the life or death of Christ. Then he asked, "Have you been shown your living quarters?"

"I have, Your Eminence."

"Fine. Let's talk about your new duties."

The two men talked for an hour. During their discussion, the cardinal told Father Stephen that he had been sent to the Holy See because of his background as an investigator with the Vancouver police before he resigned and joined the priesthood.

The cardinal then said, "You have been sent to us for a very important task because of your investigative ability and intuition."

"Yes?" replied the priest in a quizzical tone of voice.

The cardinal continued, "As you are no doubt aware, a young orphan boy called Russell Hendrix lived in a small city in your country.

"The city was Nelson in the province of British Columbia, your Eminence." then he added, "And, your Eminence, I am aware of the stories about the boy."

"Then you are also aware that many of the people in that small city believed that he was Jesus Christ, our Lord who had returned to Earth to preach amongst us again."

"I am aware of that also, your Eminence but I seem to remember being told that the clergy in Nelson didn't believe that Russell Hendrix was Jesus Christ."

The cardinal smiled and said, "And I concur with their findings."

"Then, Your Eminence, why have I been sent to serve in the Holy See?"

The cardinal got up from his desk and walked towards Father Stephen and then said, "Let's go outside, my son and walk in the gardens. The air is fresh and the sun is warm."

The cardinal replaced placed his skullcap with his red platter hat with the gold trim on the edge of it onto his head. Father Stephen followed the cardinal out of his office, then along several long hallways and then down the wide stairs leading to the entrance to the gardens. They passed several groups of four Swiss Guards who were always patrolling the buildings and gardens. They walked out of the building and towards the gardens of the Vatican. They walked past the Art Gallery and then into the gardens and along a path near the western wall of the Vatican. Stephen noticed that all of the buildings were of the same colour; deep yellow. The cardinal motioned to a marble bench under a large shade tree. Father Stephen noticed that he couldn't hear the sounds of the busy city on the other side of the wall. After they both sat down, the cardinal began the conversation again.

"What do you think is the best way to disprove the rumors that the boy is Jesus Christ?"

The priest thought for a minute and then said, "Make him a saint."

"That's very good, my son." laughed the cardinal. "Did you read my mind?"

Father Stephen smiled and said, "No, Your Eminence. I read the words above the doorway leading to your office."

The cardinal laughed again and then said, "They said that you were intuitive."

The priest then continued, "Obviously if he were considered by the Church as a saint, the people of Nelson would be hard pressed to then believe that he was also Jesus Christ."

"Now, I know we have the right man for the job." said the cardinal. Then the expression on his face turned very serious. "You understand, my son that we cannot just automatically make him into a saint."

For the next hour, the cardinal explained to Father Stephen what the duties of a devil's advocate would be. He told Father Stephen that good works and reputations for holiness are indispensable to any canonization cause. He also said that a life of exemplary virtue and piety is hardly enough. He said that after the candidate has died, the first prerequisite his or her supporters must be prepared for, is an agonizingly long, often frustrating trek towards having their candidate becoming a saint. It begins a minimum of five years after the potential saint's death, at which time a petition can be submitted to Rome appealing for a 'cause' which is the term used to refer to each case to be opened.

"But," interjected Father Stephen, "There is no evidence that Russell Hendrix is alive or dead. No one seems to know."

"That is what you have to find out." responded Cardinal Bellini. "If he is alive, sainthood is moot. However if he is dead, then perhaps he will be eligible."

"Your Eminence." began the priest. "You realize that if Russell Hendrix is alive, the Church will still be faced with the bigger problem of trying to convince the people of Nelson that Jesus Christ didn't return to them as a young boy."

"That will not be your task. Your task is two-fold. First, find Russell Hendrix if he is alive and find his body if he is dead. Second, if you find his body, then investigate everything you can about him, be it good and bad. Once my office declares it has no objections to the petition for the cause moving forward, a formality that includes the bestowal of the title "Servant of God" upon the candidate, then the real research will begin. Every nook and cranny of the boy's life must be examined in minute detail, and for good reason; the pope's decision to canonize is considered infallible, and a mistake could prove incredibly embarrassing. We don't want to go back afterwards and find out that Russell Hendrix had a mistress and entertained thoughts of becoming an atheist."

"Your Eminence." said the priest. "Are you aware that Russell Hendrix was not a Roman Catholic?"

The cardinal asked, "Was he a Christian?"

"Yes, Your Eminence. I heard that he was."

After a minute of thought, the cardinal continued. "If witnesses are alive, they will be called to testify before a tribunal of bishops, priests, and nuns. Obtaining testimony can be extremely difficult. Many witnesses will be by now aged or ailing, or must travel far to attend the tribunal."

"Surely," said the priest, "no one will take the cause of the boy being considered as a saint seriously considering our real motive for this purpose?"

The cardinal replied, "My son. Canonization in the Catholic Church is quite a serious undertaking. The Catholic Church canonizes or beatifies only those whose lives have been marked by the exercise of heroic virtue. An heroic virtuous person is considered if he was consistently of good conduct that had become a second nature to that person and at the same time, he possessed a motivation that was stronger than all corresponding inborn inclinations, capable of rendering easy a series of acts each of which, for the ordinary man, would be beset with very great, if not insurmountable, difficulties." The cardinal paused and then said, "And of course, there has to be a miracle."

Father Stephen knew what his task was. It too would be beset with surmountable difficulties. Then he said, "I understand that he may have brought about miracles including raising someone from the dead. Wouldn't that be sufficed?"

The cardinal said in reply, "Unfortunately, it is not. You must find a miracle that occurred after the boy died and that the person who was cured of his or her illness, has to convince you that the miraculous cure is a direct result of praying to Russell Hendrix's spirit for intervention by God. This will not be an easy task for you."

The cardinal paused for a moment and then added. "You must show that the wonders were performed by a supernatural power as signs of some special mission or gift and explicitly ascribed to God."

Father Stephen said in response, "That is an enormous task."

"Yes, it is," replied the cardinal, "and if you succeed in your task, I will send you on another similar task... as Monsignor Stephen, an appointment I have been told, is long overdue."

Father Stephen began to interject and was interrupted by the cardinal who then said, "I know that you turned down the offer in the past because you wanted to remain a simple priest but my son, you are now serving the Holy See and you must no longer think of yourself as a simple priest."

Father Stephen replied, "I understand, your Eminence."

He returned to his room and looked out the window at the folds of land in the distance, the hills touched with gold, bronze and purple and the orange colored roof tops of the thousands of houses, all as a reflection of the setting sun. The scent of lilac and roses from the gardens below, wafted into his room. He thanked God for permitting him to come to the holy city and take on such a task.

He remained at the Vatican for two weeks while he studied previous reports of other investigations. A few days before he was to return to Vancouver, Cardinal Bellini summoned him to his office.

"Good morning, Father Stephen." said the cardinal with a cheerful voice. Then he continued. "His Holiness has summoned us to meet with him a nine this morning."

Father Stephen was elated. The closest he had been to Pope John XXIII was a few days earlier when the pontiff was carried past him while seated in the *sedia gestatoria*, the throne that is carried on the shoulders of priests while on his way to conducting mass in St. Peters Basilica and even then he was more than a hundred feet away from him. He later learned from the pope himself that when he was carried about the shoulders of those carrying the *sedia gestatoria*, he was always in fear that because of his weight; (he was overweight) the burden would be too much for them and they would fall and he would tumble to the floor most ignominiously.

Father Stephen had earlier learned that Pope John XXIII was born Angelo Giuseppe Roncalli at Sotto Monte, Italy, in the Diocese of Bergamo on 25 November 1881. He was the fourth in a family of 14. He entered the Bergamo seminary in 1892. Here he began the practice of making spiritual notes, which he continued in one form or another until his death, and which have been gathered together in the *Journal a Soul*. From 1901 to 1905 he was a student at the Pontifical Roman Seminary. On August 10, 1904 he was ordained a priest in the church of Santa Maria in Monte Santo in Rome's Piazza del Popolo. In 1905 he was appointed secretary to the new Bishop of Bergamo, Giacomo Maria Radini Tedeschi. He accompanied the

Bishop in his pastoral visitations and collaborated with him in his many initiatives. In the seminary he taught history, petrology and apologetics. He was an elegant, profound, effective and sought-after preacher. When Italy went to war in 1915 he was drafted as a sergeant in the medical corps and became a chaplain to wounded soldiers. In 1935 he was named Apostolic Delegate in Turkey and Greece. In 1919 he was made spiritual director of the seminary, but in 1921 he was called to the service of the Holy See. Pope Benedict XV brought him to Rome to be the Italian president of the Society for the Propagation of the Faith.

In 1925 Pius XI named him Apostolic Visitor in Bulgaria, raising him to the episcopate with the titular Diocese of Areopolis. On March 19, 1925, he was ordained Bishop and left for Bulgaria. He was granted the title Apostolic Delegate and remained in Bulgaria until 1935. In December 1944 Pius XII appointed him Nuncio in France. In 1953 he was created a Cardinal and sent to Venice as Patriarch. At the death of Pius XII, he was elected Pope on October 28, 1958, taking the name John XXIII.

The pope was considered an anomaly in papal history. He even infuriated many of the members of the College of Cardinals, some with doctorate degrees, when he ordered that a doorman in the Vatican was to be given more in his monthly wage than the prelates because he had a large family to feed. Father Stephen was nervous. He never envisioned that he would ever meet the pontiff face to face and he made his feelings known to the cardinal.

Cardinal Bellini after listening to Father Stephen express his concerns, said, "The pontiff is a human being disguised as a pontiff. He is not anything like Pope Pius XII, a pontiff who personally struck me as being alien and aloof."

The cardinal paused and then said, "Let me give you three examples of just how friendly and caring our present pontiff is. When he was elected as the pope in 1958, his personal belongings and some of his furniture was moved into the papal palace. One of the workers was bent over carrying a heavy container and was chastising a fellow worker by saying, 'Cut the nonsense and help me.' Unbeknown to him, it was the pope who had been talking to the other worker. The pope obediently started to lend a hand. When the worker turned and realized that he had been chastising the pope, he was most apologetic by exclaiming, 'Holiness! Holiness!' The pope smiled to him and said, 'Think nothing of it. After all, we all belong to the party of the strong, squarely built men.' Then he invited all the workers to have lunch with him."

Father Stephen was impressed. Cardinal Bellini continued,

"After he had moved into the papal apartments, one day he was working in his study and he heard a lot of profanity being spoken by the plumbers on the other side of the wall. They were working on some pipes and were having difficulty with one of them. The pope opened the door of his study and said to them, 'Do you have to say that? Couldn't you just say shit or damn it like the rest of us do? Of course the men were astonished but needless to say, they didn't swear at all while they were in his presence after that."

Father Stephen laughed and said, "And the third example?"

Cardinal Bellini smiled and then said, "Well as you know, many people visit the Vatican and they like to explore. Well one day, a visitor found himself in a large room of mirrors in one of the suites of the Apostolic Palace. The entire walls were mirrored. And the door he entered the room from, closed behind him and he didn't know where it was when he went to leave the room because it just look like one of the many panels of mirrors on the walls. Suddenly one of the panels opened and who should appear but none other than Pope John. The visitor was embarrassed and he said in a most profuse manner, 'Forgive me, your Holiness. I am lost." The pope smiled and replied, 'So am I. Lets leave the way I came in before we are both hopelessly lost.' So as you can see my son, you have no reason to be afraid to meet his Holiness. I have met him a number of times and trust me; he makes everyone feel at ease."

The two men headed towards the Apostolic Palace. The Palace was not originally intended to be built as a residence. Only a comparatively small portion of the palace is residential; all the remainder serves the purposes of art and science or is employed for the administration of the official business of the Church and for the management of the palace. The residential portion of the palace is around the courtyard of San Damaso, and includes also the quarters of the Swiss Guards and of the gendarmes that is situated on the ground floor of the building. Of the thousand rooms in the palace, two hundred serve as residential apartments for the pope, the secretary of state, the highest court officials, the high officials in close attendance on the pope, and some scientific and administrative officials. Because Father Stephen was a guest of the Vatican, it was here that he was lodged. He didn't know at the time that his room was fairly close to the Pope's private apartments.

At five to nine, they reached the main door of the pope's apartments. In the eastern wing (facing towards Rome) of the residential section, the pope occupied two floors. On the upper floor (the third) he resided with his two private secretaries and some servants; on the second floor he worked and received visitors. One suite of rooms receives the morning sun, and the others, the midday and afternoon sun.

Cardinal Bellini and Father Stephen were on the second floor when they approached the pope's offices. Nearby were a number of Swiss guards specifically stationed there for the purpose of protecting the pope. Father Stephen observed that the walls of the hallways were not dingy and dark like those elsewhere in the Vatican, instead they were a soft cream-like colour and the area was lit indirectly by incandescent lighting and partially shaded windows that faced southeast and looked over St. Peter's Square and down the Borgo Angelico leading towards the Castle of Saint Angelo. Most of the walls were covered with priceless floor-to-ceiling masterpieces. They walked through the Salon of Gendarmi (where the pope sees special guests) and then led directly towards the pope's private study.

The two men were ushered into the pontiff's study. The room was large with dark brown wall coverings. His large ornate desk close to a wall was of a medium colored wood. A masterpiece showing Christ's crucifixion was hung on the wall behind the desk. The room was lit by three windows including an overhead lamp and the one on his desk. In the middle of the room was a large mahogany table. Hundreds of books lined the four walls and in between the bookshelves were pictures of animals. He always loved animals.

The pontiff was standing by his desk when the two men were ushered in. There were two chairs previously placed in front of his desk and he motioned to the two men to be seated after they knelt and kissed the pope's papal ring.

The Pope's ring, known as the Fisherman's Ring, is used as the personal and unique seal of that reigning Pontiff. His ring was a gold signet ring with the name of Pope John XXIII engraved around the circumference, and the figure of Saint Peter casting his net from a fisherman's boat engraved in the center. This ring, more than any other single item, signifies the Papal authority. Father Stephen knew that the papal ring had no gem in it because after the popes die, their rings are ceremoniously smashed.

The pontiff was wearing his white papal robes without the cope (cape) normally seen around his shoulders and the white cincture around his waist with one end of it going down his left side almost to the floor. He also was wearing his white zucchetto, a skullcap that was never removed from his head except when bathing and sleeping.

Father Stephen mused to himself that the pontiff must feel greatly relieved not having to wear the sixty pounds of gilded investments he wears on some ceremonial occasions in the Basilica. Because the pontiff didn't speak fluent English, his private secretary, being a fluent Italian/English translator, translated the words being uttered.

The Cardinal said, "Your Holiness. It gives me great pleasure to introduce you to Father Stephen from Canada."

The pontiff smiled and turned to Father Giovanni, his private secretary and spoke in Italian.

The secretary then said, quoting the words of the pontiff, "Father Stephen. We are pleased to have you in our presence. We believe that our brother, Cardinal Bellini has told you of your task that faces you."

"He has, your Holiness." replied Father Stephen.

This was the first person he talked to who referred to himself as 'we' instead of 'I'. But then kings, queens and popes have used those august pronouns when referring to themselves for centuries.

The pontiff continued, "We are faced with a great dilemma. There is a story that has reached our attention that Jesus Christ our Lord and Savior has returned to Earth as a small child and has subsequently vanished."

"So I have been told, your Holiness."

The pontiff paused and then said, "You must try and find this child."

"I doubt very much, Your Holiness that this person, whoever he is, is still a child, if he is still alive." replied Father Stephen.

"Of course, you are right, my son. I mean you must find this person, if he is still alive."

The pope then said in a serious tone of voice, "Your investigation into his possible beatification is a subterfuge. It is our wish that you find this young man and talk with him and help us determine as to whether or not this young man really is Jesus Christ, our Lord and Savior who has returned to Earth."

"Your Holiness." said the priest. "I understand from His Eminence that one sure way to debunk this rumor is to make him a saint."

"I agree with Cardinal Bellini's thoughts on this issue but there is a small chance that this young man may very well be alive and may be Jesus Christ and if he is, it would hardly be appropriate to make him a saint, do you not agree?"

The priest thought for a minute uninterrupted and then said, "Let me get this straight in my mind, your Holiness. If I find Russell Hendrix alive, then the Church will want me to investigate further to determine if he really is Jesus Christ, our Lord. However, if I find only his body, then the Church will still want me to investigate his past so that the Church can still determine if he really was Jesus Christ."

"You are partially correct so far." replied the pontiff. Then he said, "You have another task given to you by my brother Bellini. If the boy is dead, you will investigate him as the Devil's Advocate.

"Your Holiness. If I cannot find him alive or his body, what determination will the church make then?"

The pontiff looked to Cardinal Bellini who then said, "Your Holiness. The church will then be in a very difficult position. If the young man is deceased and we can't find his body, we will have no evidence of his existence at all."

The priest raised his hand slightly to get the pontiff's attention. He then said, "When I was a police investigator, we got convictions against murderers who killed people even when we couldn't find their bodies. That is because we had evidence that they existed. I doubt that there wouldn't be some record of the existence of Russell Hendrix somewhere."

The two men agreed with him.

The pontiff looked at Father Stephen again and said, "You should not concern yourself with our problem of making a final determination as to whether the young man, if he is alive today or the young child if he died as a child, is or was Jesus Christ. If he is deceased, we still want you to investigate him with respect to his possible beatification. We will later decide when or if the other the aspect of your investigation should cease. I will make that determination on whether or not I am convinced that he is or was Jesus Christ who has come or came again to be amongst us after I have studied your report. I will be relying a great deal on your own judgment in this matter."

The priest acknowledged his instructions with a nod of his head.

The pontiff then said, "It is very imperative that you do not discuss with anyone other than Cardinal Bellini what the purpose of your search for the truth in this matter of whether or not Russell Hendrix is or was Jesus Christ. As far as anyone else is concerned, your investigation is to determine if he qualifies to be beatified and nothing else."

The pontiff then asked, "How is your Latin?"

Father Stephen replied, "I am proficient, Your Holiness."

"That is good. So am I. For this reason, I want your report on the second aspect of your investigation to be in Latin only." Then he paused and then smiled and said, "Please. Don't make your report longer than two pages. I don't like reading lengthy reports. I am sure you can get your message across to me in two pages."

"Of course, Your Holiness." replied Father Stephen.

The pontiff motioned his private secretary to hand him a small leather case. Then the pontiff handed it to Father Stephen. He said. "Your authority to commence this investigation is in this leather case and is signed by me. It states that all who serve our Church and who are shown it are to assist you in any way that they can without questions being asked. That should be sufficent to assist you in your quest for the facts that we need in order to complete the special task we have given you."

Father Stephen asked, "Your Holiness. When or if I have come to a conclusion on my own on the question pertaining to Russell Hendrix being or not being the Son of God, who shall I send my report to?"

The pontiff paused for a moment and then he replied, "As the Devil's Advocate, you are directly answerable to Cardinal Bellini but on the issue of whether or not Russell Hendrix is or was Jesus Christ who returned to us in his reappearance, you will be answerable directly to me and me alone."

"When shall I communicate that information to you, Your Holiness?"

Pontiff paused for a moment and then said, "We will expect your report on this special issue within ninety days. In your report, you will refer to Russell Hendrix as 'our friend' and any report you send must be couriered by a priest to me." Then he added, "After we have read your report, we will send for you. We will make the arrangements with my private secretary that you will have access to me at any time."

Cardinal Bellini and Father Stephen thanked the pontiff and the pontiff than raised his hand and said, "May the blessings of our Lord Jesus be upon you both." Then he motioned to them that they could leave.

When the cardinal and the priest returned to the cardinal's office, the cardinal said, "I have your plane tickets for your trip back to Vancouver along with an initial sum of ten thousand Canadian dollars. If you need more, ask your archbishop in Vancouver for more.

I would like you to send me your first report of your progress as the Devil's Advocate in thirty days. Do not mail it to me. Give your sealed report to the bishop in Nelson who in turn will have it couriered to the archbishop in Vancouver who in turn will have it brought to me personally by one of his priests. I will then expect monthly reports from you."

As Father Stephen knelt and kissed the ring of his immediate superior, the cardinal said, "Good luck, my son. You have a formidable task ahead of you. Remember however, that secrecy with respect to the other important aspect of your task is absolute. No one is to know your findings, not even I am to know. Only His Holiness is to know. May our Lord Jesus bless you."

As Father Stephen was flying back to Canada, his mind was filled with trepidation. He wondered if he was really up to such an enormous task. He would soon discover that his task was far harder to deal with than he originally envisioned.

Peter, chapter 5, 5: Likewise. Ye younger, submit yourselves unto the elder. Yea, all of you subject one to another and be clothed with humility for God. Resisteth the proud and giveth grace to the humble.

Chapter Twelve

When Father Stephen's plane arrived at the Vancouver International Airport on Sea Island, he was paged. A young priest from the Archbishop's office was sent to pick him up and take him to the chancery.

When they arrived at Archbishop Duke's office, his secretary led him into the office. The archbishop was waiting for him while standing at the side of his desk.

"Father Stephen." said the archbishop with a smile. "I am pleased that you have returned safely. How did you like your stay in the Vatican?"

Father Stephen laughed and replied, "It appears that I wasn't destined to stay there very long but I presume that you knew that before I even went there."

"I'm afraid so, my son." said the archbishop as he motioned the priest to sit on one of the chairs in front of his desk after the priest kissed his ring. After sitting in the chair across from his visitor, the archbishop then asked, "Were you given written instructions?"

"No, Your Grace. My instructions given to me by the cardinal were entirely verbal."

"That's strange, indeed," said the archbishop, "considering that your instructions were from a cardinal. They usually like everything in writing, preferably in Latin if at all possible."

"I know what you mean, Your Grace however in this case, it wasn't only the cardinal who gave me my instructions."

After Father Stephen studied the surprised look on the archbishop's face, he continued, "My instructions from the cardinal are to search for Russell Hendrix and see if he died. If he did, then I am to investigate his past with a view of him being beatified."

The archbishop growled, "The boy wasn't even a Catholic."

"He was a Christian and that is what counts."

"No one is going to recommend that a non-catholic be beatified." said the archbishop with a snarl in his face.

Father Stephen responded with, "I will be making the recommendation myself if I am convinced that he meets all the other requirements to be beatified."

The archbishop laughed and said, "My son. I don't think the Holy See will be taking you very seriously if you make that recommendation."

"Your Eminence. If I find sufficient justification for Russell Hendrix being beatified, he will be beatified. It will probably take a few years for this to come about but it will happen, of that you can be sure."

"The archbishop was losing his patience with the priest sitting across from him. He snarled, "Father Stephen. You seem to think that you alone have the authority to beatify a non-Catholic in a few years but that isn't going to happen. It can take many years, even a hundred years for a person to be beatified and many people are involved."

"I understand that, Your Grace but in this particular case, we will be fast-tracking Russell Hendrix into beatification as soon as possible if he is eligible."

The archbishop was beside himself. He didn't intend to sit still and listen to one of his priests argue with him on something as important as the beatification of a non-Catholic. He rose from his chair, followed in suit by the priest and said, "Now that you are here in my archdiocese, you will obey me. When I say that you will stop this foolishness at once, I mean now!"

"Perhaps, Your Eminence," said Father Stephen, "you should read this document." He pulled it out of his leather case and handed it to the archbishop.

The archbishop reached for his glasses, put them on and then began reading the one-page document. It was addressed to all the clergy in the Catholic Church. The pope himself signed it. It said;

From Pope John XXIII, the servant of the servants of God, to the Bishops and Brethren of all the Churches. We give to you my brothers in Christ, Greetings and Our Apostolic Blessing.

It is our wish that you bestow upon Father Stephen, the bearer of this document, your assistance in any manner he so requests of you without question. He has been given by me a task of the utmost importance to our Church and with respect to this task; he is answerable only to me and Cardinal Bellini in the Holy See.

May the blessings of our Lord Jesus be upon you. Yours fraternally in Christ.

At the bottom of the letter was the Apostolic seal below the pope's signature. The archbishop's face gradually turned from scarlet red to a pinkish colour before he said anything. Then he said, "What is it you wish of me, Father Stephen?"

"I understand that Bishop Martin Johnson who was the bishop in Nelson in 1945 has retired. I would like to speak with him if he is still alive. I would like your office to trace his whereabouts for me."

"Unfortunately, my son, he died several years ago." replied the archbishop. "Is there anything else I can do for you?"

"I would appreciate having a car made available to me and I also need a place to spend the next couple of days."

The archbishop smiled and said, "One of our cars is at your immediate disposal and if you wish, you may stay at my residence as my personal guest."

"That will be just fine, Your Grace" replied the priest. He liked this new power given to him. He no longer had to fear the old 'Iron

Duke' anymore. With the document with the pope's signature and seal on it in his possession, it gave him powers even above that of a cardinal. The thought of being able to make demands upon cardinals excited him to no end.

Within a few days, he was in Nelson after spending a good part of a day driving 394 miles to get there. When he arrived at the Catholic Diocesan Chancery in Nelson in the late afternoon, he asked for the bishop.

The receptionist asked. "Can I say who wishes to speak with him?"

"Please tell him that Father Robert Stephen wishes to meet with him."

The receptionist left the counter and after a minute, she returned and said, "I'm sorry, Father Stephen. The bishop says he doesn't know who you are and he wasn't expecting you and asks that you leave a phone number where he can reach you and he will arrange for an appointment sometime this week if he has the time."

Father Stephen replied angrily, "Tell him that he is to meet with me later today." Then he turned and left the building abruptly.

He drove to the rectory and parked the black Cadillac lent to him by the archbishop, in the driveway and then, with his suitcase in his left hand and his briefcase in his other hand, he rung the bell of the front door of the rectory. A housekeeper appeared and asked, "Good afternoon, Father. Can I help you?"

Father Stephen smiled and brushed passed her and after putting his suitcase on the floor, he turned and said, "I will be staying here in the rectory for a week or so. Please show me to my room."

The housekeeper paused and then said, "The bishop didn't tell me that he was expecting a guest."

"I'm sure he didn't. Are you going to show me to my room?"

"Of course, Father. Please follow me."

She picked up his suitcase and led him upstairs to the second floor and showed him to the guest room. Then she went downstairs.

Father Stephen walked to the top landing of the stairs and called out to her. "Please phone the bishop and tell him that I am here and that I will expect him to meet with me within the hour."

"You can be sure that I will." replied the housekeeper in a haughty tone of voice.

He listened with amusement as the woman was speaking to the bishop on the phone. He overheard her say, "He just walked in here, just as you please and demanded that I show him his room." There was another pause, and then she said, "He said that I am to tell you that you are to meet with him within the hour."

Father Stephen had hung his clothes in the closet and was sitting at the desk in his room for about fifteen minutes when he heard a knock on his door. It was the housekeeper. She said, "Father Stephen. The bishop is downstairs. He would like you to join him in his study. Let me take you there."

Father Stephen followed the housekeeper down the stairs and to the door of the bishop's study. The housekeeper motioned him inside. When he opened the door and walked into the study, he saw the bishop standing beside his desk next to two police uniformed officers.

The bishop said angrily. "Are you the man that came earlier to the chancery to meet with me?"

"I am." replied Father Stephen in a normal tone of voice.

The bishop retorted angrily, "I told my receptionist to tell you to leave your phone number and I will call you when I have some free time." Then in an angry tone of voice, he yelled, "How dare you barge into the rectory and order my housekeeper to show you to the guest room?" Then he paused for some breath and then said, "Remove your things from this house this instant."

Father Stephen was enjoying himself immensely. He didn't like getting into verbal altercations with snotty people. All his life, he had to contend with people who were full of themselves and on many occasions, he had to take it. Now, it was payback time. He said rather casually, "I am afraid, Bishop Boyle that I will be staying here for a week….perhaps even two weeks. You will just have to adjust yourself to this intrusion upon your privacy."

One of the police officers then asked, "Is that your car in the driveway?"

Father Stephen smiled and replied, "I am not the owner of the car but I do have the owner's authority to use it."

"Do you have some identification with you?"

"Such as my driver's licence?"

The officer said, "That will do."

"Yes, I do." said Father Stephen as he pulled it out of his pocket.

The officer looked at it and then gave it back to him. He then asked, "Do you have written authority from the owner of the car to drive his car?"

Father Stephen smiled and said, "We didn't think it was necessary considering the fact that it was being lent to me and no one was intending to report it stolen."

"And who is the owner of the vehicle?" asked the officer in a snarly voice.

"Not who, but rather, what." responded the priest. Then he continued. "The ownership of the car is in the name of the chancery of the archdiocese of Vancouver."

The bishop exclaimed, "You stole a car belonging to the archdiocese of Vancouver?"

Father Stephen responded angrily. "Bishop Boyle. Unless you are a trained investigator in matters of crime, I suggest that you keep still and let these officers do the questioning. That's why you brought them here, is it not?"

The bishop retorted, "Don't you begin to....."

Father Stephen interrupted him when he placed his forefinger against his lips. Then Father Stephen sat down on one of the chairs and said to the officer who was doing all the talking. "I will give you the phone number of Archbishop Duke's rectory in Vancouver and you can phone his Eminence and tell him that you want to know if Father Stephen has his permission to drive one of his diocese's cars, specifically, the black Cadillac."

The officer just stared at the priest in awe. Then the other officer asked, "Please give me the number, Father."

When Father Stephen told him what the number was, he said, "The bishop won't mind if you make the call from here." Then he added, "Don't make the call collect. "The bishop will be paying for the call himself."

The bishop shouted angrily, "Don't you tell me whose going to pay for the call."

Father Stephen put his forefinger back to his lips again and then said, "Hush!"

The bishop face began to turn bright red as the blood was rushing to the surface of his face. Then he said angrily, "And don't you hush me!"

Father Stephen smiled and said softly. "Bishop Boyle. As time goes by, you will learn that when I give instructions to a bishop of our Church, I expect to be obeyed. Now don't say another word unless you are asked to speak."

The bishop was almost apoplectic. No one had ever spoken to him in this manner before.

The young officer got through to the rectory of the archdiocese in Vancouver and asked to speak with the archbishop. Within seconds, the archbishop was on the line. The officer then said, "Sir. I am officer Billings with the Nelson Police Department. I am in the office of Bishop Boyles and a Father Stephen is with us." There was a pause as the officer was listening to the archbishop at the other end of the line. Then the officer held out the phone to Father Stephen. The officer said, "He wants to talk to you, Father."

Father Stephen took the receiver in his hand and after putting it to his ear, he said, "Good afternoon, Your Grace."

The others could hear remnants of the archbishop's voice and then Father Stephen began to laugh. Then he said, "I didn't realize that you were in the lemon industry, Your Grace. The car's brakes need repairs and the transmission is slow in reaction. I should have taken your personal car. I'm sure that one is just perfect for my needs."

The others in the room could hear the laughter of the archbishop faintly and then Father Stephen said, "I will have the vehicle repaired here in Nelson and have the bishop pay for the repairs and then he can look to you for the money." After a few seconds, he handed the phone to the bishop. A minute later, the bishop said, "I understand, Your Grace." Then he hung up the phone and sat down at his desk.

Father Stephen smiled and then said rather firmly, "You will instruct your chancery to pay for the repairs just as I said otherwise I will instruct your staff to write the check to the garage myself."

The bishop replied, "I will see to it myself, Father Stephen."

The older officer looked at the bishop and asked, "Do you want us to remove this man from your rectory?"

"No. He may remain. I'm sorry that I called you. It was a mistake. I am satisfied that Father Stephen is an official of the Church and as such I am to give him what he wants."

"Which will be a check from your chancery to pay for the repairs to my car." said Father Stephen.

"Of course, Father Stephen."

When the police officers left, the bishop said to Father Stephen, "You should have told me who you are and why you are here when you came to the chancery."

"I would have, Bishop Boyle if you hadn't been so uncooperative at your chancery when you instructed your receptionist to turn me away."

"You could have told her."

"I am not in the habit of disclosing to receptionists, my instructions from the Holy See." retorted Father Stephen angrily.

Bishop Boyle then turned to Father Stephen and asked, "What is it that you wish me to do for you?"

"Why don't we wait until after supper?" replied the priest.

After supper, the two men went into the living room and after they were seated for a few minutes while sipping some wine, Father Stephen asked the bishop. "Do you know how I can get a hold of the records and writings that Bishop Martin Johnson may have left behind?"

The bishop asked, "Why would you particularly want to look at those documents?"

Father Stephen paused and then asked, "Does the name, Russell Hendrix ring a bell with you."

"Of course. He was the young boy who lived in Nelson in the late nineteen forties and early fifties whom people around here kept referring to as Jesus Boy."

"Did you ever meet him?"

"No. He disappeared before I came to Nelson?"

Father Stephen then said, "That is why I would like to study the notes and writings of your predecessor. I understand that he met the boy."

"Why are you interested in knowing about the boy?"

"The Holy See has sent me here to investigate his background and advise as to whether or not he should be considered for beatification?"

The bishop said rather sarcastically, "Why on God's Earth would anyone seriously consider Russell Hendrix as being a servant of God?"

"Bishop Boyle!" said Father Stephen firmly. "Surely you are not questioning the Holy See directives, are you?"

"Oh, no. Of course not." replied the bishop meekly. "I'm just curious as to why this boy has been even considered for sainthood."

"Well, Bishop Boyle." said Father Stephen. "Since you didn't know the boy, this is a matter that you don't have to concern yourself with at all."

The bishop shifted uneasily in his chair and then said, "I am afraid my son, that the views of a bishop supersede that of a priest in the Roman Catholic Church."

"In this instance," replied Father Stephen, "they don't.

"Then," said the bishop, "I will give my views to the archbishop, and that way, the office of the Devil's Advocate in Rome will have an opportunity to study my thoughts on this matter."

Father Stephen smiled sadly at the bishop and then said, "Unfortunately, Bishop Boyle, your views will not reach the office of the Devil's Advocate through the office of the archbishop."

"And why not?"

"Because I will instruct the archbishop to destroy any document you send to him that expresses any view that you may have with reference to Russell Hendrix."

"And you think that the archbishop will obey any instructions you give him

Father Stephen smiled and replied in a harsh voice, "Explicitly and without question!"

Father Stephen then stood up and said, "I have had a long day, Bishop Boyle considering that I had to drive from Vancouver this morning. I am going to turn in. Tomorrow, I will expect you to locate the documents I am seeking. I will call upon you in the chancery in the late afternoon." Then after turning his back on the bishop, he said, "Good night, Bishop Boyle."

After Father Stephen walked out of sight, the bishop wondered to himself, 'Who is this priest who can tell archbishops what to do?'

The next morning, Father Stephen got up and had breakfast. The bishop was up earlier as he had to give Mass in the church next door. From there, the bishop went directly to his chancery.

At nine in the morning, Father Stephen went to the bishop's desk in his study and phoned Archbishop Duke. When the archbishop got on the phone, Father Stephen said, "I am going to ask a favour of you, Your Grace."

"Of course, my son. What is it you would like me to do for you?"

Father Stephen replied, "The fewer people that know about the existence of the letter of direction given to me by his Holiness, the better it will be for him and me."

"I understand." said the archbishop.

Father Stephen began again. "This is why I didn't show it to Bishop Boyles." He paused and then said, "When he calls you, and he will, will you instruct him that he is to follow my directions without question or debate with respect to my work here?

"I have already informed him accordingly, my son."

"Also, if he sends you his views on Russell Hendrix, please destroy them since I am not interested in his views on this matter at all and the pope has told me that he is only interested in my views at this time."

"Consider it done, my son."

"Thank you, Your Grace and may the blessings of our Lord Jesus be upon you."

"And upon you, my son."

The two men hung up their phones simultaneously.

At four in the afternoon, Father Stephen arrived at the chancery and was led into the bishop's office as soon as he arrived. The bishop was standing by his desk and when he saw the priest enter his office, he approached him and held out his hand saying, "Forgive me, Father Stephen for being so abrupt yesterday. I realize now how important your task is and I will assist you in any way that I can."

"Thank you, Bishop Boyles." replied Father Stephen. "Do you have the documents I seek?"

"I do, Father Stephen."

The bishop handed a number of packets to the priest. Father Stephen then said, "I have had the Cadillac towed to a garage and have been advised that it will be repaired within three days. Meanwhile, I don't want to be hiring taxis…"

The bishop interjected, "One of our cars will be available to you until then."

"Thank you, Your Excellency."

The bishop was pleased that the priest was now addressing him respectfully and concluded that he was being afforded this courtesy because there wasn't any more animosity between them. He would make it a point to keep the relationship between them on a friendly and respectful basis. Besides, he knew it wasn't smart to antagonize a representative from the Holy See, despite the differences in their ranks in the Church.

Psalms chapter 25, 5: Lead me in thy truth and teach me for thou art the God of my salvation; on thee do I wait all the day.

Chapter Thirteen

Father Stephen stayed in Nelson for three weeks. During that time, he met with many of the people who were in Nelson between 1945 and 1951. Quite a few of them remembered Russell Hendrix so he was satisfied in his own mind that the boy really did exist and wasn't simply the figment of the Church's imagination.

He met with Theresa Davis' mother also. Her husband had died five years earlier. She told him that they were sorry about the way they treated the boy. She and her husband didn't approve of Russell having sex with their daughter but they realized that he wasn't the father of her child. There were two regrets that they would have to live with for the rest of their lives; the first being, not comforting their daughter when she needed them so desperately before she took her own life and the second; not asking for Russell's forgiveness before he disappeared. They were also aware that sometime in the spring, Theresa and Russell had climbed to the clearing at the top of Granite Mountain. It was probably the one place that the two of them were closer to each other than they had ever been before.

Their sorrow was so great that they gave seventy thousand dollars to an Italian sculpturer to sculpture a monument depicting Russell being held in the arms of the young girl who was the first to come to his aid after he was crucified in the barn. The sculpturer chose as his model, Michelangelo's *Pieta* depicting Christ in his mother's arms, the original being in the Vatican. At first they were going to have the copy placed on their property and then the City of Nelson asked if it could be placed in its main park by the lake. Finally, Theresa's parents decided that the best place for it would be in the clearing on top of Granite Mountain where Russell was last known to be. They believed that if his spirit was in that clearing, then their daughter's spirit would be there with him.

Despite his efforts, Father Stephen couldn't find any evidence of Russell Hendrix being deceased. Everyone presumed that he simply left Nelson on his own and moved elsewhere.

Father Stephen kept hearing the names of Beatrice and William Hampston during his enquiries. He learned where their farm was but when he got there, he learned that the farm had been sold as the couple had died in 1953.

He did learn from the people who were currently living in the farm that there was a Larry Henderson who lived a short distance west of the Hampston farm and that he was friends with Russell Hendrix. Father Stephen visited the Henderson farm but learned that Larry's parents had died years ago and Larry's son was running the farm.

The son suggested that he speak with his father in Vancouver where he is an Anglican priest, as he could give him far more information about Russell than he could.

When he returned to the bishop's rectory, he phoned Larry Henderson at the phone number given to him by his son and a minute later, he was on the phone with him.

Father Stephen began. "Reverend Henderson, I am Father Stephen and I am here in Nelson on behalf of the Vatican. I am conducting some research with respect to Russell Hendrix, whom I understand you knew personally."

Larry replied, "What is the purpose of the research?"

"The Vatican is seriously giving some consideration of him being beatified."

"No kidding?"

"I am wondering if I could meet you in Vancouver?"

Larry replied, "Why don't you stay where you are for the next four days. I will be returning home for a week to visit my son and his wife and we can meet then."

"That will be just fine." replied Father Stephen. "I will be at the bishop's rectory. Call me the day after you arrive and we will meet." He gave Larry the phone number of the rectory.

Four days later, Father Stephen received the call and he drove to Larry's home and arrived just before lunch. He was invited to stay for lunch and after lunch they went out to the patio behind the house to talk.

Larry told him what he remembered about his life with Russell except he said nothing about Russell's death. When he spoke of the clearing at the top of the mountain where he said Russell was last known to be at, Father Stephen asked him if he would mind taking him to the clearing. Larry told him that he would be pleased to do so.

On the way up the mountain, both men agreed to call each other by their first names. When they got to the top, they walked through the forest a short distance and then arrived at the clearing. In the middle of the clearing was the beautiful statue Theresa's mother had described.

Larry said, "This statue was created and brought here at the expense of and request of a rich family living just outside of Nelson. It was their way of doing penance for the manner in which they mistreated Russell shortly before Russell disappeared from them forever."

Father Stephen responded, "I know who you are talking about. I met Mrs. Davis last week."

Larry hadn't been in the clearing for several years and was pleasantly surprised to see that someone had built some concrete benches at the edge of the clearing. Both men sat on them and began to talk.

Larry began, "Russell and I used to hike up here and spend the night in this clearing."

Father Stephen looked about and said, "It is a beautiful spot." Then he looked at the sign at the edge of the clearing. After reading it, he said, "The people of Nelson must have a great deal of respect for the boy."

"We did." replied Larry. "In fact, it was his teachings that inspired me to enter the service of our Lord."

Father Stephen said, "I have had an opportunity to study the teachings of this incredible boy. I read documents that were left to the Church in Nelson by the previous bishop and apparently, he cut out articles from the *Nelson News* which included excerpts of his sermons."

Father Stephen then asked, "Larry. In your mind, is there any possibility that Russell Hendrix was the Son of God who had come back for a reappearance?"

"I was wondering if you were going to ask me that question." laughed Larry. After a pause of few seconds, he said, "I have often asked myself that question. After he was crucified by the Ballards, he died in the hospital but though some miracle which I cannot explain, he came back to life again."

Father Stephen then asked, "Did he bring about any other miracles that you can recall?"

Larry thought for a few seconds and then said, "Robert, he brought me back to life when I died in the hospital but I am not sure of what happened in the auditorium of the Civic Centre can be called a series of miracles. An evangelist came one day and talked Russell into standing beside him on the stage. Russell began to pray to God and he asked God to take away the pain that the people in the audience may have been experiencing and suddenly a number of people began crying out that they were no longer suffering from pain. I don't know if they were hypochondriacs or whether it was the power of suggestion or whether in fact, God answered their prayers and it was a miracle from God, but it was amazing to see."

Father Stephen said, "I imagine it was but you didn't answer my question."

"Quite frankly, Robert, I don't know. When I was with Russell, I really believed at that time that he may have been Jesus who had come back to preach amongst us again. But as I got older, I began to have my doubts. Still, he might have been Jesus who had returned and left Nelson to preach elsewhere."

"Did he ever tell you he was Jesus?"

Larry laughed. "On the contrary, he denied being Jesus. He simply wanted to live the life of an ordinary boy." Larry paused and then said, However, I have to admit that if Jesus did come back to preach amongst us again, he would have come back as Russell Hendrix."

"Why do you say that?"

"Robert. You had to be here at the time, being with Russell Hendrix like I was. If Russell had told me that he was Jesus, I would have believed him and followed him anywhere he chose to take me."

Father Stephen asked, "You had that much respect for him?"

"I would have followed him anywhere at any time. I have never felt this way about anyone before or since. Russell Hendrix was the closest to being Jesus Christ than any other human being I have ever met or heard about."

Father Stephen then asked, "Do you have any idea where Russell Hendrix went after he arrived at this clearing?"

Larry thought for a minute and then said, "All I can say Robert is that there is no way that I saw Russell alive again and no one in Nelson or anywhere else for that matter ever saw him alive again. I do know that he originally came from Vancouver."

The two men talked for another hour before climbing down the mountain. Before they parted, Father Stephen gave Larry his address at the Vatican in Rome and asked that they keep in touch. Larry in turn gave Father Stephen his address in Vancouver.

The following day, Father Stephen drove back to Vancouver and the day after that, he flew back to Rome. Within half an hour of arriving in Rome, he was in Vatican City.

He contacted Cardinal Bellini and after they met for supper, they went into the Vatican Gardens and upon finding a bench to sit on, Father Stephen began discussing his mission.

"Your Eminence. I have prepared two reports, both in Latin. My report to you deals with the prospect of beatification of Russell Hendrix and the other deals with my views as to whether or not Russell Hendrix was or is Jesus Christ."

After he handed the first report to the cardinal, he asked him, "Would you like to read the second report, Your Eminence?"

The cardinal asked, "Is it directed to his Holiness?"

"It is, your Eminence."

"Then I have to presume that it is for his holiness' eyes only."

"Of course, Your Eminence. You are quite right."

The cardinal began reading the report he was handed. After a few minutes he asked, "Is there anything else I should know?"

"Not unless his Holiness wishes to share with you what is in the report I have prepared for him, Your Eminence."

"Very well, my son." said the cardinal. "You have done a fine job in your initial investigation with respect to the issue of the beatification of Russell Hendrix." The cardinal paused and then said, "I suggest that you contact the pontiff's private secretary and let him know that you are here and no doubt he will schedule you to meet his Holiness sometime tomorrow."

"Yes, Your Eminence." replied Father Stephen. "And after I have met with him, Your Eminence?"

"I want you to take a week off before you begin your new assignment. Enjoy the sights and sounds of Rome, my son. And when you come back, you will be taking on your new assignment as Monsignor Stephen."

"Thank you, Your Eminence."

With that said, the two men parted and Father Stephen returned to his room. Father Stephen wondered how the pontiff would react to his report. He was restless all night thinking about it.

The next morning, he received a call from the pontiff's private secretary and was instructed that he was to come to the papal apartments at nine that morning.

When he arrived at the pontiff's apartments, he was ushered into his study by the pontiff's private secretary. The pontiff, who was in his white robes with the silk sash around his waist and his white platter's hat on his head, got up from his chair and with his private secretary who acted as an interpreter now beside him and approached Father Stephen.

Father Stephen knelt on one knee as he kissed the pontiff's gold ring and then when he stood up, he said, "Thank you for seeing me on such short notice, your Holiness."

The private secretary quoted the pontiff. "We are pleased to see you, my son. Please be seated and tell us about your investigation."

After Father Stephen sat down, he opened his brief case and pulled out a leather packet and handed it to the pontiff. When the pontiff opened it, he commented. "Just what we like. A two-page summary in Latin." Without reading it, he placed it on his desk and then looked at the priest and said, "We are going to go on our morning walk in the gardens. Please accompany us and we will talk about your investigation."

The three men left the pope's office and walked along a narrow hallway leading out of the Apostolic Palace to the Vatican gardens. Father Stephen was surprised to learn that although very few people ever walked along this private hallway, there were beautiful pictures and tapestries on the walls that were protected by glass.

When the three men were outside and walking on one of the many garden paths that are occasionally bordered with stone fragments of ancient cultures, the pontiff began the conversation. "In your opinion, have you completed your investigation into the matter of Russell Hendrix."

"I have, your Holiness."

"My first question to you is; is Russell Hendrix alive?"

Father Stephen replied, "I don't believe that he is, Your Holiness. I don't have conclusive proof one way or another but I met an Anglican priest in Nelson who just happened to be Russell Hendrix's best friend and from the manner in which he spoke, I got the impression that Russell Hendrix died in 1952 as a sixteen-year-old boy."

"What gave you that impression?"

Father Stephen paused in his walking and faced the pontiff directly and said, "Reverend Henderson said to me, and I quote, 'There is no way that I saw Russell alive again and no one in Nelson or anywhere else for that matter ever saw him alive again.' unquote. Your Holiness. If Russell Hendrix had merely disappeared, the Anglican priest would have simply said that he hadn't seen the boy again but when he inserted the word, 'alive' into his statement, I think he accidentally let it slip out that he knew that the boy was deceased."

The pontiff began walking again and for a minute while he kept his thoughts to himself. Then he said, "We think your interpretation of the words of the Anglican priest are correct, my son. We don't see how they can be interpreted in any other way."

As they rounded the northern rear corner of St. Peter's Basilica, they heard shouting from the base of the 75 million pound dome that is forty-stories in height. The pontiff stopped and waved at the tourists standing at the railing of the dome and then he gave them the sign of the cross. He smiled at Father Stephen and said, "My faithful following. Bless them. Every morning, a hundred or more of the faithful climb the stairs leading to the base of the dome knowing that if the day is mild outside, I will pass by at this time of the morning and they will get an opportunity to see me." Then the pontiff began to laugh. "Of course, there is another equally important motive for making that long and difficult climb." He paused and then said with a chuckle in his voice, "I have been told that the view of the city of Rome from the dome is superb and unequalled."

Father Stephen and the pontiff's private secretary smiled. It was true. Pope John XXIII was a human first and a pope second.

As the three men continued to walk, they walked past the Church of Saint Stephen with the basilica still on their left. Then the pontiff asked, "Tell me what you think about the boy as a candidate for sainthood."

Father Stephen began his oral report on that issue he was to look into also with the pope's secretary doing the interpretation for them both. "From what I learned, Your Holiness, Russell Hendrix was an extremely remarkable boy. He had a photographic memory. Not only could he quote the entire *Bible* word for word, but also his understanding of the passages and his interpretation of them were unequalled. Even the clergy in Nelson, both Catholic and Protestant alike, were in awe."

The pontiff listened intently. Father Stephen continued. "I had an opportunity to read the private notes of the bishop of Nelson who was the bishop there until 1958. In one passage, he said, and I will quote as best as I can. *'Never have I had the good fortune in the past of having listened to anyone who could interpret the meaning of the passages in the Holy Book like this boy can. It is almost as if he was there when all the events took place.' unquote."*

The pontiff didn't respond for quite a while. While the three men were walking on the pathway behind the Vatican City's three-story Administration Building, the pontiff said, "Tell me something about the boy's character.

Father Stephen responded. "From my talks with many of the people in Nelson, he was like none they had ever known. He was considerate to others; he was brave and never said a bad word about anyone."

The pontiff noticed a change in the expression of Father Stephen's face. Then the pope said, "But…?"

Father Stephen replied, "Apparently, when he was sixteen-years-old, he had sex with a sixteen-year-old classmate."

"A girl, I hope."

Both priests laughed and Father Stephen replied, "Yes, Your Holiness. From what I heard, she was very pretty."

The pope smiled and said, "You know what Jesus said about casting the first stone."

Father Stephen replied, "I am not condemning the boy, Your Holiness. However I would be remiss that if I didn't mention that the girl was pregnant."

"Was it his child?"

"No, Your Holiness." Then after a pause, the priest said, "It was said however that the girl hanged herself because the boy wouldn't give her moral support."

"Oh, dear. How sad." responded the pontiff. "Tonight, I will offer a prayer for her soul."

"Apparently her parents were initially very angry at him and they blamed him for their daughter's death. The girl's parents later realized that they were wrong in the manner in which they treated Russell and regretted that they didn't have an opportunity to ask him for his forgiveness"

The pontiff looked at Father Stephen rather sadly and said, "It is unfortunate that they found themselves in a position of wanting to express their forgiveness towards the boy but in not being able to do so, they were no longer in peace."

The pontiff then asked, "Father Stephen. Do you think that Russell Hendrix qualifies to be considered for beatification?"

Father Stephen thought about that for about a minute and then said, "No, Your Holiness, Not at this time. However, I should like to suggest that your Holiness has the authority to declare the boy as a Venerable Person. That by itself is a very respectful title that can be given to someone whom your Holiness believes lived a life of heroic virtue."

"In your opinion, Father. Do you believe that the boy while he was alive, lived a life of heroic virtue?"

"Very much so, Your Holiness." replied Father Stephen.

"Then please give Cardinal Bellini your report as to why you believe this and he will give it very serious consideration."

"I have already done that, Your Holiness."

The pontiff' secretary held out his left wrist and pointed to his watch. The pontiff then turned to Father Stephen and said, "Father Giovanni has just reminded me that we have an important meeting to attend." Then after a second or so went by, he added, "Come to my study a week from today at nine and we will walk in the gardens again and we will discuss the issue as to whether or not, Russell Hendrix was Jesus our Lord who came back for a second appearance. Feel free to lengthen your report on this issue if you wish and bring it with you."

With that said, the pontiff turned and he and his private secretary headed back to the papal apartments.

The priest had a real task ahead of him. Father Stephen visited Cardinal Bellini again and sought his advice with respect to his other report. The writing of his report on the prospect of Russell being named as a Venerable Person had been easy. The other issue on whether or not the boy was Jesus Christ, who reappeared to preach, required a lot of thought on his part.

John, chapter 3, 4: How can a man be born when he is old? Can he enter a second time into his mother's womb and be born again?

Chapter Fourteen

Father Stephen had spent all of the seven days allotted to him by the pontiff, working on his report. He later arranged with Father Giovanni for the meeting with the pontiff in his study at nine in the morning on the eighth day.

When he arrived, he handed the pontiff his forty-two-page report. The pontiff placed it on his desk without looking at it and then said to Father Stephen. "Walk with me in the gardens, my son."

The two men, accompanied by the pope's secretary, took the elevator to the ground floor and stepped into the first of three small courtyards that run along side the Sistine Chapel. When they emerged from the third courtyard, the pope led them to the path leading to the Vatican gardens.

After they had been walking in the gardens behind the Basilica in the company of Father Giovanni for a while, they found a bench to sit on at the Italian Gardens. Then Father Stephen faced the pontiff and spoke in Latin, a common language they both spoke fluently. Then he said, "I have sinned father and I wish to make my confession."

The pontiff waved his private secretary away and Father Stephen then began his confession. He told the pontiff how he had abused his authority by being disrespectful to his archbishop in Vancouver and especially towards Bishop Boyle in Nelson.

The pontiff asked, "Have you asked them for their forgiveness?
"I have not, Father."

"Then your penance will be that you will go to them and ask them for their forgiveness, my son."

"I shall. Thank you, Father."

With that having been settled, the pontiff blessed him and then the two men walked towards Father Giovanni who was waiting for them nearby and when they reached him, the three of them began walking on the pink-pebbled walkway in the direction of the Pontifical Ethiopian Seminary.

The pontiff asked Father Stephen, "Do you believe that the Hendrix boy was Jesus Christ our Lord?"

"I do, your Holiness."

"On what basis have you made that determination?" asked the pontiff.

Father Stephen summarized what he had written in his report. The pontiff listened intently without interrupting the priest and when Father Stephen had finished giving his reasons, the pontiff was silent for two minutes as they continued to walk along the walkway.

The pontiff looked at the priest walking beside him and then said, "So, my son, you are saying that Jesus Christ came to Earth again when he was born as Russell Hendrix. That would mean that he returned to Earth in approximately nineteen thirty-six.

The pontiff then added, "In Matthew, chapter twenty-four, verse thirty-six, it says, 'No one knows about that day or hour, not even the angels in Heaven, nor the Son, but only the Father.' The pontiff paused and then said, "Only God knows when Jesus will return, my son." He then added, "Let me quote Pope Benedict, one of my predecessors, He said, 'God demands that we be clever; he doesn't demand that we be prophets.' So since I am not a prophet, I cannot give you a definitive answer as to when Jesus Christ will return again. Let me ask you this question however. Did God tell you and you alone that Jesus returned in nineteen thirty-six?"

This question caught the priest off guard. He began thinking of an answer in rebuttal. Then he replied, "I don't know how God will make that event known to us but I know that at first the Christian community expected an imminent return of Christ, but it has adjusted itself with remarkable ease to the notion of an indefinite postponed second coming. When the return will occur, the Christian community simply doesn't know absolutely."

The pontiff then replied, "The *Bible* says that the disciples asked Jesus, that same question and I will quote, *'Tell us when this will happen, and what will be the sign of your coming and of the end of the age?' Jesus answered: 'Watch out that no one deceives you. For many will come in my name, claiming, 'I am the Christ, ' and will deceive many.'* unquote. Perhaps Father Stephen, the boy came to deceive you and the others."

Father Stephen, replied, "From what I learned in my investigation, he deceived no one. He even denied being Jesus Christ."

"Then," responded the pontiff with a smile, "If the boy denied being Jesus, then why do you claim that he was Jesus?"

Father responded with, "I don't think the boy knew that he was Jesus Christ who had returned to Earth."

"How can that be if he was Jesus?" asked the pontiff.

"Because, Your Holiness." replied Father Stephen. "Just as Jesus as a child in Nazareth didn't know that he was going to be the expected Christ until he was much older, Russell Hendrix died before he was old enough to know who he really was."

"That proposition is thinner that a wafer being given to a celebrant at Mass, my son."

After the three men had walked on the pathway behind the Ethiopian Seminary and were walking across the grass towards the Grotto of Lourdes, the pontiff paused for a minute and then said to the priest, "If you read *Thessalonians*, it says in part, *'Concerning the coming of our Lord Jesus Christ and our being gathered to Him, we ask you, brothers, not to become easily unsettled or alarmed by some prophecy, report or letter supposed to have come from us, saying that the day of the Lord has already come. Don't let anyone deceive you in any way, for that day will not come until the rebellion occurs and the man of lawlessness is revealed, the man doomed to destruction.'* unquote."

The pontiff paused to think for a few moments and then said, "Father Stephen, we have not reached that period in time where we have been doomed to destruction. Further, Thessalonians reveals that the destruction of the Antichrist, and goes on to say that the second coming of Jesus Christ, will occur simultaneously. Do you have evidence that the antichrist has been destroyed?"

Father Stephen knew he couldn't answer that question and said so.

The pontiff then added, "In *Thessalonians*, it says, '*For the Lord himself will come down from Heaven, with a loud command, with the voice of the archangel and with the trumpet call of God, and the dead in Christ will rise first.*' This means, my son, that the whole race of man will die and then the dead will be raised, and the living changed simultaneously. Can you show me evidence that when Russell Hendrix was born, he came down from Heaven with a great command with the voice of the archangel and the dead rose to meet him?"

The priest couldn't answer that question affirmatively either.

The three men, led by the pope, walked eastward past the Administration building of the Vatican that was on their left and the Mosaic workshop building on their right until they reached the white-walled Abyssinian Church of St. Stephen. The late morning sun on their left was now warm at this time.

The pontiff motioned the two priests to a marble bench close to the church. After they were seated, the pontiff continued with his views "In *Thessalonians*, the writer goes on to say, '*This will happen when the Lord Jesus is revealed from Heaven in blazing fire with his powerful angels.*' unquote. Even Mark said, and I quote, '*At that time men will see the Son of Man coming in clouds with great power and glory.*' The pontiff paused for a moment and then said, "Can I presume that you cannot state for a fact that when Russell Hendrix came into the world as a newborn, he was seen descending from the clouds with great power and glory?"

Father Stephen nodded his head in the affirmative.

The pontiff looked sadly at Father Stephen and said, "Your belief is in complete conflict with the tenets of the Holy Scriptures, my son."

Father Stephen paused for a few minutes before he replied. Then he said, "Throughout the history of our Church, it has steadfastly insisted on the reality of the reappearance of Christ as a settled belief, but at the same time, it has granted liberty on the question of when it will occur."

The pontiff responded, "Unfortunately, much of modern Christendom has succumbed to divisive speculation regarding Christ's return."

Father Stephen spoke most adamantly in response. "My understanding of the reappearance of Christ is clear: the Lord Jesus Christ truly did return. His second advent was not a myth, nor an empty promise, nor was it simply a metaphor."

The pontiff then replied, "Our Church believes that the *New Testament* revelation of the second coming of Christ is meant to stimulate our preparation for it, not our speculation about it."

Father Stephen was quick to point out to the pontiff that the *New Testament* never uses the term 'second coming'. He said that it refers only to Christ's arrival. He added, "Personally, I prefer to refer to his reappearance on Earth as his second coming within this century."

The pontiff replied, "I find logic with your first theory but your reasoning doesn't support your second theory."

Father Stephen responded, "For almost two thousand years, Christians from all walks of life during their days on Earth; have looked for the reappearance of Christ. As we approach the end of the second millennia, millions of Christian believers still speak of hope of his return to Earth. Never before has the world heard so much talk about it—from the backwoods preacher to the most renown television evangelist and while the Christians continue to search the *Bible* for further clues to the second coming, scoffers also continue to mock the idea saying, 'Where is the promise of his coming?' It seems to me, your Holiness, we must take a stand and recognize the fact that Jesus may be amongst us, even to this day."

The pontiff asked, "In body, my son or in spirit?"

"Both, Your Holiness." replied the priest. "For those of us who do believe that Jesus is amongst us, no proof is necessary. For those who don't have this belief, no proof is possible." He paused for a moment and then he faced the pontiff directly and said, "I read two of your sermons, your Holiness and please forgive me for using the words of your own sermons to propel my own views forward on this issue but I feel that I must."

The pontiff replied, "If I said them, I will have to live with them, my son."

Father Stephen continued, "Your Holiness. In nineteen forty-six, when you were the nuncio in France, you gave a sermon in the Cathedral of Bourges and you said and I quote, *'We are the disciples of Christ who has been dwelling among us for two thousand years.'* unquote. Your Holiness. I believe as you did then, that Jesus has been dwelling with us on Earth ever since his original resurrection. At another sermon, your Holiness, you said and again I quote, *'We believe that God is at work in the conscious of the individual person, that he is present in history, because Christ has not left the world that he redeemed.'* unquote. Should I not use these two statements stated by Your Holiness to strengthen my own belief?"

The pope liked this priest. He had wit and he had courage. He wasn't afraid to pick out sermons from his pontiff's past and throw them right back in his face.

The three men began walking towards the Basilica and a moment later, the pontiff stopped walking and invited the two priests to sit with him on a marble bench nearby where they could look at the copula of the Basilica.

After a few minutes, he said, "Perhaps, my son, no proof is necessary to substantiate your belief but real evidence must be submitted to the Holy See if you are to propagate your theory to its ultimate world-wide acceptance. Do you have a theory that will withstand the onslaught of skepticism?"

Father Stephen by now suspected that even if the pontiff really believed as he did that the soul of Jesus returned to Earth time and time again, it was also obvious to him that the pontiff wasn't going to stick his neck out and make the proclamation on his own. The reason was obvious. If the pope said that Jesus was on Earth at this time, many would claim to be Jesus. If there was to be a public statement made to this effect, it had to come from someone else and not the pope.

He replied to the pontiff' question, "Yes, Your Holiness, I do have a theory." After having said that, Father Stephen pondered his next comments. Then he continued, "The definition of man is best described as an entity on our planet composed of body and soul and made in the image and likeness of God. Man, then, is composed of a material element, the body and a spiritual element, the soul and not as two independent elements that just by coincidence, happen to be joined together while the body grows but rather as two separate elements that by God's will, are joined together from inception and as such, they need each other to form a complete whole, namely, a human being." The priest paused and then continued, "I believe that if Jesus returned to Earth, he appeared both in spirit and in body, as a human being, as he did when he first appeared on Earth almost two thousand years ago."

"And you think that he appeared as Russell Hendrix, as a complete human being with a body and soul?" asked the pontiff.

"Well, Your Holiness." replied Father Stephen, "You may not believe that he was Jesus Christ but I think you will agree with me that the boy had both a body and a soul and that it isn't the figment of my imagination."

The pontiff smiled. He knew that on that point, he and the priest were in agreement.

"The soul of man, though unseen, is just as real as the body." began Father Stephen. Then he continued, "It is conceivable that the body of Russell Hendrix, his mind that is, while he was on Earth may not have believed that he was Jesus but his soul may very well have been that of Jesus."

"If that is true, then," asked the pontiff. "why didn't his soul communicate that information to Russell's mind?"

Father Stephen responded, "Probably for the same reason that almost two thousand years ago, the soul of Jesus Christ didn't disclose to him when he was a child that he would some day be Christ our Lord. When he was Russell Hendrix's age, he probably thought he was going to be a carpenter, just like his father was."

"You don't know that for sure, do you?" replied the pontiff.

"Not any more than you know for sure that the soul of Russell Hendrix was not the soul of Jesus Christ, Your Holiness."

The pontiff smiled. The priest wasn't afraid to speak his mind. He stood steadfast in his position and made his thoughts clear. He liked that in scholars like this priest.

Father Stephen continued. "Your Holiness. I believe that God sent his son back to Earth as Russell Hendrix to test us as to whether or not we were ready for his son's return."

The pontiff asked, "Do you think we are ready?"

"No, Your Holiness. We are not and the proof of that is, if you will forgive me for saying this, neither are you ready for his return."

The pontiff realized that the priest had just one-upped him on that point. The priest was right, If the Vicar of Christ wasn't going to accept Russell Hendrix as Jesus Christ, and he wasn't, then he wasn't ready to accept any human being on Earth at this time in history, as Jesus Christ. He would want more evidence than that which had been given to him by Father Stephen.

The priest asked, "Your Holiness. Do you believe that when we die, our souls will live on?

"Of course, my son."

Father Stephen continued, "That is also my belief too, Your Holiness. It is my belief that souls, like atoms are indestructible. When we die, our souls do not die but instead they take their places in the bodies of other human beings. I believe that when Jesus Christ died and then was resurrected and later ascended into Heaven, his soul remained with him because he was still alive in Heaven. I also believe that when God decided that his son should return to Earth, his soul then took its place in other human bodies and that the soul in those human bodies was still the soul of Jesus Christ who had returned to Earth, time after time."

The pontiff remarked, "Your belief is in the extreme, my son."

"Most beliefs are when it comes to religion, your Holiness."

The pontiff asked, "But if the soul in those human beings was the soul of Jesus Christ, why didn't it make itself known to those in whose bodies the soul existed?"

"That goes back to my earlier statement when I implied that two thousand years ago, Jesus didn't know when he was a child that he had the god-given soul of God's only son." replied the priest.

The pontiff said, "Then you are saying that our souls will be placed in the bodies of human beings after we die."

"That's correct, Your Holiness." replied Father Stephen. We know that there have been since the beginning of history, no more than fifty billion human beings on the planet, and if everyone of them had a soul, then where would the souls go after they died?"

"To Heaven or Hell, my son," replied the pontiff.

Father Stephen then asked, "Then where did the souls of human beings on Earth today come from?" He paused and before the pontiff could reply, he continued, "Most religious people believe in life everlasting for the faithful, a continuation of the life force that reaches far beyond the limitations of our mortal flesh. In such belief systems, death is not an end but a transformation where we as human beings shed our corporeal selves at the moment of our demise and that our souls live on to rejoin our Creator. I believe as many do, that once our souls are free from our corporeal selves, our Creator causes them to enter other human beings again at the moment of their conception and live within those human beings until they too are deceased and their souls are transformed again to other human beings being born."

"And you have evidence to support this, my son?" asked the pontiff.

Father Stephen smiled and replied, "The difference between fact and belief, your Holiness, is not unlike seeing the same object from two different directions. If the object is a round ball of the same colour throughout and two people are looking at it from two different directions, then what they see are the same. They would regard their observations of the ball as an undisputed fact of its existence. If however, after standing in different locations, the object they see is a house of different dimensions throughout, then what they each see is obviously different. They may not agree in their interpretation of the description of it but that doesn't alter the fact that the house they see is still a house even though they differ in their interpretations as to what they saw, and for this reason, their observations of the house is nevertheless, an undisputed fact of its existence and not merely a belief of what they saw."

The pontiff motioned him to continue.

The priest then said, "As much as we believe in the concept of the existence of souls, this life spark remains strictly an article of faith.

It is my faith that makes me believe that God sent his only son Jesus back to Earth again in another reappearance in this century, in the form of Russell Hendrix."

The pope responded with, "You are saying then that if the boy is dead, then the soul of Jesus is now in the body of another human being."

"That is what I am saying, Your Holiness." Father Stephen continued, "The boy, unbeknown to him, had the soul of Jesus inside him and when he died, his soul returned to our Creator to be sent back to Earth again at a later time. It is for this reason that I don't believe that when Jesus appears in front of us again, he will look anything like he did almost two thousand years ago or even what he looked like in the early nineteen fifties just before he died."

"Why do you say that, my son?" asked the pontiff.

Father Stephen opened his *Bible* and searched for the passages that would strength his position.

"The *Bible* itself, states this, Your Holiness. For example, on that very day in which Jesus Christ was resurrected and he appeared to Mary Magdalene, she saw him as a man whom she originally thought was a gardener. If Jesus had returned from the dead in the exact form he was in when he was carried to the cave where he was entombed, she would have seen him as Jesus and not as a gardener whom she had never met before."

"But, my son," responded the pontiff. "she later realized that she had spoken to Jesus."

"That is true, Your Holiness but only after he spoke to her and implied that he was Jesus. Her willingness to believe that Jesus had risen from the dead was so strong; she accepted the man before her as the Jesus she remembered in her mind and not the man she thought she saw as a gardener with her eyes."

As the pontiff got up from the bench to walk again in the garden, Father Stephen continued with his dissertation on his position. "I refer you to another so-called appearance of Jesus before two of his disciples who were fleeing north after the crucifixion of their master. On the road, they were talking to each other about all the things that had recently happened in Jerusalem, and about the suffering and death of their Savior. While they were talking about all that had happened, the *Bible* states that Jesus Christ himself drew near and walked with them, but their eyes were kept from recognizing him at all as Jesus. In Mark, chapter sixteen, verse twelve, it actually says, '*After this, he appeared in another form to two of them, as they were walking into the country.*' unquote. Now surely, Your Holiness, these two disciples who had been with Jesus for years would have recognized him when he walked with them after his resurrection, would they not?" Before the pontiff could reply, the priest said, "They didn't recognize him because his soul was in another body—in another form."

"But my son," began the pontiff in reply, "they did eventually believe him to be Jesus soon after they talked."

"I agree, Your Holiness but not as the man they remembered him as he was while they were both in his service but rather, they recognized him as Jesus in the body of another human being."

"So what you are saying, my son," responded the pontiff, "supports your position that Jesus Christ returned to Earth in the body of Russell Hendrix."

"That is my position, Your Holiness." Father Stephen then added, "And the same thing happened again after the resurrection when his disciples were fishing and they saw a stranger on the shore who told them to cast their net on the other side of the boat and it was subsequently filled with fish. The other disciples called out to Peter, 'It's the Lord!' believing that Jesus had return to them. As you know, Peter swam to shore and when the others saw him on the shore at a fire he had built, they saw him with a stranger whom they later believed was Jesus. In fact, it was Jesus but none of his disciples dare ask him, 'Who are you?' when they really didn't know who he was. What I am saying, Your Holiness, is that Jesus returned after the resurrection in another bodies and not in the original body his soul had been previous in after his death on Goglatha and before his resurrection."

The pontiff walked some distance and was almost in the centre of the small group of trees on the northern part of the grounds of Vatican City when he asked another question.

"And what about Thomas who doubted that the man who stood before them was Jesus? asked the pontiff.

Father Stephen replied, "Just another example of Jesus' soul returning to Earth in the body of another man."

The pontiff smiled and then said, "A body that had the same wounds as Jesus did after he was carried down from the cross."

Father Stephen responded, "That aspect of Jesus' return has always puzzled me, your Holiness. But I am mindful of the fact that the reason why Thomas doubted that the man before him was Jesus was because he didn't recognize his face." He paused and then said, "What is really puzzling is that each time Jesus appeared before his disciples after his resurrection, he appeared to them as strangers, not as one stranger, but as several strangers. I believe that God decided to place the soul of Jesus into the bodies of several human beings in the same time-frame. It was a message that the souls of all of us live forever and in the bodies of other human beings that come after we are deceased."

"What happened to those humans in that same time frame when the soul of Jesus shifted from one human being to another?" asked the pope.

"I can't answer that question, your Holiness." replied the priest. Then he continued, "My quarrel with being told that I will be born again, though, at least in its current usage, is that it gives the mistaken impression that transformation is a one-time affair. It predisposes that once you are on Earth as a human being and die, your soul will either go to Heaven or hell. End of story. I don't believe this is an accurate representation of the scriptures." The priest paused and then continued, "On this issue of being born again, I come down on the side of the Unitarian poet, Edward Cummings, who once wrote: '*We can never be born enough.*' Your Holiness. We can never be born enough. The soul—the curious soul, at least, the live soul—always longs to be made new. To be ever more whole. To be reborn. Not because we were born wrong the first time, but because God has created our souls to live forever in the bodies of human beings. And so my wish for all of us is that we be born again—and again—and again."

The pope said nothing during the time Father Stephen was presenting his submission so the priest took that to mean that the pope was prepared to listen to him a bit longer. He then said, "Your Holiness. "Life is an endless series of rebirths. Semper Reformanda. Always forming and reforming. Always ready to receive a new soul. According to Hinduism, a soul reincarnates again and again on Earth until it becomes perfect and reunites with God. During this process, each soul enters into many bodies, assumes many forms and passes through many births and deaths. This concept is summarily described in the following verse of the Bhagavad gita: *Just as a man discards worn out clothes and puts on new clothes, the soul discards worn out bodies and wears new ones.* According to Hinduism, a human being has to live many lives and under go many experiences before it attains perfection and becomes one with God.

"Father Stephen. "What you have told me is possible but it requires a great deal of thought on my part before I can even begin to seriously consider your theory."

Father Stephen asked, "If you decided in your own mind, your Holiness, that Russell Hendrix was in fact Jesus Christ who had really returned to Earth in the year, nineteen thirty-six, will you consider empowering a Commission to study this issue in greater depth?"

The pontiff placed his hand on the priest's shoulder and said sadly, "We are afraid, we cannot, my son. Time would make that impossible. We are already in our eighties and it is unlikely that we would ever read their findings. We could not in all honesty, create a Commission of cardinals and learned religious scholars to enter into such an enormous undertaking without our presence involved to some degree to guide them along. Pope Pius could have pulled it off but after his harsh rule of twenty years, the current cardinals, in which fifty-one of the cardinals are older than we are, do not want their pope to govern them with an iron hand. Admittedly, we are the

Vicar of Christ, but the effectiveness of our decisions is limited by the cooperation and obedience of our fellow bishops. We promised them that the Holy See would work in an atmosphere of calm and reflection. In that kind of atmosphere, we would have to muster at least two-thirds of our prelates to support such a position. They in turn would have to convince the forty thousand celibate priests and their following worldwide that Christ has been with them on Earth all along."

The pope paused for a few seconds and then said, "My son, we are already faced with the preparation of the upcoming Second Vatican Council and the issues in those meetings will probably go well beyond our own presence on Earth. The issue of birth control which is on the agenda alone will go beyond the day when we meet our creator."

The pontiff paused for a moment and after studying the expression of sadness that was creeping on the face of Father Stephen, he continued, "If we were to place this issue of the boy being Jesus Christ on the agenda, it would act as an ice jam and everything on the agenda would end up in one horrendous pileup. It would take years to get the original topics on the agenda flowing again."

Father Stephen wasn't a stupid man. This was something he could understand.

The pontiff continued, "The weight of this important issue is a heavy cross to bear because we too would like an answer to this most important enigma. Unfortunately, we alone would not be able to sway the thinking of our most eminent and reverend fathers of our Church at this time. It is something that should be put off to another time when the Church is willing to compare science with religion and do so on the understanding that they are not incompatible. Meanwhile, my son, do not be afraid to continue to believe what you honestly believe in your heart. We relish contradictions and respect all who differ with the views of their pope, providing that their views are honest and sincere even though in the past and no doubt even in our present time, there have been and still are false teachings and dangerous opinions. Our Church has in the past, condemned those who advocate such radical thinking within our Church. We prefer to apply the medicine of mercy rather than use the weapons of sanction. We think it is more in keeping with the demands of today to adjust to change, even if the change conflicts with what we have been taught in the past."

The pontiff paused and then said, "It is not the Gospel that has changed. It is we who are simply beginning to understand it better and that is why we seek counsel even from religious scholars such as you whose beliefs may be the antithesis of our earlier teachings. As to your theory—when we have read your written report, my son, we will submit our own views in response and place both our documents into the secret Vatican Archives. Perhaps Father Stephen, when both of us finally meet together in Heaven, we can discuss this matter further but until then, it is a closed issue for me at this time."

With that said the pontiff held out his hand so that the priest could kiss the papal ring and after smiling at the priest, the pontiff and his private secretary parted from Father Stephen. The priest returned to his quarters and the next morning, he reported to Cardinal Bellini for his new assignment as Monsignor Stephen.

"Mister Cunningham. Are you still with me?" The young reporter opened his eyes and smiled at Larry when he replied, "At this stage of your story, Reverend, I never would have gone out on my own. I was always close beside you as I listened to your every word."

After Larry handed Cunningham another beer, the young reporter asked. "What ever happened to Father Stephen?

"He continued on for the next ten years as a monsignor while serving as the devil's advocate with respect to other applicants and after he served the Holy See during those ten years in that capacity, he was returned to Vancouver as a bishop. It was then that we became good friends. We would have lunch together once a week and it was during these lunch meetings that I learned about his discussions with Pope John when he served as a devil's advocate in the Vatican. I also learned that the pontiff was so impressed with Monsignor Stephen, that he offered him an open invitation to visit him any time he was staying in the Vatican. Pope John realized that Monsignor Stephen was a man of the world. He realized that he didn't begin his service as a young priest just out of the seminary but as a police officer, knowledgeable in the ways of men and women. The pontiff often asked him for his views on secular issues rather then just spiritual issues. They met many times and had long talks about many things but they never had talks about Russell Hendrix again. For a while, every time they met, Monsignor Stephen would go down on one knee and kiss the papal ring until one day the pontiff said to him, "If you want to go down on your knee, then go to my chapel and kneel before the Blessed Sacrament. From now on, when we meet, my son, the kissing of our ring will suffice." The only other persons he said that too was his valet and his private secretary."

Cunningham asked, "Did the pope ever leave the Vatican?"

"Of course. Every summer he would go to his summer villa outside of Rome and once in a while, he would slip out of the Vatican and visit an old friend of his in Rome."

"Slip out of the Vatican?"

The bishop told me that one day when he was a bishop and was having lunch with Pope John; the pontiff asked him if he would like to join him for a trip into the city to see an old friend. The bishop was pleased at being asked and so the pontiff arranged for his private secretary to secretly fetch the pope's chauffeur so that Vatican officials wouldn't ask for a police escort and have the streets closed off. When they arrived at the old age home for the priests where he was going to visit his old friend, the doorman was surprised to see the pontiff at the door."

"Did he do this often?

The bishop told me that the pope once appeared unannounced at a children's hospital just after Christmas Mass. The next day, he visited the prisoners in the Roman prison Regina Coeli unannounced. He was like that."

Cunningham asked, "Did the bishop ever learn what the pontiff's views were with respect to Russell Hendrix being Jesus Christ?"

Larry replied, "From what the bishop told me, as far as the pontiff was concerned, he had written his own views on the matter and placed them in the secret Vatican Archives along with those of Bishop Stephen when he was a monsignor and the matter was closed for further discussion by him to anyone after that and that included Bishop Nichols. The pontiff did mention to him one day however that he expected that some day both of their views would be published in the *Acta Apostolicae Sedis*, where papal documents are collected and printed and added that neither he nor Bishop Stephen would ever see that day."

"Was Father Stephen, I mean Bishop Nichols not in the least curious about the pontiff's views on the issue?"

"Immensely but he cherished his personal relationship he had with Pope John so he kept his curiosity to himself." Larry paused for a moment and then said, "I think the pontiff let his thoughts on the matter slip on May twenty-second, nineteen sixty-two when he spoke for the last time to the crowd in St. Peter's Square. I will quote him as best as I can remember. The pope said, *'Happy Ascension Day. Let us hurry to the Lord who goes up into Heaven. And if we cannot follow him and we remain on Earth, let us do what the apostles did, who gathered in the hall of the Lord's Supper and prayed for the Holy Spirit…Saluti, Saluti'* unquote. This, in my opinion was his way of saying that both our Lord and Heaven is here on Earth."

The reporter asked, "Isn't that what Russell Hendrix said?"

"It was."

Cunningham then asked, "But if the pope spoke about Jesus going up into Heaven and the rest of us remaining on Earth, doesn't that mean that Heaven and Earth are in two separate locations?"

Larry responded, "I believe that, like Jesus, the pope spoke those words as a riddle. I believe he meant that we should hurry to meet God in Heaven which is on Earth and that if we can't follow Jesus because we don't believe in Him, then we will remain on Earth beyond the presence of God and Jesus and as such, not be in Heaven which is here on Earth."

Before Cunningham could interject, Larry continued, "Some 30 years before Paul wrote his letter to the Ephesians, on the *Feast of Shevuot*, the very occasion when Jews were bringing to the temple the first fruits of the grain, oil and wine, a mighty wind had blown through the place and Jesus' disciples were filled with the Holy Spirit. This event, the pouring out of the Holy Spirit without measure, marked the inauguration of the last days. Heaven had pulled off the grandest invasion of Earth. From that time forward, Heaven would not be confined to a garden or to one nation; Heaven had come to invade the entire Earth."

Larry got out of his chair and excused himself as he headed back into the house. Moments later, he returned carrying with him a red-leather-bound *Bible* in his left hand. He hand it to Cunningham.

"This was Russell's *Bible*. The cloth cover was very much worn so I had it rebound with red leather. It is now our family's *Bible*."

When Cunningham opened it, he read the inscription. The words written in long hand said, '*To Russell Hendrix, the son we never had but love as if he is our son.*' It was signed by William and Beatrice Hampston and dated, August 1946, six years to the month before Russell died.

Cunningham flipped open the book and noticed a small black and white photograph inside the book. Larry said, "That is the last known photograph ever taken of Russell. I took the picture a few weeks before he died. He was reading his *Bible* at that moment." Cunningham handed the *Bible* back to Larry.

He opened it and after thumbing through it, he began reciting from one of the pages. "Let me quote from the book of Hebrews. '*You have come to Mount Zion and to the city of the living God, the Heavenly Jerusalem, and to myriads of angels, to the general assembly and church of the first born who are enrolled in Heaven.*' "Now surely that can be interpreted to mean that since Jerusalem was referred to as being Heavenly and the first born were enrolled in Heaven, then Heaven, just like Jerusalem must be on Earth."

Cunningham made no comment. He hadn't thought of this prospect in this manner before.

Larry continued, "The people in the past, like many alive today, spoke of Heaven as being in the sky or beyond. Heaven, according to ancient Judaism and Christianity, was merely the sky. But then they also thought of Earth as being flat. To them, the term 'the kingdom of Heaven' was the same as 'the kingdom of the sky.' Modern thinking like the thinking of the past, considers Heaven as the abode of God and the location of the blessed afterlife but it has undergone a hasty retooling in light of modern knowledge, namely that there is no absolute up or down, that the sky and outer space are not up there but out there and Heaven can be out there and even here on Earth. In other words, it is everywhere."

Cunningham asked, "Could Heaven be another dimension?" "That is possible." replied Larry, "but if it is, we can't define it in a way that it is easily discernable from Earth. For example, air is present with us and yet we cannot see it. Because we can't see air, doesn't mean that it is not with us on Earth. Pope John the second said, *'In the context of Revelation, we know that the Heaven or happiness in which we will find ourselves is neither an abstraction nor a physical place in the clouds, but a living, personal relationship with the Holy Trinity. It is our meeting with the Father which takes place in the risen Christ through the communion of the Holy Spirit.'* unquote. Russell gave us the same message when he was asked where Heaven was. He said when speaking to the clergymen in Nelson, *'If you envision Heaven being a place where angels sit on clouds and play harps, no. I don't believe that is what Heaven is.'* He then went on to say, *'I don't think that Heaven is in any particular place. I think it is everywhere on Earth.'* I concur with both Pope John the second and Russell on this point."

"Is there any chance that I could meet the bishop?"

"Perhaps after you have died. He died several years ago."

"And I don't suppose he kept written records of his discussions with the pontiff?"

No, he didn't and this brings me up to the point where I said earlier that some of what I told you today; would be off the record."

The young reporter was uneasy at this point of his meeting with Larry. He replied, "Yes, I remember."

Larry said, "I don't want you writing or publishing anything about what I said to you about Bishop Nichol's conversations with Pope John the twenty-third."

"But this is such an important part of the story of Russell Hendrix."

"I appreciate that but neither Bishop Nichols or Pope John are alive and you would be quoting what I was told by one of the parties to those conversations between the two men and publishing second-hand quotes at best is always risky, especially when I would be forced to then deny that this conversation between us and the conversations I had with the bishop ever took place in the first place."

The young reporter knew that Larry was right because he hadn't recorded the second session he had with Larry after supper. He then replied, "It shall remain unpublished."

Cunningham asked, "Do you believe in reincarnation?"

Larry thought for a minute and then replied, "Since there is no absolute scientific proof of reincarnation, and none against it, I feel that it is up to each of us to decide as to whether or not we really believe in it."

The reporter asked, "But how do you think a person would come back to life?"

Larry responded, "Reincarnation could come about as the souls of deceased persons move from humans at their moment of death to others at the moment of being conceived.

"But," asked the reporter, "would they know that they lived in a past life?"

Larry smiled and replied, "As I said earlier, the concept of children's past lives coming to the fore are quite remarkable especially in western countries, where children have seldom been exposed to the beliefs of reincarnation.

Larry paused before he continued, then he spoke. "Let me give you an example. Back in the early nineteen hundreds, when India was still a dominion of England; there was a boy of about five years of age living in a small village in India. One day, he and his parents went to visit some relatives in another small village that was several hundred miles away. This was the first time they had ever been in that village. When they arrived, their young son began talking with the elders in the village. He asked them questions about certain members of their families and about their health. He appeared to know all of them and what they had been doing five years earlier."

Cunningham said, "This must have been a real shock to them"

"It was." replied Larry. "Although many of the people in India believe in reincarnation, experiencing something like this was rare indeed so a big thing was made about it. The governor in that area arranged for British scientists to interview the boy and the villagers.

They finally concluded that in all likelihood, he was the reincarnation of an old man who had died five years earlier in that village. As the boy grew older, he remembered less and less of his previous life in the village until finally, all memory of his past life was gone from his memory."

Cunningham asked, "Do you think that the boy on the sidewalk remembered you and your life together?"

Larry replied, "If the boy was the reincarnation of Russell, I think any memory of what his life was like in his past life was for the most part gone but there were probably some remnants of his memory of his previous life left in his mind that made it possible for him to at least recognize the structure of my face as a familiar one he had seen before but couldn't remember where. Of course that was many years ago and if he were to see me now, he may not recognize me at all."

Cunningham asked, "Is it possible that the boy you saw on the sidewalk, has the soul of Jesus within him?"

Larry replied, "I don't know. However, I don't think God intends to let the world see Jesus as the world saw him two thousand years ago. I believe that the soul of Jesus will continuously inhabit the bodies of humans beings on Earth perhaps for centuries until God is satisfied that the time has come for Jesus to fulfill his role as Christ, the Son of God. When that time comes, the world will really know that Christ, the Son of God has arrived."

Larry smiled at Cunningham when he said that there was one more treat for him to look at. He told him that after he climbs the mountain to look at the statue of Russell, he should look at one of the stained windows in the Anglican Church in Nelson.

"It took some influence on the part of the archbishop of our church to permit me to design and have installed a window in the Nelson Anglican church that would best depict the role Jesus played in Russell's life and the fate they shared together. I won't explain it to you. You will see for yourself what the message is."

Cunningham then asked, "Could you tell me how I can go to the top of Granite Mountain so that I can see for myself the clearing you have spoke of?"

"It's easy to find. There is a sign half a mile east of here. It says Russell Hendrix Trail. The people in Nelson know that that is the beginning of the trail leading up to the clearing where Russell was last known to be. The trail is easy to follow after that."

With that having been said, Larry and Cunningham parted company.

The next day, Cunningham drove to the sign and parked his car on the shoulder.

While he was climbing up the mountain, he realized why there was a well-beaten path leading to the summit since so many people had climbed the mountain to visit what they believed was Russell's accession into Heaven which by itself, was a sign of the great respect they had for him when he was among them.

When he got to the clearing, he saw what so many people who climbed the mountain saw. The clearing was beautiful and serene. He sat on the concrete bench at the edge of the clearing and looked down at the lake far below and appreciated why Larry and Russell visited the clearing so often. And like those who visited the clearing before he did and those that visited it after he did, the bell that Larry brought to the top of the mountain rang loud enough in the distance for him to hear.

When he stared at the statute of Russell in the arms of the girl against the reddish clouds of the late afternoon, he began to appreciate the significance of the statute. It told the people of Nelson that as a community, they should have cared for Russell like the girl who held him in her arms after he was crucified. It they had, he might still be among them.

Later, he went to the Anglican Church to look at the stained glass window Larry had spoken of. As he stared at it in awe, he realized that there was a strong message in the design of the window with it depicting only two figures on crosses and not three. One of them was much smaller than the other. The message as he saw it, was that many people sacrifice themselves in the service of Jesus and God and that, Russell had done that also during his own lifetime, as short as it was, and he shared the same fate as Jesus did; both having been crucified at a young age.

The following day, Cunningham visited the *Nelson Times* to look up the past editions in 1945 through 1951. He wanted to photograph some of them and bring them back to his editor in Vancouver. However, when he got there, he discovered that there had been a fire in the building in 1952 and all prior editions of the paper had been burned to ashes.

Nevertheless, Dave Cunningham believed Larry's story. He knew that it is possible for people to exist and never be spoken of. It was as if they never existed at all. He figured however, that if Russell did exist and he lived his young life in Nelson amongst them, the way Larry described it, then many of the people there at that time probably never forgave themselves for abandoning him like they did and were too ashamed of themselves and would be too embarrassed to discuss with strangers, their previous association with Russell. The reporter believed however that Russell's spirit is also with those in Nelson who listened to his teachings and continue to live the life of righteousness and at the same time, love Jesus.

The reporter wasn't absolutely sure about whether or not human beings are reincarnated but he wanted to believe in his own mind that Russell Hendrix, by whatever name he was now going under, or whatever human form he was in, was currently alive somewhere in the world. He hoped that Russell loves Jesus as he did in his past life, follows his teachings, and as such, is living a righteous life like the one he lived in his past life in Nelson.

The young reporter also believed that if Russell's soul did return to life again, then when the young boy was dying on the top of Granite Mountain, he was shown a brief glimpse of Paradise on Earth in his final moments of his previous life. He also believed that Russell is currently living with Jesus and God and with everyone else on Earth, and at the same time, experiencing the joys and pleasures of the Paradise that he was shown just before he died so horribly in his previous life.

On August 14, 1995, exactly seven years after he first learned of the existence of Russell Hendrix, Dave Cunningham and his seven-year-old son, Russell were overnight camping near the summit of Grouse Mountain, the mountain that overlooks Vancouver to the south of it. As they sat by their campfire that night while admiring the city lights of that large city far below them, a warm breeze suddenly encompassed them. It was then that Dave began thinking of Russell Hendrix again.

As his mind began going back to the events in Russell Hendrix's life, Dave muttered to himself, "If you really are alive, I hope that someday we will meet."

"Daddy!" cried out his son. "Are you talking to yourself again?"

Dave looked at his son and laughed and then said, "It beats talking to the trees, Russell."

As he looked at his son, he asked, "Would you like me to tell you a story about a nine-year-old boy?"

"Oh yes, Daddy. Please do." said the boy excitedly.

"Then turn over onto your back and pick out star to look at and I will tell you a story of a young nine-year-old boy who lived in a small city many years ago."

Dave and his son Russell turned onto their backs and as they stared into the night sky and the bright stars above them. Dave began telling his son his promised story.

"By December 1945, the Second World War had been over for four and a half months. It had been a five-year global war that cost almost fifty-five million lives—"

If our spirits live forever and is within each of us in our lifetimes, is it not conceivable that we were here before and that after we are gone, we will be here again?

Dahn A. Batchelor